Suarez l
edge of the v.....
print. It was a hiking boot of some type, fairly new with
a lot of tread. Suarez explained they noticed it on the
way back, and followed them from a point in the
middle of a meadow back toward the crime scene. We
marched slowly forward, picking up the tracks evenly
spaced. I got the sense whoever it was had been
walking steadily, not running or jogging. I glanced back
over my shoulder, trying to get a bearing on the
willows.

"This is farther than we went before," Suarez said.

We moved into a cluster of trees. The sunlight was
dappled here, not as bright as in the meadow. The grass
was overgrown with weeds and shrubs. Something
didn't feel right. Suarez moved another step in front of
me, trying to squeeze between two fallen trees. I saw a
glimmer of light reflect off something just ahead.

"No!"

Suarez plunged forward. I shoved him to the right.
And just that quickly, I was knocked off my feet, flying
backward.

Praise for Mark Love

"A fast-moving police procedural, *WHY 319?* crackles with authenticity. The author knows his investigative methods, and pulls the reader along at breakneck speed as Jefferson Chene leads a team of detectives in a race to catch a serial killer before the body count rises. The chase is suspenseful, sexy, deadly, and always engaging."

~Donald Levin, author

~*~

"Mark Love writes in a style reminiscent of Dashiell Hammett or Robert Parker, projecting a smoky, dark, cool atmosphere. The Detroit setting is unusual and provocative and his detective Jefferson Chene a brooding man, clearly hefting significant baggage. Which makes the back love story even more tantalizing. Will he let her in? Will he keep her at arm's length?"

~M.S. Spencer, author of
The Penhallow Train Incident

~*~

Also by Mark Love
and available from The Wild Rose Press, Inc.
Why 319? A Jefferson Chene Mystery

Your Turn to Die

by

Mark Love

A Jefferson Chene Mystery

Your Turn to Die

Cover Art by *RJ Morris*

The Wild Rose Press, Inc.
PO Box 708
Adams Basin, NY 14410-0708
Visit us at www.thewildrosepress.com

Publishing History
First Mainstream Mystery Edition, 2019
Print ISBN 978-1-5092-2410-4
Digital ISBN 978-1-5092-2411-1

A Jefferson Chene Mystery
Published in the United States of America

Dedication

For Kim,
another chapter in our story

Acknowledgements

I don't know everything. Never have, never will.

That's why I turn to people with different backgrounds for information that can be crucial to making my stories realistic. With that in mind, here's a note of thanks and appreciation to the following for their patience with my crazy questions:

Fred Wheeler for his expertise on firearms.

Paul Wirth for everything related to technology.

Olivia Sholtis for being so anxiously willing to research Prohibition whisky.

And to Kim Love, Meredith Ellsworth, Helene Love Snell, and Jerry Sorn, who read the earlier drafts of this novel and whose feedback made it so much better.

Prologue

It didn't look like the kind of morning for murder. The mist burning off with the sun revealed a gregarious crowd, struggling for some semblance of order. Green and brown camouflage fatigues, plastic goggles and leather boots adorned many of the participants. Some were clothed in sneakers, jeans and sweatshirts, mostly black or dark in color. Others wore heavy plastic helmets that covered the face. From a distance it looked like a raiding party from Selfridge ANG base.

Up close was another story. These were not the lean, mean physiques of true military men and women, but the various shapes of weekend warriors, seeking a little fun and games. Much of the clothing was worn and mismatched, probably from an army surplus supplier. The group was quickly separated into four divisions, designated by colored armbands. An elaborate version of capture the flag was about to begin. But one participant was after much higher stakes.

The sun was quickly warming the area when the target was spotted. It took him a while, since he didn't want to get too close and risk being recognized. Surprise was going to be a major part of his game.

As luck would have it, he was part of the black team. The plan was to defend against blue and attack yellow. But his target was on the red squad. As the players dispersed, he drifted toward the trees, keeping his quarry in sight.

With patience, the target would be eliminated before noon.

This was the first of four rounds scheduled for today. According to the rules of engagement, if a paint pellet struck you, you were eliminated from that series. Those hit were instructed to head back to the neutral area, where cases of beer, soft drinks and bottled water were already chilling under ice. Deli platters would be offered between the second and third rounds of play. After the final rounds, the grills would be fired up and a feast would be served. Since each squad used the paint colors to match their armbands, one inept soldier could be a splattered rainbow by the day's end.

During the initial round, he kept to the sidelines, trying to elude any potential attackers and maintain visual contact. With less than twenty minutes remaining in the game, a warrior from the blue team sprang from a low tree limb and nailed him with a shot to the stomach. Instinctively, he flinched and clutched his gut. After a moment he smiled, then wiped the smear of paint on his fatigues and headed for the neutral zone. He had lost sight of his quarry, but was unconcerned. Patience would be its own reward. If he struck too soon, the target may be discovered before he could make his escape. And that was not part of his plan.

At the neutral zone, he pulled a Vernors from the ice then leaned against a picnic table. On the far side of the area he spotted his man, a large blotch of yellow paint adorning his neck and right shoulder. His eyes never left the target. The man was slumped on the ground, breathing heavily, with his back braced against a tree. Sweat beaded his face. He pulled off his hat, wiping his face with his bare hands. The camouflage shirt and pants were also darkened with sweat, which seemed odd, since the temperatures were in the low seventies.

A whistle sounded repeatedly, signaling the end of the first round. The rest of the players straggled in and received their assignments for game two. Some switched to other teams, but many remained where they were. After all, it was the game, not the enemy you faced, that counted.

This time, the target was going to be engaged. Black was to defend against yellow and attack red. That was precisely what he had in mind. As the battle began, he slipped over to a cluster of willow trees, adjusted his equipment and made his way slowly through the low hanging branches. The game went on around him. His eyes remained narrowed and focused. Nostrils flaring, he was searching for the scent of his prey. His ears were attuned for the slightest clue of his target. He checked each area cautiously before moving on.

There!

He was just up ahead on the left. The man was making this too easy. He had isolated himself from the group. Now he had straddled a fallen log and was holding his head in his hands. The hunter gently lowered the bulky paintball gun to the ground. From one of the cargo pockets of his pants, he removed a revolver. From another, he pulled out a long metal tube. Deftly, he fastened it to the muzzle of the gun. Then he moved closer, still cautiously checking his surroundings before taking even a single step. He was less than ten feet away when the target looked up.

"Go away. I don't want to play today."

"This game's for real." He brought the gun up and extended it toward his quarry.

"What kind of paint gun is that?"

"I don't play with paint, Morrissey. I use the real thing."

Morrissey raised the goggles from his face and squinted at the hunter in the sun-dappled shadows. Recognition finally registered. "What the hell are you doing here?"

"Taking care of business."

"Okay, shoot me and get it over with. I feel like shit anyway."

"Where are the jewels?"

The man squinted in an effort to focus. "What are you talking about?"

"I want the jewels. Diamonds and rubies and emeralds. Tell me."

"Just get it over with."

"Tell me!" He moved close and pointed the gun just below the target's belt buckle. "I want the jewels. You owe me that much. And more."

Morrissey shook his head. "Go to hell."

"You first." He pulled the trigger. There was a soft coughing sound as the gun fired. As a precaution he dropped to his knees and clamped a hand over Morrissey's mouth to muffle any noise. Morrissey struggled, clutching at his groin.

"Diamonds and rubies and emeralds. Tell me now and I'll end this quick."

Morrissey continued to moan beneath his gloved hand. He knew the chances of getting the information from the wounded man were slim, but it was worth a try. He shifted the gun to the right side of Morrissey's chest and fired again.

Morrissey jumped as the bullet slammed into him. A crimson spray coated his shirt. The shooter glanced around, making sure no one else had entered the shelter of the trees. He'd doubted the jewels even existed. They were secondary to everything else. He rocked back on his heels and got to his feet. Morrissey was gasping now, blood forming little bubbles on his lips. He lowered the gun until it was close to the dying man's forehead. Steadying his hand, he squeezed the trigger one last time. Morrissey was gone.

He picked up Morrissey's paintball gun and fired a red pellet at his own left leg. The killer jumped in surprise at the pain of the impact at such close range. The paint was a brighter shade than the stain spreading on the ground below the body. Satisfied, he turned away and out of the willows toward the neutral zone.

"Game over."

Chapter One

Graymaker propped one elbow on the bar and studied me over the rim of his Salty Dog. "You know what you need, Chene? You should spend some time with a very qualified, experienced psychologist."

I leaned against the cooler and let my eyes wander over the thinning crowd in the saloon. "Like I'm going to take advice from anyone drinking gin and grapefruit juice?"

He wobbled on his stool. "Don't knock therapy. You could work out a lot of your problems with a good head doctor."

"What makes you think I've got problems?"

Graymaker grinned and slugged down half of his drink. "C'mon, Chene, I've known you a long time. You've been with the state PD ten years and now you're back here tending bar. You must have problems."

Cissy, a skinny brunette with the high squeaky voice of a cartoon character came to the waitress stand to get a drink order filled. Two draft beers, one rum and Coke and a frozen margarita later, I returned to my position across from Graymaker.

"Just because I'm helping Ted out doesn't mean I've got problems."

He shook his head slowly and pushed his empty glass across the counter. "It goes deeper than that.

Probably all the way back to your childhood. Want to tell me about it?"

"Sounds like you're trying to drum up business. Having trouble making your malpractice payments or are you behind in your alimony again?"

The old man shook his head and wobbled again. "My practice is thriving. But I can spot the signs of someone who needs to resolve matters in their personal life. You're a textbook example. You can't commit to an emotional relationship. You have a problem dealing with people in authority. That's just for starters."

"I have plenty of relationships, thank you very much." Abandoning my spot against the cooler, I began to wipe down the mahogany bar with a towel.

"We're talking about the opposite sex."

My eyes landed on a petite blonde across the room. "My favorite kind. I enjoy the company of women."

"One night stands are not relationships."

I flicked the bar towel a few centimeters from his knuckles. "Maybe I'm just more selective than you at finding the right woman."

"No need to bring my divorces into this." Graymaker waggled a forefinger at me. "We are talking about you."

"You're the only one talking. Course, you do enough for both of us."

Ted appeared on the stool beside Graymaker. "I miss anything?"

I shrugged. "Graymaker is trying to drum up new patients. He's getting so desperate he wants to analyze me."

"Forget it, Gray. The guy's got enough problems without getting hooked up with the likes of you."

"I don't have any problems."

Ted and Graymaker stared at me. I poured Ted a cup of coffee and turned my attention to a trio of late arrivals at the opposite end of the counter. The two cronies were awaiting my return.

Graymaker pounced. "You were saying?"

"I have normal relationships. Friends. People I enjoy spending time with. People I have feelings about."

Ted snorted into his coffee mug. "Name six."

"What the hell is this? Analyze Chene night? I've got better things to do—"

"Name six," Ted repeated, in case I'd forgotten the subject.

"Six?"

Ted and Graymaker were taking turns, like a couple of geriatrics watching a tennis match. "Yeah. Six. Half a dozen people you have feelings for."

"Ted. McDonald. Kozlowski. Cantrell. Frank Powell…"

"Dead guys don't count," Ted interrupted.

"Why not?"

Graymaker raised his eyes toward the ceiling. "You can't even name six live people. Let's not start into problems saying farewell to the dead."

The antique ship's clock behind me chimed out the hour, sounding as loud and welcome as the gong at the end of a round at a boxing match. I nodded at the two old timers and headed for the open hatch on the end of the bar.

"Where you going?" Graymaker called.

"My shift's over. I told the old coot beside you I'd cover until eleven. He's closing. Maybe you two can analyze each other for some laughs."

Before either one could respond, something caught my attention. The flat screen television that was up on the far corner went from the highlights of the earlier Tigers game to the evening news. The banner across the bottom read "War Games Murder" in six-inch type. I snagged the remote from under the counter and moved to the corner of the bar, closer to the screen, cranking up the volume as I went. One of the anchors was already into the introduction when he threw the focus to Olivia Sholtis, the reporter at the scene.

"We have just been informed that the victim has positively been identified as Kyle Morrissey, the successful entrepreneur behind a number of businesses throughout metro Detroit. While the police investigation has only begun, it will be a difficult undertaking. According to the operator of the war games, over a hundred people participated in the event today. Morrissey was a regular at these games, where people from all walks of life engage in mock battles using paint guns to simulate military weapons. Morrissey's body was found only a short time ago."

She did a quick interview with the guy who operated the games. No one from the local sheriff's department was willing to get in front of the camera. I lowered the volume as Olivia threw it back to the anchor.

Ted was behind the bar now. He cocked a raised eyebrow at me.

"Does that look like a case for you?"

I shrugged. "Too early to tell. But if it's complicated, we may get the call. You know this guy?"

"I met Morrissey a couple of times. He was a

hustler. A pretty sharp businessman, he started out buying up those old theaters around town, fixing them up and drawing people in. He'd show classic films, bring in some minor Hollywood types for plays and such. I heard he was doing the same thing with bookstores. He liked to get his name in the papers."

"Where did you meet him?"

Ted thought for a minute while pulling a couple of drafts for another waitress. Without being asked, he poured another Salty Dog for Graymaker. Ted held the cocktail in one hand and extended his other, palm up to the shrink. He grumbled for a moment before he gave up his car keys. Only then did Ted relinquish the drink. The psychiatrist made a rude remark about Ted's heritage before taking a healthy slug of the concoction, slurping kosher salt off the rim.

"Probably at one of those charity events. He was big in the local communities. When he reopened the old Shores Madrid Theater, he donated the proceeds from the first week to cancer research. He sponsored a Little League and a Pee Wee hockey team as well. The guy spread it around." He narrowed his gaze at me. "What makes you ask?"

"Curiosity. It goes with the territory."

"Maybe it was an accident."

I didn't say anything. It was late. If I started speculating, Ted and Graymaker might see it as an opportunity to return to the earlier conversation. The last thing I wanted was to be interrogated by them. I waved two fingers at them and headed out. As I exited the bar I couldn't hold back a grin. There was someone I definitely had feelings for, but I'd been keeping that to myself. I wasn't quite ready to have her suffer through the scrutiny of Ted and his cohorts. We'd met three months ago when I was investigating her roommate's murder. When we started dating, a little piece in the back of my mind kept me cautious. Losing someone close to you could easily cloud your judgment. I was reluctant to move too quickly with Simone. The last thing I wanted was for her to suddenly realize that we would never have met if her roommate was still alive.

Home was a small square house on a dead end street about five miles north of Ted's saloon. It was on a narrow canal that flowed into Lake St. Clair. The place had three good sized bedrooms, a roomy kitchen and a small living room with a working fireplace. Out back was a three season room that overlooked the canal. I'd found it a couple of years ago when the housing market crashed. It was a foreclosure that needed a lot of work. While I'm comfortable with cleaning and painting, I left the serious projects for professionals. There's a one car detached garage that backs up to the seawall for the canal. As I swung into the driveway my lights reflected on Simone's car. There were a couple of lights on low in the kitchen. I locked the car and came through the side door.

"I'm out back."

"Need anything?"

"No, I'm good now."

The storm windows were up and a nice breeze was flowing in from the lake. Simone was reclining on the cushions of a rattan sofa, a thick novel in her hands. She marked her place with a length of ribbon and closed the book. I started to walk past her toward one of the matching chairs. She reached up and caught my hand. Dropping the book, Simone swung her feet to the

11

floor and stood. Her arms went around me. I watched as she tipped her head back, offering me a kiss. No one would ever confuse me with Casanova. But I'm not one to pass up a kiss from a beautiful woman.

"Did you like my message?" she asked timidly.

"Yeah, it was a pleasant surprise."

Simone was supposed to be gone all day with family obligations. I hadn't expected to see her. An hour ago she sent me a text, asking if it was okay if she stopped by. Swamped behind the bar with patrons, my response had been an exclamation point. I didn't have time to elaborate. Simone lives in an apartment out in Berkley, about a forty-minute drive from my place in St. Clair Shores. It was only a couple of weeks ago that I'd given her a key. This was the first time she'd used it.

"Should I ask about your day?" she whispered.

"No. Tell me about yours."

"It was mother-daughter stuff. A couple of nice meals, some shopping and plenty of conversation. We're thinking about a week in Paris in September, after the summer tourists are gone."

"Sounds like fun."

Simone pressed her cheek against my chest. "You could go with us."

The idea of a family vacation took me by surprise. I'd met her mother twice. The reception was a little strained both times. I doubted she'd warm up to me during a trip to France. But as Graymaker guessed, I have issues with relationships.

After being in the saloon for eight hours, the summer air felt invigorating. Taking her hand, I guided Simone out the back door and down to the seawall.

Leaning against the garage, I pulled off my boots and socks. The water level in the canal was down enough so I could dangle my legs over the edge and only my toes would get wet. She gave me a curious look.

"I am *not* going skinny dipping."

"Neither am I. But it's peaceful out here and the breeze feels good." I settled on the dock and lowered my legs. The cool water splashed over my feet.

She was wearing a tailored pair of navy shorts and a white silk blouse with short sleeves. The blouse had tiny darts of green and gold throughout. Simone hesitated before stepping out of her sandals. As she sat beside me, she leaned her head on my shoulder. I caught a whiff of perfume. The water splashed up her leg and she gave a little start.

"It's freezing."

"Lake Michigan is colder. Lake Superior still has ice cubes in it."

"Is that supposed to make me feel better?" In the starlight I could see her eyes. They twinkled with their own power.

"Well, I will do my best to keep you warm."

My arm was around her waist. I was leaning in for a kiss when my phone rang. It had the insistent tone signifying it was work related. Simone recognized it as well. Quickly she darted in and pressed her lips to mine.

"Chene," I said, answering the line but refusing to let her go.

"Y'all see the news?" Cantrell's rough country voice scratched my ear.

"The war games bit?"

"Yeah. That un's ours now."

"You got a plan, Pappy?"

"Nah. Meetcha all at Lil Nino's at eight. Y'all can work it out."

"You call the squad?"

"Yup."

"Later, Pappy." He was already gone.

I turned and flipped the phone in the general direction of my boots. Simone had a look of curiosity on her face. I could feel a tremor of tension in her body as it rested against me.

"A morning meeting. Seems like we have a new case."

She relaxed slightly. "I thought you might have to leave right away."

"No, it will keep."

"I'm getting cold." She pulled her feet from the water and pressed them against my jeans.

"Maybe we should go inside."

"I seem to recall a comment about keeping me warm."

"It's a standing offer."

Her eyes sparked with laughter but she struggled with what I guessed was a look of disappointment. "Well, I suppose that will have to do. Come along, Jeff."

Gracefully she swung her legs up onto the seawall and rose.

Images of warming her swept through my mind.

****

Lil Nino's is a diner that staked its claim on Gratiot and Eleven Mile Road fifty years ago and has taken on all neighborhood competition ever since. Everything from a restaurant specializing in French crepes to an organic bakery and a vegan café tried to compete without success. As a sign of surrender, the last owner sold Nino the property. He waited all of ten minutes before converting it into a banquet hall. Nino understands the area and knows what works.

Sunday morning, we gathered around a large round table in a far corner. Pappy arrived early, judging by the spread of the newspapers around him. Steam from a mug of coffee swirled up in front of him. He nodded and went back to his paper. I took a seat across from him as a waitress appeared with menus and more coffee. I was fifteen minutes early but expected the others momentarily. It had been tempting to stay curled up in bed with Simone, but I knew better than to be late. Pappy is a man of many traits. Patience is not one of them.

Captain Prescott "Pappy" Cantrell was the leader of our group of detectives. Officially known as Squad Six, the five detectives under his domain handled major cases that cross into multiple jurisdictions around the large tri-county area that made up the metropolitan Detroit territory. Cantrell was a gangly country boy from the hills of Tennessee, but his backcountry ways were more of a disguise than anything else. He was sharp. A veteran of the politics and machinations that went hand in hand with an operation within the Michigan State Police, Cantrell knows how to get things done. He folded the last section of the paper as movement caught my peripheral vision. The rest of the squad had arrived.

"Morning, Pappy," boomed a voice so deep it could have come from underground.

"Kozlowski. Where's yer partner?"

Cameron Kozlowski jerked his head toward the

restrooms. Koz, as he was affectionately known, stood just over six and a half feet tall and packs over two hundred and fifty pounds of muscle onto his frame. He'd been on the squad for over five years. "Making a pit stop. Asked for herbal tea."

Cantrell made a clicking noise. "Cops ain't supposed to drink tea."

Koz raised a hand that could easily palm a basketball. "You tell her that."

"Ah will."

Three other people joined us. As they settled with menus, my eyes flicked around the table. Beside me was Donna Spears, recently promoted to detective from the patrol division of the State Police. Donna had been instrumental in helping identify a serial killer who had been wreaking havoc on the area three months ago. She had good instincts and was eager to learn. Across from her was Laura Atwater, the other female member of the squad. Pappy recruited Laura about a year ago, drawing her away from the Ann Arbor PD. She and Kozlowski hit it off immediately. When the opportunity presented itself, they usually partnered. I watched her playfully slug Cantrell's shoulder when he expressed his opinion about herbal tea. My eyes shifted to the last person to join us.

Ramon Suarez settled into the chair between me and Koz. It was an unspoken rule that Pappy liked the females on either side of him, no matter where we gathered. Suarez was a short, stocky guy with thick black hair and the Latino features of a 1950s matinee idol. He'd joined the squad two weeks ago and was still trying to fit in. I checked out today's ensemble and had to bite back a grin.

Cantrell was an easy going guy. He had an aversion to suits and ties, unless we were appearing in court, at a funeral or some other official function. Despite explaining this to Suarez, he had yet to take the hint. He was decked out in a lightweight tan suit, with a navy blue shirt and striped tie. New Italian shoes gleamed beneath the table. I wondered if he dressed like a dandy when he was on the Detroit PD.

We ordered and settled back. Cantrell pulled the front section from the paper and tossed it into the middle of the table.

"Y'all gonna be gettin' real familiar with this guy fast. Ah'm already gettin' calls from Lansing, so ya know what dat means."

"The governor knew this guy?" Koz asked.

"Stands to figger. Morrissey had money. The governor likes his money." Cantrell cut his eyes to me. "Whatcha got, Chene?"

Before the meeting, I'd gone online and read the newspaper accounts of Kyle Morrissey. There was some background information that added to what Ted described last night. On the drive over, I'd roughed out a plan of action. Cantrell was expecting it. And I didn't want to disappoint him.

"Let's start the day at the crime scene. I'll contact the county sheriff who caught the original call. We can meet him there. We need to know everything about this war games operations, how many people were in attendance, the crew who run the place and more. Then we need to start looking into Morrissey's activities."

Cantrell nodded as the waitress appeared with our food. No two orders were alike. Kozlowski was having stuffed French toast with bacon and sausage on the side.

Donna had scrambled eggs with Canadian bacon and rye toast. Laura was having a white egg omelet and a side of fruit. I'd opted for a Denver omelet. Suarez was having pancakes and bacon. He cast a curious eye at Cantrell's plate.

"What's that, Pappy?"

"Eggs over easy with a side of grits."

Suarez looked squeamish as Cantrell stirred the bowl. "Grits? This is Motown, man. There can't be three restaurants around here that serve grits!"

"There's nine. And ah knows where each one is."

"Any concerns about the media?" Kozlowski asked, smoothly transitioning the conversation back to the case.

"Not at the moment. I don't think they're aware of our involvement yet," I said.

"Will be soon 'nuff," Pappy said. "Governor wants a statement made."

Cantrell was normally the spokesman for the squad. I knew he would stage a ten- minute press conference from behind the podium at the post which served as our headquarters. He tolerated the media. There were a few reporters who had quickly learned over the years that if you asked direct, pertinent questions, Pappy would give you a good sound bite. He could silence a crowd with a glare. He'd give them just enough to fill a few lines of type or a thirty second blurb for the newscast. When he had more, he'd share it.

We ate quickly. The waitress appeared with refills of coffee and trained her gaze at Cantrell. He nodded once. She gave him a quick squeeze on the shoulder, dropped the bill on the table and set a large carryout container of coffee by his hand. He shot her a wink as she wiggled away. Apparently she knew Pappy well. He glanced across the table at me and scowled.

"Ain't y'all got a crime to solve?"

"We're gone. Thanks for breakfast, Pappy."

The others pushed away from the table and headed for the exit. Koz and I each threw some cash down for the bill and a tip. Pappy was generous, but he expected to see us chip in. As the two senior members of the squad, we knew what he liked.

Outside the others gathered around their cars. I didn't want a parade going to the crime scene. Since it was on the way, we would swing by the post and drop off three vehicles. Kozlowski and I would drive.

At the post Laura pulled a bag from her car and threw it into Kozlowski's trunk. She jumped in beside him and they took off. Donna carried a nylon backpack with her and slid into the front seat of my Pontiac. Suarez parked his car at the far end of the lot, as if someone would bother his four-year-old Charger. He ambled over to the car empty handed. I looked over my sunglasses at him as he reached the back door.

"No gear?"

"Nah, Sarge, I got everything I need."

Donna snickered beside me. "Almost."

"Let's go. We've got a killer to catch."

Chapter Two

Something about this area was vaguely familiar. It was a rural setting, north and west of New Baltimore, which was about a forty- minute drive north and east from the post in Mount Clemens. The crime scene was part of a large parcel, more than ten acres of property set well back from the road. There was a sprawling farmhouse off to the side, one of those ancient two story structures that projected the image of wide open rooms with creaky floorboards, big picture windows and a stone hearth and fireplace. I could see a wraparound porch and a number of wicker chairs evenly spaced about. It looked comfortable.

About two hundred yards beyond the house were a couple of barns. A number of four wheeled motorcycles were lined up there, along with a couple of pickup trucks and a farm tractor. There was a gravel parking area off to the left. I parked besides Kozlowski's BMW sedan. Beyond us were two sheriff cruisers and a couple of guys in uniform. Koz and Laura were leaning against the rear bumper of his car, swapping street shoes for heavy boots. Laura had even gone so far as to pull a pair of nylon pants over the slacks she was wearing. A navy blue baseball cap with the state police insignia rested on the roof. She pulled her dark hair into a pony tail and worked it through the band on the back of the cap. Koz grabbed an identical cap and tugged it in place.

I went to my trunk and removed a pair of work boots. As I was pulling them on, Donna appeared beside me. She had already changed footwear. From her pack, she removed a pair of latex gloves, then grabbed a small spiral notebook and a ballpoint pen. She tucked them into pockets of her jeans. Her blonde hair was short, and she swept it back and tugged on an official ball cap. She shouldered the pack and shot me a grin.

"What about Mr. Fancy?"

I continued lacing up my boots. "We'll see what shape he's in by the end of the day. Guess you could say this is part of his orientation."

"This could be fun."

"Or at least worth a few laughs."

Suarez came around the back of the car as I stood up and pulled my pack into place. Donna pushed the trunk lid shut.

"Where the hell are we, Sarge?"

"The scene of the crime. We're going to check it out."

In the distance I could see a grove of trees. Strung across them was a weave of yellow plastic, indicating the crime scene. As a group we began walking toward the sheriff's cruisers. Suarez glanced down at his shiny street shoes and grumbled. Kozlowski clamped a meaty hand on his shoulder.

"Always have a go-bag."

"What the hell is a go-bag?"

"A bag filled with gear, so that when you need to go, you're ready. Heavy boots, gloves, crime fighting gear, extra clothes, whatever else you may need." Koz threw a nod in my direction. "Didn't Chene tell you that when you came onboard?"

I could see Suarez shoot me a look in my peripheral vision. "Yeah, but I hadn't gotten around to it."

"Bad move, rook."

"I ain't no rookie." His voice quickly went indignant.

"Then stop acting like one. When the boss tells you something, you'd damn well better do it. Or you'll have to make do. So until you get with it, you're a rook."

The conversation died. We stopped in front of the cruisers. Both men were in uniforms. One had lots of stars across the shoulders. He was a lean guy in his late fifties, with gray eyes and a day's worth of gray stubble on his chin. I introduced the crew.

"Ray Craddock. I'm the sheriff. Sure glad you guys are taking over. This is way beyond our abilities."

"We haven't had an opportunity to read the reports. Why don't you fill us in?"

Craddock gestured toward the grove of trees. "Let's talk and walk."

Sometime during the night out here, a steady rain had fallen. The ground was a mixture of dirt and mud, worn down by vehicles driving back and forth and countless footprints from the people involved in the war games. Craddock narrated the events as we walked along.

The games usually wrapped up around four in the afternoon. What followed was a gigantic barbecue, with burgers, dogs and bratwursts sizzling on the grill. There was a large tent offering shade to about twenty-five full sized picnic tables. The grill was a brick structure on the east side, large enough to handle a crowd of two hundred. The owner and his crew would be busy cooking and serving. It was part of the package for the warriors. By six most of the people were tired and happy and fed and on their way home. By seven the place was empty except for the workers. That was when they noticed the one car still in the lot.

"It was no big deal at first," Craddock said. "Apparently there are a fair number of women who like to play. The competition gets their motors running. Mix in the beer with the food after the games and it's not uncommon for a couple to go off on maneuvers of their own."

"Shit happens," Kozlowski said.

Craddock nodded. "Roger that. Anyway, Kenneally had his crew do a sweep of the area to get it ready for the next day's games. They use those four wheelers and cover the game site, picking up trash and such. It was just about dark when one of them swung over to check that grove. That's when they found the body. They called us right away."

We reached the cluster of willow trees. I was pleased to see that not only was the area roped off with the crime scene tape, but someone had gone so far as to erect a small tent over where the body had been. I thanked Craddock for his efforts.

"We don't have a big budget or a lot of equipment. Once the victim was identified, I knew we wouldn't be handling the investigation. But I wanted to preserve as much of the scene as I could. Between last night's forecast and the morning dew, we did what we could."

Two of Craddock's deputies had responded to the call from Kenneally's house. Upon arrival they ran the details on the car and called Craddock. He was there ten minutes later. We remained outside the grove as Craddock finished his report.

"I took some pictures of the victim and called the New Baltimore MSP post for forensics and a coroner. They scrambled here right quick. I don't have their reports yet. Chances are, you'll get them before we do."

"Did you interview whoever found the body?"

Craddock nodded. "Yeah. Guy freaked out a little. Actually got about five feet away before he tossed his dinner. I taped it. One of my team transcribed it this morning." He handed over a thin envelope. I tucked it in a pocket of my backpack.

I nodded to Koz. He led the team into the grove. I held back in case Craddock had anything else to offer.

"Tell me about the operator here."

"Kenneally has owned this place for ten years or more. Used to work in the city in the automotive sector. Got tired of all the politics and crap that went with it. Came out here with his wife and daughter. He was from somewhere up north, small town, liked the peace and quiet. The wife was a city girl. She lasted about two years."

"Divorce?"

"Oh yeah, big time. Turns out Kenneally owned a lot of stock and played the market well. Even dodged a bullet when the economy went bad. Hedge funds or some such crap. Anyway the wife bugged out about the time he was getting this war game thing going. She missed the city. Rumor had it she also missed one of his poker buddies." Craddock shrugged. "Women. Can't live with them, can't figure out why."

I returned the shrug. "I've heard a lot of variations on that."

"Haven't we all."

"Anything else you know about Kenneally?"

"Guy pays his taxes, does a nice business up here. The daughter still lives with him, helps run the show. He employs four men full time and a couple more on the weekends when the players are in. Well liked. Brings some decent money in. No previous calls or problems."

We ducked under the crime scene tape and joined the others. Craddock showed us how the victim had been positioned. We could see the darker spot on the ground where the blood had leaked out of the body. Laura pulled a digital camera from her bag and took a series of pictures. Kozlowski used a tape measure to track the distance from the edge of the grove to the scene. Donna was busy making notations in her book. I watched them work. Suarez was off to the side, taking it all in. If there were any wrappers or trash, the forensics guys from the post would have gathered them. I noticed the remnants of plaster casts on the ground. Apparently they had found a number of different footprints. I turned and looked back the way we had come in. To the east was the farmhouse. The property extended quite a way in every other direction.

"What's next, boss?" Laura asked.

"Take a walk. You go south get a feel for the property. Koz, go north. Suarez, take the west. Don't go beyond the property line."

Craddock stepped up. "I know the boundaries. I'll go with your fellow north. Granger can go west. The road is the boundary south."

Suarez dipped his eyes at his feet and gave his head a slow shake. Without a word, he began to follow the deputy out of the grove.

"How about me, boss?" Donna asked.

"Let's go interview the owner."

Gary Kenneally was an ordinary, average guy. He was standing on the wraparound porch, leaning against a support column for the roof, arms folded across his chest, watching us approach. Beyond him on the porch was a grouping of four wicker chairs with brightly colored cushions. A wicker table was in the center.

"You the state cops?" Kenneally's voice had a rasp to it, like a rusty nail on a cracked chalkboard.

I introduced us. Kenneally undid his arms and extended a hand. We both shook it.

"I got coffee or iced tea. Too early for a beer."

Donna flicked her eyes at me. I nodded. "Coffee sounds good."

"Have a seat. I'll be right out."

True to his word, Kenneally came back a moment later with a pot of coffee. Behind him was a young woman in her early twenties. She wore tight cutoff jeans and a tighter tank top. Long black hair was worn in a braid that hung over one shoulder and brushed the top of her breast. She carried a tray with ceramic mugs and a bowl with sugar and cream packets. I watched as she bent to place the tray on the wicker table. Her eyes were on Donna. The braid swung with her movement and she flicked her head, throwing it over her shoulder.

"This is my daughter, Jenna."

"Detectives Chene and Spears," I said.

Jenna moved to a chair beside Donna and sat, tucking her bare legs beneath her. We helped ourselves to coffee. Donna placed her digital tape recorder on the table and identified each of us.

"What can you tell us about Kyle Morrissey?"

Kenneally shrugged. "He was a decent guy. Liked coming out here about once a month in the season. Played hard. Got along well with the others. I knew he was from money, but he didn't flaunt it. Seemed like a regular guy."

Jenna looked like she was about to interject but changed her mind.

"How long are we talking?"

Kenneally glanced at his daughter. "Jenna manages the records. Did you look him up in the system?"

"Yes, he's been coming here at least five times a year for the last eight years. We've been in business for nine. The first year we weren't very sophisticated. It was more by happenstance than anything else."

"How's that?"

"A group of guys who used to work with Dad came out for a picnic. They started talking about the property and how it was perfect for a paintball camp. There was nothing else around like it. We did a little research and decided to give it a try."

"How many players were here yesterday?"

Jenna pulled a smart phone from the back pocket of her shorts. She worked the screen. "One hundred and twenty-eight registered and paid for."

"How does this work?"

Kenneally spoke up. "You can register in advance on the website. That requires payment with a credit card, but it guarantees you a spot in the action. The price includes lunch and a barbecue at the end of the day, along with the liquid refreshments. We have a crew of six who monitor the games and keep things going. A lot of people are repeat customers. Some companies use it as a team building exercise. Others have a tendency to gang up on the boss and blast away."

A smirk quickly crossed Donna's face. I chose to ignore it.

"So everyone registers and pays in advance?"

"Most of them. I think we had about a dozen who reserved and paid cash when they arrived Saturday morning."

"We're going to need a list of the players from yesterday."

Jenna bobbed her head, the braid swinging back around. "No problem. Do you want a print out or a digital copy?"

"Digital will work just fine. Detective Spears has a flash drive you can load it on. We're going to need whatever information you have. Names, addresses, phone numbers, email and methods of payment."

"I can give you the details from each account. It will also show how long they've been coming here and how often."

"We're also going to need information on all of your crew."

"That's not a problem," Jenna said.

"We appreciate the cooperation."

"Dad says if we help, you're more likely to let us reopen. We lost a lot of business today, since the sheriff won't let us do anything until you figure out who did it."

"Once we release the scene, you'll be able to resume operations."

Kenneally sat back and blew out a breath. "That's good news. We've got a couple of groups scheduled for tomorrow. I didn't want to cancel if we can help it."

I looked over my shoulder toward the barns. "What's over there?"

"Those are for storage. We keep the equipment in there, barricades, hay bales and whatever supplies we need."

I set my coffee mug on the table. "Mind if I take a look?"

"Not at all. I'll show you the layout."

As I got to my feet, I nodded at Jenna. "Thanks for the coffee. Detective Spears will go with you for those files."

Kenneally led me out to the barns. There were a couple of old pickup trucks inside, along with a number of wooden props in the form of houses and storefronts. He explained that the crew would place these around different areas on the property for that day's games. Players could use these as places to defend or capture. Details were crudely sketched on a whiteboard by the barbecue area each day. The variations kept people coming back. We circled back to the porch as Donna was coming out of the house. I thanked Kenneally for his help. He went back inside as we moved to the parking lot. In the distance, I could see the others were headed toward the vehicles.

"Got the files?"

"Oh yeah, and then some."

"The girl shared a few tidbits?"

"Morrissey hit on her a couple of times. She wasn't interested."

"Rich white men aren't her type?"

Donna flashed me a grin. "She'd prefer rich white women."

"Well, well, well."

"Don't feel bad, boss."

"She's too young for me anyway."

"Not for me."

"Didn't know you were rich."

That brought out another grin. "Working on it."

We waited by my car. Koz, Craddock and Laura joined us first. Suarez and the deputy seemed to be in a hurry.

"Nothing out of the ordinary in the south," Laura said.

"Same with the north," Koz said.

"Think we found something weird, Sarge," Suarez said. "Looks like some boot prints around the perimeter. I think they were made after the crime scene guys were here."

I looked at Craddock.

"I put two guys on guard here last night."

"Regular deputies?"

He shook his head. "I had to use reserves. My budget's already stretched pretty thin. Couldn't abandon the road patrols and afford to pay overtime."

"Chances are they stayed in their cars," Laura said.

"Where's Morrissey's car?"

"It's at the impound yard," Craddock said. "I wanted to make sure it was secured. We ran the plates, but nobody looked inside."

"Whatcha think, Chene?" Kozlowski asked.

"Take Atwater and Spears. Go check the vehicle and have it towed to our lot. We'll need an inventory of everything in it. If there's a phone, download the call logs and whatever other information you can find." I turned to Donna. "Start working that file. There may be a few people registered who don't exist. Break the players by territory. We're going to have to interview them all."

"Got it, boss," she said.

"I'll have Granger lead them to the impound yard," Craddock said.

Suarez had been silently watching. As the others dispersed he stepped forward. "You want to see these tracks, Sarge?"

"Yeah, let's see where they go."

Craddock went to talk with Kenneally and see if anyone was around last night. Suarez led the way. We stopped just at the western edge of the willow trees and he showed me the boot print. It was a hiking boot of some type, fairly new with a lot of tread. Suarez explained they noticed it on the way back, and followed them from a point in the middle of a meadow back toward the crime scene. We marched slowly forward, picking up the tracks evenly spaced. I got the sense whoever it was had been walking steadily, not running or jogging. I glanced back over my shoulder, trying to get a bearing on the willows.

"This is farther than we went before," Suarez said.

We moved into a cluster of trees. The sunlight was dappled here, not as bright as in the meadow. The grass was overgrown with weeds and shrubs. Something didn't feel right. Suarez moved another step in front of me, trying to squeeze between two fallen trees. I saw a glimmer of light reflect off something just ahead.

"No!"

Suarez plunged forward. I shoved him to the right. And just that quickly, I was knocked off my feet, flying backward.

Chapter Three

"Sarge! What the hell was that?"

I was on my back, trying to draw a breath. It took a moment. At that point Suarez was crouched beside me, his gun in one hand. He grabbed my shoulder with his free hand and yanked me upright.

"Take it easy, Suarez."

"I think you got shot, Sarge. You're bleeding!"

I pushed him away. My right arm felt okay. My back was making creaking noises, as if the vertebrae were moving back to where they belonged. I raised my left arm. There was a stream of blood flowing down the outside from the elbow to the wrist.

"Shit," I muttered.

"We need to get you to a hospital, Sarge." Suarez wasn't looking at me. Instead he was facing the way we'd been headed. He kept sweeping his gun back and forth.

I rolled to my knees and stood up. My chest was sore but it was no worse than a recent collision playing softball. Slowly rotating my head, I worked the kinks out of my neck. Suarez kept fidgeting beside me.

"Stow that gun before you hurt somebody."

"But Sarge…"

I forced an edge to my voice. "Put it away."

Reluctantly he holstered his weapon. I could sense eyes upon us, but didn't see anyone at first. Then a branch moved ever so slightly and a guy materialized from behind it. In his hands was an automatic rifle, pointed at the ground. He didn't say a word, just stood there. On my right I saw a faint flicker of movement and another guy stepped forward. He held a large caliber revolver. Both guys were in camouflage gear, complete with caps. Suarez jumped when he spotted them.

"Relax," I ordered. "We're with the State Police. We're investigating the homicide from last night."

The guy on the right nodded. "You're on private property. Kenneally's place ends about twenty yards behind you."

"No disrespect, but we were following tracks found at the scene."

He squinted at me. "You got ID?"

"Sure."

"Slow and easy."

I pulled out my shield and held it up. Suarez did the same. The guy with the revolver stepped a bit closer. He barely glanced at Suarez's creds but stared closely at mine. What might have been a grin crossed his face.

"Thought that was you." He tucked the revolver into a web holster and waved two fingers at the ground. The other guy slung the rifle over his shoulder. "Call the chief. We got company."

A minute later I heard the throaty rumble of a four wheeled yard cart. Just beyond the trees it rolled to a stop and a stocky fellow in fatigues jumped from the seat. He pushed through the branches as if they were mere raindrops in a spring shower. As he cleared the last tree he pulled a pair of sunglasses off and let them dangle from a cord around his neck. He had a barrel chest and short blonde hair that was going gray at the temples. His pale blue eyes studied me.

"Damn, Chene, maybe you ought to just join up. You're getting to be a regular visitor out here."

It took me a second to place him. "John Perryman, the militia guy. I thought this area looked familiar."

Perryman offered his hand. As we shook he grabbed my left wrist and carefully turned it over.

"You boys didn't bother to offer first aid?"

The two men shrugged. Apparently my injuries hadn't raised much concern.

"C'mon, Chene. We've got a first rate medic on duty today. Let's get you patched up." Perryman looked at Suarez for the first time. "Ace, bring the other officer along."

As I followed Perryman to a path through the trees I thought back to our previous meeting. It was in March when we were chasing the serial killer. There had been a deadly altercation with a new member of the militia group. I had come here to interview Perryman and his crew, trying to piece things together. The meeting had been a little tense, but ultimately helped us solve the case.

His mode of transportation had two seats and a small cargo bed. It was more of a yard buggy than a motorcycle. Conversation over the engine noise was impractical. We bounced across a meadow and headed for the old Quonset hut that served as the group's headquarters. Perryman slid the buggy to a stop right beside the door.

"Ace called for the medic."

"I appreciate that."

"Hey, if you hadn't tripped our wire, you wouldn't need a medic."

I didn't say anything as we stepped inside. Perryman studied me for a moment and a grin spread across his face.

"You didn't trip it. The other guy did. That's why you're the one got bloody."

"I saw the wire at the last second."

"And you pushed him out of the way. Hey, corpsman, here's the patient."

A slender young woman in fatigues pants and a tight black T shirt came forward. I wasn't sure if she was old enough to have finished college, let alone medical school. She had jet black hair pinned up at the back of her head. Hazel eyes appraised me. A hint of a smile played at her lips. She donned a pair of latex gloves. Gently she took my left hand and rotated it. She made a clucking noise with her tongue and teeth and tenderly probed the gash.

"You got a lot of dirt and debris in here. We need to get this cleaned out. Come over by the sink."

"Anything I can do?" Perryman asked.

"Bring me the device from the far cupboard."

"What's your name?" I asked.

"Emmie. Yours?"

"Chene."

"Nice to meet you, Chene."

"Same here. You really a doctor?"

She cranked up the smile a bit. "I am today. No worries. You got lucky. No broken bones, just a nasty laceration from that tree. The guys set those booby traps with enough tension, they could launch a satellite into orbit."

"It definitely launched me."

Perryman brought over a small square box and set it on the counter. He plugged it into an electrical outlet and stepped back. I watched Emmie open a compartment on the top and fill it with water. She switched it on and grabbed a small wand from the end. Immediately a steady stream of water pulsed out. She began to move it slowly down my arm from the elbow to the wrist, flushing out the cut. Small bits of debris dropped into the sink. Emmie took her time. Only after careful scrutiny did she switch off the machine. With some sterile gauze, she blotted the excess water from my arm. Then she picked up a pair of forceps and gently eased the flaps of skin back together. Emmie deftly put a few sterile strips of tape across the wound. She covered it all with another gauze pad and more tape. Satisfied, she stepped back and peeled off the latex gloves.

"Keep it dry for a day or two. Give it some time to heal and you'll be fine. There might be a scar."

Perryman snorted a laugh. "Don't think a little scar will bother Chene much."

I ignored him. "Thanks. I get the impression you've done this before."

Emmie drained the remaining water from the machine and unplugged it. As she was wrapping up the cord, I realized it wasn't a specialized medical device, but a home dental kit, the kind people use to blast food from between their teeth. She laughed lightly as she handed it to Perryman and pointed at the cupboard.

"We get a lot of scrapes and cuts up here. Guys getting carried away with training or maintenance. That's the most useful piece of equipment in our medical supplies."

Emmie handed me a pack of aspirin and a bottle of water. "You're all set, Chene. Take some aspirin a couple times a day. That may help with the aches and pains."

I shook hands with Emmie and thanked her again. She flashed me another smile. Perryman led me outside. We settled at a picnic table. Perryman chose a spot where he could lean back against the table and gaze out at the property. In the distance we could see Suarez walking between the two militia men. I sat beside him but shifted to study his face. It didn't seem to bother him.

"Those tracks led from your property to the crime scene and back. You know anything about that?"

"Yeah, those are mine. I saw the lights and the commotion last night. We had a team up here yesterday for exercises and most of them left around seven. I like to stay up here on the weekends. I got close and watched the action with binoculars. When they took the body away and everyone cleared out, I hiked down for a closer look."

"Anybody around that can verify that?"

Perryman shifted and looked right at me. "You remember that I'm a defense attorney by trade?"

"I know. So you understand the importance of having a solid alibi."

"There were fifty guys here training all day yesterday. I was right in the thick of it with them. You got time of death yet?"

"Not exact, but the body was found around seven."

"From what I hear, he was long dead by then."

"So you stayed here overnight?"

He nodded. "There's a room in the far corner. Nice big bed, a wardrobe closet, plenty of hot water. It can be very…tranquil."

"You alone for all this…tranquility?"

A chuckle escaped him. "Fuck you, Chene. Emmie was with me."

"Which explains the need for the hot water."

"It's a weekend thing. We're both single. We have some…common interests. She's up here a couple of times a month. Beyond that, we go our separate ways."

I shrugged. "She's a bit young for you."

"I don't have daddy issues. I'm just drawn to mature men."

Perryman and I looked over our shoulders. Emmie stood in the doorway, hands on her hips like a mother scolding a child. Something in our expressions must have gotten through. She gave her head a shake.

"Before you bother asking, yes, I was here all night. There are soiled clothes in the hamper in the back room and two towels by the shower. My body wash, shampoo and cosmetics are in the bath as well. You want to look?"

"No, I'll take your word for it. John's been straight with me before."

"Smart move." Then she turned on her heel and went back inside.

Perryman and I sat there quietly as the others approached. I had a lot to think about. No matter how many times I tried, there was no plausible reason for Perryman to be involved in Morrissey's killing. His curiosity with the crime scene made sense. I pushed to my feet as Suarez and the others stopped in front of us. Perryman stood up.

"Ace, grab one of the trucks and drive these officers back to Kenneally's place."

The guy with the revolver snapped off a salute. "Yes, sir."

We shook hands and went to the truck. Ten minutes later we were standing in the parking area behind my car. I popped the trunk and began to pull off my hiking boots. I glanced at Suarez. His fancy shoes were trashed. Mud and debris coated his slacks from the knees down. It looked like the material was snagged and torn just above the knee on the left leg.

"What now, Sarge?"

I knocked the mud off my hiking boots and set them inside a plastic crate in the trunk then pulled on the motorcycle boots I'd been wearing earlier. There was a box beside the crate. It held other supplies, including emergency crime scene equipment. Suarez was about four inches shorter than my five foot ten, so I knew none of my gear would fit him. But there was a clear plastic rain poncho inside. I dug it out and handed it to him.

"Put that on my seat, so you don't slime the upholstery. Dump your shoes in the trunk."

Grumpily he accepted the poncho and worked his feet out of the shoes. I watched as he struggled to walk across the gravel to the passenger door. I slammed the trunk lid and got behind the wheel. Suarez was silent all the way back to the post. I didn't feel much like talking, considering the various angles of the investigation. And I didn't want to cheer him up. That wasn't my job. Neither of us spoke until we were parked in the lot.

"I'm sorry, Sarge. I was unprepared today."

"As Cantrell would say, 'sorry don't feed the

bulldog'. You've got people that need to know you'll have their back. Preparations are a big part of that."

He nodded and reached for the door handle.

"I'm not done. You were told two weeks ago to build a go-bag. Where is it?"

Suarez's eyes were locked on the floor. "I forgot."

"Well, that's your assignment for the afternoon. Get out of here. There's an army surplus place a few miles south on Gratiot. You saw what would have been useful today. Go build two bags."

"Why two?"

I bit back the response of 'because I said so'. Cantrell had recruited this guy from the Detroit PD. He must have some smarts. But maybe they never got involved in cases where they got their shoes dirty.

"One bag goes in your car, just in case you're on route to a scene and get redirected. The other goes in your locker here. Keep in mind that not every crime happens in the city or during the day. It wouldn't hurt to have a change of clothes available too. Leave the Armani at home."

"Got it. I won't let you down again, Sarge."

"I hope not."

He retrieved his muddy shoes from the trunk and left. I shook out the poncho, folded it and stuck it back in the box. Kozlowski was waiting when I came inside. He followed me down to the break room. We each got a mug of coffee. He hooked a thumb at my arm.

"What the hell happened to you?"

"Ran into an old friend. What did you find with the car?"

"A possible gold mine of crap. Laura found his smart phone on the console. There was a briefcase in the trunk, along with clothes, shoes and some file boxes. We had it towed to the lab. They will inventory everything else tomorrow and get us a list. I kept the briefcase. Laura's working on the phone. She's making a list of contacts and calls."

I leaned against the counter and sipped my coffee. Koz had something else on his mind. After working together for so long, we knew each other's moves well.

"How late are you going to push it today?"

"Got a date?"

He flashed me a wide grin. "Damn, Chene, I've always got a date. But it wasn't me I was asking about. Today's Laura's first wedding anniversary."

"What the hell is she doing here?"

"You know how it is. Pappy calls, we come running."

"She could have told him she had plans. He'd cut her some slack."

"Yeah, but we both know better."

Cantrell can be a real taskmaster. Once we get a major case like this, he prefers to keep everyone involved, sort of the 'all hands on deck' mode. Since this was our first day on the case, some leeway would be appropriate.

"Did she have anything set?"

"Nothing specific. I know she likes the water. They talked about going on one of those riverboat cruises."

I dug out my phone, scanned through the directory and made one call. When it was done I nodded to Kozlowski. He made a call, kept it short and sweet. Then he asked again about my arm. I spent the next twenty minutes filling him in on the discovery of John Perryman and his militia group at the adjoining property. Satisfied, we moved out to the bullpen. Laura and Donna were at their desks, focused on the computers. Laura was about to fill us in when the desk sergeant escorted a guy into the room.

Laura scrambled to her feet. "What are you doing here?"

The guy did one of those shrugs where he raised his palms. "I was given specific instructions to, and I'm quoting, 'get my scrawny ass over here immediately or suffer dire consequences'. There were a few other comments, but that was the gist of it."

Laura looked at Kozlowski. He tried to look innocent and nodded toward me.

"What's going on?" Donna asked.

Laura introduced her husband, Eric. He shook hands with us, while keeping an arm around Laura's waist. I handed him an envelope.

"Get out of here. Take that to the Grosse Pointe Yacht Club. Ask for Judge Larabee. He and his wife are old friends. They have a nice cabin cruiser there. Once you're onboard, they will take you for a relaxing ride along the lake. The club has a gourmet chef and a four-star restaurant. You'll have dinner there."

"Why?" Laura was skeptical.

"Even Cantrell would give you time off for your anniversary. Get out of here. We'll meet in the morning."

"Did you bring the gear?" Koz asked Eric.

He nodded. "Shorts, tank tops and her bathing suit. Might as well get some sun while we're out on the lake."

"Get out of here," I repeated.

Laura and Eric practically ran out the door. Koz

chuckled and dropped his bulk into his chair. I leaned a hip on my desk. Donna sat back and crossed her arms on her chest, flashing a wide grin.

"That was a sweet thing to do, boss."

I waved it off. "The timing was right. How's your search going?"

"I transferred the file to a spreadsheet. Then I broke it into zip codes, so we can narrow it down by territory. I'm also doing a name search on the server for any criminal histories. We might get lucky and get a hit."

"I would not be surprised if we get a few names that don't exist," Koz said.

"What are you working on?" I asked him.

"I'm going to take over from what Laura was doing on the phone. We'll need to see if any of those contacts match up with the players from yesterday."

"Good idea."

"What about you, boss?"

"I think it's time to pay a visit to the widow."

Chapter Four

Donna and I drove to the Grosse Pointe Park address for Morrissey. The house was a miniature castle, probably built in the late thirties. It was three stories high, with a gabled roof and lots of leaded glass windows. The block was tree-lined, with oaks and maples towering beyond the rooflines. We parked at the curb and studied the dwelling for a moment before exiting the car.

"Check out the garage, boss. I'd swear that's a classic Camaro ragtop in there. Right next to the Jaguar."

The two-car garage was separate from the house, set back toward the rear of the lot, at least fifty yards from the street. "How old are Morrissey's kids?"

Donna checked her notebook. "Dale, a boy, is sixteen. Janice is fourteen."

"All they need is Scruffy the dog to complete the All-American family portrait."

As I spoke the side door of the house banged open and a gangly boy stepped out and turned toward the garage. Behind him bounced a large, furry dog.

"I didn't know you were psychic," Donna said as she opened her door.

We went up the front steps and knocked discreetly. I was expecting a relative or maybe a neighbor to respond. But I recognized the woman framed in the doorway from the publicity photos I'd studied a few hours ago.

"Mrs. Morrissey, I'm Sergeant Chene and this is Detective Spears with the Michigan State Police. We're part of the team conducting the investigation into your husband's death. I know this is difficult, but if we could ask you some questions—"

She frowned in annoyance. "I was expecting someone hours ago. The governor assured me this was being taken care of. I also spoke with a man named Cantrell. I don't appreciate being kept waiting."

"My apologies." I didn't think it was necessary to explain where we'd been.

She fluttered a hand at me. "Come in."

Mrs. Morrissey ushered us into a formal living room and gestured toward a pair of stiff upholstered chairs. I pocketed my sunglasses inside the sport coat I had slipped on when getting out of the car. Donna tucked hers into the V neck of her blouse. When we approached the house, she had switched on the digital recorder tucked into her jacket pocket. This was Donna's first interview with a victim's family. I wanted to see how well she'd follow my lead and what observations she made.

As the widow settled herself onto one end of the sofa, I let my eyes sweep over the room. There was a plush area rug by the sofa in a soft rose color. Beyond the rug hardwood floors gleamed with multiple layers of wax. Pale gray marble surrounded the fireplace hearth and the two columns that supported the mantel. The plaster walls had been recently painted an eggshell white, then touched up with a sponge to set an unusual pattern, accenting the color of the carpet. Other than the sofa and two upholstered chairs, there was only a teak coffee table, strategically placed in the center of the room.

Above the mantel was a family portrait, probably done in this very room by a professional photographer. The parents were on the couch, flanked by the two kids. Both children favored his wife. According to the details I'd reviewed earlier, Colleen Morrissey was thirty-eight, the high school sweetheart of the victim. She had worked with him during the early years, slaving together to get the business up and running. Morrissey had named the company Vagabond Enterprises. Once it began to flourish, she stayed home to raise the kids. While Donna made some comforting comments to put the widow at ease, I took a good look at her.

Colleen was about five four and if she weighed more than a hundred and ten pounds, I'm the greatest detective since Holmes. Auburn hair with some blonde highlights fell to her shoulders, curling gently behind her ears. Her green eyes were bloodshot and puffy. She was wearing skinny jeans and a sleeveless white silk blouse that was so sheer, it left little to the imagination. I could see the pattern of a lacy bra that scooped up her breasts and put them on display. Her feet were in expensive sandals, little more than ornate straps of leather around the heel and across top of her foot. The toes were exposed, with bright red polish on the nails.

Before I could begin my questions, a dark haired man stepped into the room. He moved to the sofa and sat beside the widow. "Sorry, I had to take that call. Are you the cops handling the investigation?"

"Detectives Chene and Spears. And you are?"

"I'm Nicholas Trent, a friend of the family."

Trent was probably ten years younger than the widow. The dark hair was rapidly receding. He was about five foot eight and on the border between fit and stocky When he sat on the sofa, he perched close beside Colleen, so that their thighs brushed together.

"How long have you been a family friend?"

He seemed to preen at the question. "For years. We've always been close."

"So you know about Mr. Morrissey's activities?"

"Of course."

I turned my attention back to the widow. "We need a lot of information about your husband. Did many people know he would be at the war games yesterday?

"I don't know about anyone at work, but the family knew he was going. He enjoyed it. A chance to go out and shoot people." She gave her head a negative shake in disgust. "Kyle was a big kid. He was always playing games. He worked hard, but once he became successful, he started doing all the things he couldn't do as a child."

"Like what?"

"Hunting, the war games, fancy trips. He bought that old muscle car. Originally he was going to do the work himself, but he didn't have the time or the talent. So he had someone else rebuild it. But he loved to drive it around."

"What does this have to do with anything?" Trent interrupted.

I glanced at Donna. She nodded and cleared her throat. "We have to learn as much as possible about Mr. Morrissey in order to conduct our investigation. The more we know, the better the chances are of finding out who was responsible."

"You should be focusing on the idiots who played that silly game," Trent said, "rather than bothering Colleen with this nonsense."

"Where were you yesterday?" Donna asked.

Trent snapped back as if she'd struck him. "What does that have to do with anything? Certainly you don't think I could kill Kyle?"

"Right now, we're not ruling anyone out," I said. "So answer Detective Spears's question. Where were you yesterday?"

A flush of color dotted his cheeks. I could see a sheen of perspiration across his brow. Apparently Trent was unaccustomed to being put on the spot.

"Well, I was here in town all day. I played tennis in the morning. I don't remember exactly what time we got done. Then I did some errands and had a quiet dinner at home."

"Anyone with you for that quiet dinner?" Donna asked.

"Well, I, no, that is…"

"So you don't have an alibi?"

I watched Trent get more flustered before raising my hand. Donna didn't sit back and gloat. She remained perched on the edge of her chair. I returned my attention to Colleen Morrissey.

"You get the idea. We need to know everything we can about Kyle. His business, the people he worked with, the people he socialized with, his schedule of activities, what he liked to do with his free time. Anything and everything may be vital to this case. What we really need is information. Are you still involved in the company?"

Colleen pushed off the couch and began to pace the

room. We waited in silence until she made a complete circuit and paused in front of me. I watched as she steadied herself and assumed the superhero position, hands on her hips, head tilted up with a trace of defiance. Her eyes locked on mine.

"I haven't seen the financial reports for this quarter, but as far as I know, everything is very profitable. Kyle sold off a few of the theaters but still has six throughout the area, for nostalgia sake if nothing else. The bookstores continue to grow." Behind her Trent cleared his throat. She snapped her left hand in his direction to silence him, but her attention remained on me.

"Any conquests on the corporate level? A new venture or project that your husband was working on?"

She didn't hesitate. "No. The only thing Kyle has been occupied with lately is the Glamour Train. The fourth anniversary run is set for this Wednesday."

Donna picked up on my puzzled expression. "The private railroad out in Oakland County. Mr. Morrissey staged a fundraiser every year. Boutiques and designers have models wearing the latest fashion on board the dinner train. Patrons buy tickets for the evening, have a gourmet meal, enjoying the train ride along the countryside and the fashion show. There is usually an auction after dinner. Very upscale."

I shrugged toward Mrs. Morrissey. "I'm not much into fashion or the society pages. This is a fundraising event?"

"No need to apologize. The Glamour Train was one of Kyle's pet projects. All of the clothing and the meals were donated, and all the proceeds from the auction went to several charities." Colleen seemed to warm slightly at my discomfort.

"Is there someone at the office we should talk with tomorrow? We'll have to interview all of the people who worked for Kyle."

Colleen shifted her feet and maintained her stance. "I will be going to the office at nine tomorrow morning to meet with the staff. I can instruct them all to cooperate. If you'd like, you can sit in on the meeting."

"I'll do that."

I turned my gaze to Trent. Donna picked up on it and asked him for his contact information. He made a show of pulling out a thick leather case and handing her a business card printed on heavy stock. He seemed to hold onto his end of the card for an extra beat. Donna began to ask him quietly about his work. For a moment I watched her manipulate him. Colleen Morrissey remained standing, studying me.

"Would you mind if we walked around a bit? I could use some air," I said.

"Not at all."

She led us outside. In the driveway was the Camaro, partially covered by a cloud of soap bubbles. Colleen met my eyes briefly, then strolled toward the backyard. Donna and Nicholas Trent followed, continuing their conversation. I could hear just enough to know she was charming him. Donna is about five foot six with short blonde hair. She's not thin like a fashion model, but has plenty of curves that draw the eye. I knew she was leading Trent on to gain information. So I followed Colleen Morrissey into the backyard. An elevated wooden deck ran behind the house, ending with a gazebo. Several large rose bushes were visible beside the deck. Donna efficiently guided

Mrs. Morrissey toward the flowers. She was also going to talk with Morrissey's daughter, no doubt with the widow present. I moved toward the Chevy.

The hose came to life as I approached, chasing the soap from the hood. Whether intentional or not, I got a blast in the face as well.

"Dale!" The edge in Colleen's voice was evident, even from that distance.

The boy dropped the hose. On the driveway were a couple of worn bath towels that he planned to use on the car. Sheepishly, he extended one toward me. Sprawled on the ground in the shade of the garage was the dog, an Alaskan husky with beautiful black and white markings.

"Sorry, sir." His voice was higher than I expected.

"No harm done. Everything I own is drip dry." I wiped my face on the cloth and blotted my shirt. "That's quite a ride. Sixty-eight?"

Dale was gently washing the side panels with a chamois. "Sixty-seven. My dad and I found it at a scrapyard a few years ago. We were going to rebuild it together, but it was too much for us. So he sent it to a shop for the heavy work. Once we got it back, it's been my job to wash it every week."

"How's she handle?"

"Like a dream." He flashed a smile filled with youthful enthusiasm. "You ought to see it blow the modern production cars off the line at a green light. I'd swear Dad smoked the tires a couple of times."

"You drive it much?"

"Only out to Metro Park a couple of times and up Woodward for the Dream Cruise." His smile faded. "Are you really with the cops?"

"State police." I introduced myself and shook his soapy hand.

"Jefferson Chene? That's your name? Isn't that an intersection?"

I gave my shoulders a little shrug. "What's in a name?"

"You quote Shakespeare too?"

I was surprised he caught that. "I like to read. And call me Jeff. Or Chene. I'm not nearly as formal as the rest of the squad. Were you and your dad pretty close?"

He rinsed off the last of the suds before answering. "Yeah. He made it a point of spending a lot of time with me and my kid sister. Dad never got along with his father, his parents divorced when he was five or something. Guess he wanted to set a better example than his old man did."

I used the towel to dry off the vinyl top. Dale picked up a clean chamois and began working the hood, drawing the water off. After a moment, he continued talking.

"We did a lot of father-son stuff. Movies. We were always going to see the Tigers, Lions, and Red Wing games. Neither one of us ever really cared about basketball. But we'd hit the classic car shows and concerts a lot. Played tennis and golf. Jogged once in a while. Dad's a health nut. He's really into physical fitness. We even read a lot of the same books and talked about them."

"Sounds like you two were pretty tight."

Dale wrung out the chamois and began drying the front fenders. "I think we were closer than Dad and Jan were. That's more of a mother-daughter bond. Not that they didn't get along well, but it wasn't the same, you know?"

"I get the idea."

He continued working quickly over the painted surfaces, pulling the water off the car with steady strokes. I dabbed at the taillights, letting him ramble on a bit more about the family.

"Do you know who killed my dad yet?" There was a hopeful look on his face that made me take a moment before answering. He'd been acting very grown-up during our conversation, but deep down, he was still a kid.

"We're just getting started. There aren't any witnesses. At least, no one who's stepped forward yet." I handed him the towel and watched him drape it over the fence beside the chamois he'd been using.

Dale walked into the garage. The dog raised his head off his paws and watched Dale's movement. The kid emerged a minute later and dropped several ice cubes on the dog. Two bottles of iced tea dangled from the fingers of his right hand. He passed one over.

"Didn't think you'd take a beer," he said, with a trace of a smile.

"Never on duty." We popped the tops and drank some tea. I noticed Donna and Mrs. Morrissey were no longer in the yard or on the deck.

"You know anybody with a grudge against your dad?"

"Not everybody loved him, but I don't know anyone who would go to that extreme. It's not like he was some slum landlord or drug dealer. He gave a lot back to the community. Charities and stuff."

I sipped the tea. "Yeah. I heard about the fashion train."

Dale grinned and shook his head slightly. "Glamour train. But that was just one of many. He had fundraiser nights at the movies and the bookstores all the time. Shelters for abused women. Drug awareness. Food banks. Soup kitchens. Toys for tots with the Marines at Christmas time. He didn't just pick one charity. He spread it around."

"Know much about his business? Did he ever talk with you, kind of man to man, about some of his corporate dealings? Buying up new properties, selling off a theater, anything like that?"

We were leaning with our backs against the fence, facing the Camaro. As he spoke, I swiveled my gaze so I could study him. The Husky, having chewed up the ice cubes, was sitting beside him now. Absently, Dale reached down with his free hand and scratched the dog between the ears.

"Once in a while, he'd talk about things with work. He knew I was interested. Seems like every project he got behind did really well. Like how things worked out with the theaters. God, he loved the movies. If he had his way, Dad would spend six hours a day watching movies in the theater, a barrel of popcorn in one arm and a pack of candy in his pocket. Didn't matter what kind of movies either. It could be action, mysteries, comedies, thrillers or even musicals. Just—movies. If it was a new movie and based on a book, he'd read the book after he saw the flick, see how closely they stuck to the original story line. Weird, huh?"

"I do the same thing myself sometimes, if I really like the movie. How about the people who worked for your dad? Anybody he didn't get along with? Anyone you know who left the company recently?"

Dale shook his head. "Nah. That kind of stuff I never heard about. Most of the people at the office have been with him a long time. At the stores and the theaters, the managers stay, but there's always a turnover of people working the registers and the concession stands. It's not exactly a career job."

"It's unusual that key employees stay with one company for a long time nowadays. So he must have found a way to keep good people."

"Dad was always big on loyalty. I heard him talking at one of the theaters one night, offering a manager a bonus for her efforts to clean the place up and cut down on turnover. Like I said, the permanent people usually stayed. He told me it was worth it to pay them well. I guess they were happy."

He turned to look beyond me. Coming up the driveway were two teen-age girls, wearing shorts, tank tops and sandals. They stopped in the shade at the corner of the house. At the same time Donna stepped out the side door and headed over to join us. I introduced her to Dale.

"You two partners?"

"Part of a team," Donna said. "It's called Squad Six. There are five investigators, one captain. We all work together."

"So I guess I'll be seeing more of you," Dale said, his eyes on the waiting girls.

"Count on it," Donna said. We headed down to the street. She inhaled deeply several times as we walked down the driveway to the car. "Nothing like the scent of testosterone in the air."

****

I parked around the corner where we'd left

Donna's car. This late on a Sunday afternoon, I planned on cutting the others loose. We had made some progress for the first day on what promised to be a very complex case. Everyone knew we'd be buried in the details going forward. We got out and I leaned against the hood of my Pontiac. Donna rested a hip on the trunk of her car.

"Observations?"

"Since you asked, I think Trent and the widow have been keeping each other company in more ways than one."

"Tomorrow I want you to check out his alibi. Go to the club he was at and ask around. See if anyone can tell you who his tennis partner was. Get the details."

"What about his quiet dinner at home?" Donna made quotation marks in the air with her fingers.

"Talk to the neighbors. Pull the information on the widow's Jaguar."

"She didn't mention if she was playing tennis with him."

I considered that for a minute. "Dale said his dad was into tennis, so it's possible Trent was one of his regular opponents. Colleen Morrissey strikes me more as a swimmer than a tennis player. But that club caters to both."

Trent stated he played at the Grosse Pointe Hunt Club. This was a key focal point for many in the elite suburbs, with everything from horses to tennis to swimming and camps and a top flight chef. If Trent could afford the dues, he wouldn't hesitate to use the facilities frequently.

Donna was grinning at me. "She certainly wasn't dressed as the grieving widow. So you don't think she has the body type for tennis?"

"Like I said, she looks like a swimmer."

My phone rang. Kozlowski had news. I switched it to speaker and laid it on the hood. Donna leaned forward.

"I finished the contact list and the call log then ran it against the registrations from yesterday's games. No connection."

"That would have been too easy," I said.

"Yeah, but there was something else you might find interesting."

"Such as?"

Kozlowski chuckled. "I just sent you a text. Check it out."

I flipped to the message. There were no words, but a photo was attached. We watched as the image filled the screen. It took a moment for it to download. What greeted us was the profile of a well-endowed young blonde woman, naked from the waist up. This was definitely not Colleen Morrissey.

"There are a dozen pictures on this phone like that. And no duplicates that I've seen," Koz said.

"Are you looking at faces?" Donna asked with a grin.

"I am carefully scrutinizing each photo."

"Apparently our victim wasn't the golden boy the press would have you believe," I said. "You're sure he took those photos?"

"Either he did or the girls were sending him selfies. A couple of these have shelves of books in the background. Maybe they were taken at some of his stores."

I rocked back and leaned against her car. Donna

gave me a questioning look.

"Twelve of them?"

"Yes, unless there are more encrypted," Koz said. "I had a feeling you'd want to show these to Pappy in the morning, so I'm including the photos in the report. I'll print up a couple. He'd be pissed if I ran them all through the color printer."

"Maybe photography was just a hobby," Donna said.

"There is one more thing I found."

"What's that?"

"Morrissey's phone is synched to his business email account. There was a strange one in the spam folder that caught my eye."

Donna and I exchanged a glance. "What did it say?"

"The subject line said 'today' with a question mark. The message read 'Your turn to die.' Kozlowski said quietly. "The sender was gibberish, just a string of what looks like random numbers."

"You tip the geeks?"

"Cyber squad has been notified. No one's on duty, but I left both a text and a voice message for Yekovich to see what they can find."

"Anything else you can do there?"

"Nothing comes to mind, boss."

"Secure everything and take off. We'll brief Cantrell early and get started on the interviews."

"That's a lot of people to get to. You got a plan?"

"Always. See you in the morning."

Chapter Five

Donna headed out. I leaned against the Pontiac's hood, letting an idea dance across my mind. One phone call confirmed it. I headed home with a quick stop along the way. Being in a relationship was a new experience for me. There have been a few others in the past, but nothing that lasted more than a month. Maybe I was changing.

Simone's car was in the driveway. She was in the tiny backyard, relaxing on one of the wooden deck chairs that I keep meaning to paint. Simone was facing west, enjoying the sunshine. Her eyes were hidden behind large oval sunglasses. There was a mischievous smile playing across her face.

"I hope it's okay that I stayed. I wasn't sure if you'd be back early or not, but it's more peaceful here than at the apartment."

"I don't mind at all."

She was wearing a gold tank top and a pair of denim shorts. Her slender legs were bare. I settled into the chair beside her.

"You have some very friendly neighbors."

"I do?"

Her laughter was light and musical. "Yes, you do. A lot of people going out on their boats, up and down the canal. Everyone waves and toots the horn."

"Two things you need to understand. One, when a

boat is leaving a canal like this and entering the lake, they are supposed to sound the horn to alert other boaters. There's only one more house at the end of the street, which puts us pretty close to the lake. So they may not have been blowing the horn at you."

A smirk crossed her face. She pushed up out of the chair and came over, settling onto my lap and sliding one arm around my neck.

"And two?"

"Two is I'll bet most of people waving were guys admiring a beautiful woman."

The kiss that followed was slow and tender. "Good answer."

Without getting into too much detail, I told her about the investigation. There was a flicker of concern when she noticed the bandage on my arm. That faded when I assured her it was nothing serious. We talked in generalities. Simone could find out most of the information from the media. After a while we moved into the kitchen. She boosted herself up onto the counter as I began putting things together for dinner.

"Have I ever mentioned how much I enjoy it when you cook for me?"

"No, but I don't remember any complaints. Hungry?"

"Starved. I was going to give you one more hour. If you hadn't called, I was going to head home and pick up a hot dog along the way."

"A hot dog?" Skepticism filled my voice. "Are you telling me I could get away with feeding you hot dogs?"

She swung a foot at me. "No, you can't. I'd eat a hot dog from Lafayette's if we were going to a baseball game or downtown for something. But if you're cooking, I expect great fare. So what are you making anyway?"

"It's shrimp with some fresh veggies on angel hair pasta."

She groaned in anticipation. "What can I do to help?"

While I put the dinner together, she took half a loaf of French bread, split it and sprinkled olive oil and herbs down the center and put it in the oven on high heat. Then she cleaned some fresh berries and grapes to accompany the meal. When the pasta was ready, I put it on two plates and garnished it with quarters of fresh avocado. Simone handed me a bottle of Reisling to complete the meal. We ate quietly, enjoying the fresh air from the lake.

"I have to go to work tomorrow," Simone said softly as we cleaned up the kitchen. I noticed how comfortable we'd become, moving together.

"Traffic can be rough in the morning." I knew it would take her about an hour to get to her office from here.

She dried her hands on a towel as the last pan was put away. "I'll need a good night's sleep. It's going to be a busy week."

Twilight arrived. We didn't have the lights on in the house. Shadows were quickly filling up the rooms.

"You could spend the night. I have to be at the post early for a briefing."

"I don't have clothes here. I'd have to swing by the apartment anyway to get dressed. I can't show up for work in shorts and a tank top."

"I could wake you before I leave, so you'd have plenty of time."

"Do you want me to stay?" Her voice was even softer now. She was right beside me, her eyes on the floor. I was straining to catch every word.

I turned her to me and tilted her chin up. "Yes, I want you to stay."

"Then why didn't you just say so?"

"Stay the night."

"But I want to get a good night's sleep."

"Then I guess it's time for bed."

****

Six-thirty Monday morning I was the second one at the post. Cantrell was in his office, feet propped on top of his garbage can, a cup of cold black coffee on the desk. A thin trail of smoke snaked its way above his head and out the casement window behind him. Cantrell raised his eyes to meet mine as I set a fresh cup of coffee before him.

"Obliged, Chene."

"Any time, Pappy. You finish the reports?"

"Ah did. This un here has all the makin's of a pooch screwin'."

"No argument there."

Late last night, I'd written a quick summary from home and updated the report. Kozlowski had started the process before he left, providing a detailed list of all the contacts on Morrissey's cell phone and the call logs. He'd printed out two of the photos and cataloged the rest as well. There was no video footage. Koz also included Donna's spreadsheet with the war game participants.

"Y'all got a plan?"

"I do. Figured we'd go over it with the squad."

Cantrell poked a gnarled finger at me. "How did

Suarez do?"

There was no mention of Suarez in the summary. I explained what happened at the scene. Just to keep him in the loop, I also mentioned Laura's early departure for her anniversary. Cantrell chuckled and shook his head.

"That girlie is dedicated. Ah woulda given her the day off."

"Yeah, but she doesn't want special treatment. None of us do."

"Whatcha think of this Suarez kid?"

It was an effort to keep the disgusted look from my face. "We'll see how he does today. Are you sure about this guy?"

"Ah am. Ah recruited him. Give'm time, Chene."

This was something to keep in mind. Cantrell was a good judge of character. Since being named to lead the squad, he'd recruited all of us over the years. I had recommended Donna Spears, after she'd been instrumental in helping us bring down a serial killer back in the spring. Cantrell knew her. Sometimes I got the feeling that she was already in consideration. Bottom line was it didn't matter. In the background I could hear the rest of the team arriving. Cantrell grabbed the cup of coffee and headed for the conference room.

The others were gathered around the table. Cantrell took his customary seat at the head. Laura and Kozlowski were on his right. Donna and Suarez on the left. I was across from him. We always sat this way. Once everyone was settled in, Cantrell got down to business. He wasn't one to waste time.

"Y'all thinkin' about them girlies on his phone?"

"We could meet any of those women in our

investigation. It may lead to some very interesting questions," Laura said.

"True dat."

Kozlowski flashed a grin. "I'll send everyone those photos from Morrissey's phone. It's better than printing out copies."

"So what's the plan, Pappy?" Donna asked.

Cantrell dipped his head in my direction. "Run it, Chene."

All eyes shifted to me. "We've got over a hundred warriors from the game that need to be interviewed. And there is Morrissey's employees, his attorney, any business associates, banker, accountant and neighbors. We need to move fast, but there's no way we can easily conduct everything ourselves."

"We might have a break there," Kozlowski said. "I noticed a number of the guys from the war games place had a code number on their account. Kenneally confirmed my hunch. There are forty-five who worked at the same company. It's a manufacturing place out in Sterling Heights."

"Good work. That makes this a little easier." I looked across the table at Cantrell. "What's our chance of drafting Squad Five for a little help?"

"It be good. Naughton likes his boys sharp. Whatcha got in mind?"

Squad Five was our version of a bomb squad. The crew specialized in weapons and explosives but they were known to assist with other investigations.

"Have them cover the interviews with the players from the war games. We can brief them on the situation. Naughton's good at asking questions. He knows how to do it right. And how to dig."

"That shop will take a good part of the day," Koz said.

"No doubt. I'll suggest he send three guys up there. The rest can begin with other players and work off the list. We'll want them to match identification."

"All them warriors for real?" Pappy asked.

Kozlowski shook his head. "Seven people registered don't show up in the databases. Probably used a fake name. Paid cash for the games. One of them may be our killer, but maybe not."

"Why would someone use a fake ID at a paintball game?" Donna asked.

Koz shrugged. "Maybe they weren't old enough. Kenneally's games are for 21 and over. He provides beer. Maybe it was a couple of kids looking for a kick and a few brews. Or maybe it was someone who didn't want their spouse to know how they spent their Saturday."

"Of the fake names, were they all guys?" Laura asked.

"No, two of them were women. What's the difference?"

She flashed a wicked smile. "There's a lot of property up there. Lots of wide open spaces and some areas that are far from view. I'm thinking it's a rendezvous."

"What are you talking about?" Suarez asked.

"If you're having an affair, maybe you can't afford a motel room or you don't want to be seen going into one in the middle of the day. Or you don't trust anyone with your secret. So you find a spot like this. You both show up, using a different name. You pay the fee, wander away from the crowd and find a place where you can get busy."

"That's a different approach," Koz said with a grin.

Laura playfully slapped his arm. "Like you've never had sex outdoors."

"Not with that many people milling around. But it could raise the excitement level with the possibility that someone can see you."

"Exactly. I'll bet they even have camouflage lingerie."

Pappy waved a gnarled hand at the group. "Y'all git on with it."

I spelled out the rest of the day's activities. Kozlowski would meet with Naughton and the Squad Five team. Laura and Donna were going to the Grosse Pointe Hunt Club to interview staff and guests. I wanted them to confirm Nicholas Trent's alibi. Then they were going to cover Morrissey's neighbors. I would take Suarez with me to meet with Morrissey's employees at their headquarters. Kozlowski would follow up with the coroner on the autopsy. He also wanted to take another look at the car and the contents.

"Meet back here at six. We'll debrief and figure out a plan for tomorrow."

"Y'all got plenty to do," Cantrell said. "Don't forget the governor be watching our asses on this one."

I pushed away from the table. "Let's roll."

****

Vagabond Enterprises main offices were not what I expected. Rather than be situated in a sterile office building in a high rent district like Birmingham, Morrissey had opted to place his headquarters on the second floor of a renovated historic building near downtown Ferndale. We got to the office a few minutes early. Suarez had been quiet on the ride out. Now he paced the small lobby area. I stood across from the reception area, reading a framed article on Kyle Morrissey. Exactly at nine, the inner door swung open. Colleen Morrissey posed in the doorway. She was dressed in black today. A demure black dress, with a thick gold necklace. Her hair was swept back and held in place with a gold clip. She was wearing a touch of makeup.

I introduced Suarez. Colleen gave him a curt nod.

"I suppose we should get started."

"If you're ready."

She led us down a hall to a small conference room. The room was dominated by a solid table. It was a beautiful mahogany piece that was almost chest high on me. The table gleamed with polish. I could see my reflection in the grain. Two men and two women were in attendance. For some reason I expected more people to be there. Colleen Morrissey stood at the head of the table. There were no chairs in the room. Suarez and I drifted to the other end.

Colleen cleared her throat and placed her palms on the table. "These are the detectives who are handling the investigation into Kyle's death. I want each of you to answer their questions and cooperate with them completely. Give them any information they want.

"In the interim, I will assume control of the operations. Any matters that you would have discussed with Kyle, you can bring to me. I will be utilizing his office and getting reacquainted with the business."

I watched all four heads nod solemnly. Colleen lifted her chin and glared at me. Maybe she was used to others backing down or knowing their place. I rested a palm lightly on the table.

"The detectives will use the conference room to interview you. I'm assuming they prefer to meet with you individually."

"That's right. This may take a while."

The glare amped up in intensity. "Take as much time as you need. But do your job. Find his killer."

With that she spun on her heel and stormed out. Everyone watched her leave then turned slowly to look at me.

"I'm Chene and this is Detective Suarez. Let's get names and titles for starters."

Suarez had placed his digital recorder on the table when we first entered. I pulled a thin notebook and a pen from my jacket. I pointed at the guy closest to me. Suarez mirrored my moves.

"I'm Steve York, Chief Financial Manager." He was short and stocky with a close shave and a rapidly receding hairline. A pack of cigarettes was visible in the pocket of his white Oxford shirt. York shifted and rested his thick forearms on the table.

I nodded at the lady beside him.

"Valerie Mann. I am the Chief Operations Manager for the theaters." She was a petite woman, even smaller than Colleen Morrissey. She had long jet black hair worn loosely that draped over her shoulders. Valerie Mann was wearing a pale yellow summer dress. One hand toyed with a beaded necklace. She gestured at the other woman.

"Tracy Wright. I'm the office manager. Basically I support all the others, schedule appointments, file documents, and cover the office when everyone else is gone." She was probably the oldest of the bunch. I guessed she was in her mid-fifties. Her blonde hair had thick streaks of gray. She wore navy slacks and a white blouse.

The last one was a young man who looked fresh out of college. "I'm Gary Andreski, I manage all the marketing and advertising for the operations." He was wearing a dark blue shirt and a red necktie. He was very nervous.

"What's the layout here?" I asked.

The others exchanged a glance. Valerie Mann spoke up. "These are the executive offices. Other than Tracy, we each have a private office. This used to be a series of loft apartments. Kyle bought them all and knocked out the connecting walls. We manage all the businesses from here."

"You three go about your duties. We'll start with Ms. Mann."

The others quickly left the conference room. Suarez looked at me but kept quiet. I waited until the door was closed. Valerie Mann retained her composure. She stayed in place with the window overlooking the street behind her. As she folded her hands on the table in front of her I noticed her nails were adorned with a French manicure.

"By the way," she said quietly, "it's Mrs. Mann."

"Congratulations. How long have you been married?"

"Four years next month." She wiggled her left hand, flashing a small diamond engagement ring and a thin gold wedding band.

"Let's start with your career. How long have you worked for Morrissey?"

"I've been with Kyle for eleven years. I started out

on the concession stand at the theater in St. Clair Shores when I was in high school. After graduation, I kept working while going to college at Oakland University. Kyle even gave me a scholarship to take business classes. When I got my degree, he made me an assistant manager for a new property in Farmington. Kyle's enthusiasm for entertainment was contagious. We shared a lot of the same strategies and values."

"Been working at the headquarters long?"

Her expression remained calm, serious. "Almost two years. When he expanded into the bookstores, Kyle needed someone to continue his plans with the theaters, so he could concentrate on the new projects. My name kept coming up."

"So you're a movie buff."

"Yes, I've always felt spellbound by the movies. I'll watch the same one several times. First for enjoyment, then for details, then for thematic messages or values that the director, cinematographer or producer might be trying to convey." She paused, perhaps bringing up a particular movie memory. "Often I completely miss the message. But I still love movies."

"You must have been an integral part of the operations and involved in many of his business plans. Did Mr. Morrissey have any enemies? People he'd forced out of business? Someone he'd given the bum's rush to?"

She didn't answer immediately. Either she was stalling, or giving the matter serious consideration. I waited. Silence can become unbearable during an interview. Especially for the person who's supposed to answer. Sometimes they grow uncomfortable and rush to fill it. But I'm patient. I've been doing this for years.

"I'm sure everyone has an enemy of some sort," Valerie said. "But I can't think of anyone who Kyle ever crossed that would want him dead."

"How many theaters are operating now?"

"Six. They run under the Nostalgia logo. Grosse Pointe, St. Clair Shores, Mt. Clemens, Royal Oak, Farmington and Birmingham." She ticked them off on her manicured fingers.

"And the bookstores?"

"Three to date. Kyle didn't care for the huge bookstores, with the espresso bars and music departments and high prices. Have you been to an Imagination Station?"

"No."

"It's a perfect tie-in with his love of the movies. Kyle wanted a place that was a little different. Something off the wall. He and Dale got hooked on fantasy books. We carry everything from the days of King Arthur and witches to space travel and distant civilizations. Rather than trying to cater to every taste like the supermarket approach, Kyle narrowed the field: mystery, fantasy and science fiction. If it doesn't fit those categories, you can't find it at Imagination Station."

"You sound like a commercial."

Valerie blushed and lowered her eyes. "I helped with the campaign. Kyle is—was, trying to do so much more than just make money. He approached teachers at the different community colleges in the areas where the stores would be. Kyle wanted local connections. He hired art students to paint murals on the walls, depicting scenes from the type of books he wanted to sell. Several students went to each location. Kyle picked out sketches that he really liked, had them done on the walls, then had the artwork redone in posters. He is— was, going to encourage local authors by offering to publish their stories in a small magazine, as long as they fit the genres. Kyle had big dreams and even bigger aspirations."

"We're going to need a list of the key people at each store. The managers, assistants, anyone who would come in frequent contact or dealings with Morrissey. We will need to interview them."

Valerie nodded. "Sure thing. I'll print it out from my office."

"What about the people outside the company? Any complaints from customers that were off the wall? Someone who gave you the creeps?"

"No. I never heard of anything wrong. Kyle was a friendly guy."

"You must have been close." I let it hang there. It was a comment that could be taken more than one way.

"Yes, we were."

"Anything other than business?"

Her eyes blazed with fury. The knuckles on her laced fingers went white. "What if there was?"

"We need to know."

"Why?"

I walked around the table until I was right across from her. "I'm investigating his murder. And right now, I need to know everything about the man and the people he was involved with. The more I know the better chance I have of finding out who killed him." I let that sink in for a moment, matching her eyes with my own glare. "So answer the question."

"And what if I don't?" Her eyes still flashed with

defiance.

"If I find out somewhere else that you withheld information that hindered the case, you can face charges. Obstruction of justice. Interfering with an officer in the performance of his duties. Shit like that. Don't you want his killer found?"

"Of course I do!"

My voice became a snarl. "Then answer the damn question."

She clenched her hands tighter. Valerie looked everywhere but at me. I kept my eyes on her face. Behind me Suarez remained motionless. We waited.

"This really sucks," she said.

I didn't respond.

"Who will you tell?"

"No one, unless it becomes vital to the investigation."

Valerie pushed away from the table and walked to the window. She toyed with the blinds, peeking out at the pedestrian traffic below. I waited some more.

"This really sucks."

"So you've said."

She kept her back to us. "It just happened. About a month ago. We were working late, going over a proposal for an old theater in Ann Arbor. Kyle wasn't sure it was right for us. It would be a nice tie-in for another bookstore. We were alone. There's always been a lot of sexual tension between us. Little hints, comments, a few double-entendres back and forth. Things like that. It was raining that night. Colleen was out of town with the kids. Toronto. My husband was in Muskegon. It just happened. One minute we were looking over the plans. The next, we're rolling around on the floor. Practically shredded our clothes."

Her forehead was resting against the cool glass.

"After all those years of being so close, the tension just got to us. It was only that one night. But it was all night. We left about six in the morning, to go to our separate homes. I called in sick and slept away the day. Kyle was back by noon. That was the only time. No one else knows." She shuddered, whether from chills or remembering the excitement of the moment, I couldn't tell. "I have never been unfaithful to my husband."

I'd forced her to dredge up some very personal memories of the victim, which must have increased her sense of loss. I wasn't particularly proud of myself. But I had to remain impartial. Cold. I maintained my position by the table. Valerie took a minute to gather her composure then faced us.

"Your husband never suspected anything? No midnight confessions when he returned from Muskegon?"

She wiped her eyes with her fingertips. "No. By the time Roger came back, it was all behind us. Kyle and I returned to our normal routine. No comments were made about that night. We both knew it was a one-time deal, even though we didn't talk about it. Now what happens?"

"Like I said, it's between us. Unless it becomes important to the investigation."

"Anything else?"

I handed her a business card. "Not for now. But if you think of anyone who might have wanted to harm Mr. Morrissey, either personally or professionally, give me a call. No matter how insignificant it might be."

Valerie nodded and started to leave the conference

room. With the door still shut, she turned back.

"Does forcing people to reveal their secrets under the guise of aiding your investigation get you off?"

I shook my head. "No. Everyone has secrets they don't want to share. It's part of the job."

"Do you like your job?"

"Usually. But there are times when it really sucks."

Chapter Six

We interviewed the others. Tracy Wright had been with Morrissey since the beginning. She'd been working as a cashier at the first theater he'd bought. Morrissey had often told her she was the voice of reason and caution as he spun ideas to grow his empire. Wright admitted that he often ignored her advice. She claimed that if she liked an idea, he would reject it, considering her blessings to be a curse. Before building the offices, Morrissey had always worked out of the backroom of one of the theaters. Once the lofts were renovated, he'd brought her along to help keep things running smoothly.

Gary Andreski was twenty-four and had been with Vagabond for two years. A graduate of Wayne State University, he handled all the marketing and promotions for the various locations. Andreski was quick with the website and the social media aspects. He bombarded the internet with details and updates. He was a high energy kid. Either that, or he was ingesting way too much caffeine.

Steve York had become the finance guy seven years ago. Prior to that, he'd worked for the public accounting firm that managed the books for Vagabond. York was a numbers guy. His people skills were poor. As a result of that, the accounting firm always kept him in the background. That suited him just fine. People had issues. He was more comfortable generating reports, working with the figures. Morrissey recruited him, offering stock in the business and a generous salary. It was a no brainer.

Before the interview with Tracy Wright, I'd confronted Suarez. "What's your problem? You didn't ask a single question."

"I thought you wanted to run it, Sarge."

"Suarez, if you're not going to contribute, I can find other things for you to do. The idea of having two people in the interview is to gain more knowledge. You may have a question that I don't think of. Your involvement may also keep the interviewee off balance. They may accidentally give us information without realizing it."

"Got it, Sarge."

I jabbed two fingers at him. "Stop calling me Sarge."

"Okay, boss."

Before retorting about that being no better, I realized it was how the others on the squad were referring to me. "You can call me that, or Chene. I want you to take the lead on this other female. You know what we're after. If there's a point I want to make, I'll jump in."

"Got it."

He led Tracy Wright through the process. I bumped in with a couple of questions, but let him run it. Suarez hit the high points and followed up on a few areas where she was being vague. I hung back. He did well with both Andreski and York. After the last conversation we remained in the conference room for a moment.

"So how come there are no chairs in here?"

I had been wondering the same thing but wouldn't let on. "What's your take?"

"Other than the wiggle time with Mrs. Mann, I think Morrissey behaved himself here. Kept his focus on the business and building his empire. Can't say I don't blame him. She's a beautiful woman."

"Did you look through those photos Kozlowski sent?"

"Yeah, she wasn't one of them."

I drummed my fingers on the table. "You think Morrissey was a patient man?"

"I dunno. Eleven years is a lot more patience than I've got."

"Yeah, but it wasn't like he was starving for attention. I'm inclined to think he was waiting for the perfect moment to make his move."

"Sort of like, he saw his chance and he pounced on it."

I smothered a grin. "Well said. What do you think of Mrs. Morrissey's behavior?"

"Maybe part of it is anger at her husband. Whatever crap he was into is sure to come out now. She could have been putting up with his bullshit as long as the money was coming in and he didn't bring the shit home."

"You know, Suarez, you might be right."

He shrugged. "Hey, it happens once and awhile. What's our next move?"

"We'll get that information from Valerie and have a quick chat with the widow."

Colleen was in the office at the end of the hall. The hardwood floors gleamed, reflecting the track lighting strategically positioned above us. The walls were tastefully decorated with a combination of classic movie posters and framed newspaper clippings. There was a professional photograph of some old historic looking residence, perhaps from the areas where the theaters were. Grand openings of the theaters, renovation projects, charitable events and more showed the climb of Morrissey's efforts. The office next door belonged to Valerie Mann. She stepped out as we approached.

"Here's the list." She handed me an envelope that bore the corporate logo. I flicked it open and saw several pages. With a nod I slipped it into an inner pocket of my sport coat. I jerked my head toward Colleen's door. Suarez kept moving. I put my hand out to Valerie. She hesitated a moment, then took it gently.

"Thanks for your help. And your honesty."

"I hope you catch whoever did this."

I nodded and released her hand. Suarez was already chatting with Colleen Morrissey as I came into the room. I closed the door. At first glance, the office was a continuation of the outer room. Only upon closer examination did I realize the photos were of Colleen and the kids. The desk was a smaller version of the conference room table. The widow sat behind it swiveling slowly back and forth in a high backed leather chair. Suarez was asking about the conference room.

"...it's a great looking table, but it's taller than you normally see. And what's up with no chairs? It must be hard to have a meeting in there."

Colleen Morrissey flashed the first true smile I'd seen. "The table was designed specifically for us. Tall enough to lean against. You put your files and paperwork right there in front of you. No meeting lasts more than an hour. Most people can't wait to give their reports and get back to their chairs."

"That was your idea," I said.

She nodded. "I have an uncle who does woodworking as a hobby. He made that for us and this desk. When it came to meetings, Kyle had a short attention span. He was always ready to move on to the next thing."

Valerie knocked at the door. Standing beside her was a short man with jet black hair and a thick moustache. Using two fingers I waved him in.

"This is Yekovich from our Cyber Unit. He's going to take Kyle's computer in so we can check it out. There may be information on it that could have a bearing on the case." There was one of those all-in-one computers with the large monitor on the desk.

"Hey, Chene." He turned to Colleen. "I'm sorry for your loss. I'll make sure you have a receipt for the computer. Did your husband use a laptop or tablet as well?"

"No, he wasn't that keen with technology. His phone was synched to the computer here, along with the calendar."

"Did he use a computer at home?" Yekovich asked.

Colleen shook her head. "Only this one."

Yekovich copied down the model and serial number on a receipt. He unplugged the system from the network cables and carried it out of the office.

"What's the arrangement here with ownership?"

Her features darkened with a frown. "You think this all comes down to money?"

"I've seen people killed for many reasons. Money is often a factor."

"Kyle owned fifty-five percent of the stock. I own another fifteen. He gave twelve percent to Valerie and Steve. Tracy got six percent. It was a reward for their dedication. Kyle was generous with salaries as well."

"Is there a partnership agreement?"

She turned a wry smile in my direction. "It sounds like you know your ownership options, Detective. Yes, if anyone wanted to leave the business or was fired, their stock reverted to Kyle. In his will, I inherit all of his stock. Some of it is held in a trust for the kids. He always hoped Dale would join the business right after college."

I jotted a couple of things down in my notebook and glanced at Suarez. He caught my eye and gave his head a minute shake. "We've completed the interviews here. But there may be other questions as we continue the investigation."

"You have my numbers. If I'm not here, I'll be in the car or at home. My cell phone is always with me."

"Mine too. If you think of anything else we should know, call me."

As if summoned to life at its mention, my phone rang. The number on the screen was vaguely familiar but I couldn't place it.

"This is Chene."

"Hey, it's Malone. You got a minute?"

"I'm kind of in the middle of an interview right now."

"If this is the Morrissey case, that's why I'm calling."

I watched Colleen swivel back and forth in her

desk chair. "Keep talking."

"Jamie may have some information that could be helpful. It would be easier if we met in person."

"Text me an address and I'll be there within an hour."

"Done."

I tucked the phone back in my pocket. Colleen rested her elbows on the arms of her chair. She was bouncing her fingertips together. Her gaze once again locked in on mine. In my peripheral vision, Suarez shifted uncomfortably.

"You don't seriously think one of our employees could be Kyle's killer?"

"We are not eliminating anyone yet. Someone knew Kyle was going to be at the games. Someone wanted to kill him. We have no reason to exclude people at this point."

Her eyes opened a bit wider. "Even me?"

"Even you. A lot of homicides occur because of sex, drugs or money."

"That sounds like a cliché."

"Funny thing about clichés. Somewhere along the line, they were based on truth." I got to my feet. Suarez stood up as well. "So what else besides the business? Are there insurance policies, stocks and bonds in a broker's portfolio, things like that?"

"The company has several life insurance policies on Kyle. We had a couple of policies privately as well."

"What's the value?"

Suarez fidgeted again. Colleen glared in my direction.

"Check with your attorney. We're going to need that information and if I have to get a subpoena, I will."

Still no response.

"We'll be back," I hooked a thumb at the door. Suarez seemed in a hurry to get outside. Colleen didn't get up as we left the office.

Suarez stayed quiet until we were out on the street. "Do you really think she could have killed him?"

"Right now, I don't have enough information to either eliminate her as a suspect or charge her with something. She's holding back, which makes me curious."

"Now what, boss?"

"We go visit a brother cop."

****

On the way across town, I told Suarez about the call. Malone is a State Police sergeant working at a post in the western suburbs. He managed the patrols for that area on the busy evening shifts. Our paths crossed numerous times over the years. I was a little skeptical about the call but knew he wouldn't waste my time.

The address he sent was for a quaint little ranch house in Livonia. Malone's Jeep was in the driveway. He had been dating a writer for a while now. I parked across the street. As we were headed up the walk, I caught a glimpse of movement in the front window. The screen door opened as I reached the porch. Out stepped a slender redhead with hypnotizing green eyes. She was wearing micro blue shorts and a white tank top. Her long, shapely legs immediately caught my attention. She flashed me a brilliant smile.

"Hello, Chene. It's been a long time."

"That it has. You look good, Jamie."

"So do you. Come on in." She swung the door wide. As we entered I heard someone moving around in the kitchen at the rear of the house. Malone appeared in the archway between the kitchen and the living room.

"Coffee's ready." He gestured toward the kitchen table.

"This is Detective Ramon Suarez, the newest member of the squad. Meet Jamie Richmond and Malone."

"A pleasure." Malone shook his hand.

"Likewise." Suarez looked closely at Jamie. "You look very familiar. Have we met before?"

"Not that I recall."

We got situated around the table. Suarez started to pull out his digital recorder. I shook my head. He and the others made small talk. I waited until it died down and turned my attention to Jamie.

"Malone said you had some information about Morrissey."

She shook back a thick lock of hair that had been dangling over her eyes. "It's a couple of years old, but it might be pertinent. Once I saw the story on the news this morning, it clicked."

"We were out of town for the weekend," Malone explained, "didn't see a paper or watch the news or even touch a computer."

"I was going through withdrawals," Jamie said wistfully.

"So how did you know Morrissey?"

"Before I started writing mysteries full time, I worked as a reporter. The last couple of years I did that, I went freelance. I was writing for all kinds of magazines and trade publications. I'd find a good subject for an interview, do the research, write the article and sell it, sometimes four or five times."

"How can you sell the same piece more than once?" Suarez asked.

She gave him a gentle smile. "It's easy. Take Morrissey. The guy was a successful entrepreneur. He had two different type of businesses going, the movies and the bookstores. A lot of magazines publish articles each week online, in addition to whatever they decide goes in the print version. So I sold a feature on him to a magazine that focuses on entrepreneurs. Then I tweaked the copy and sold it to a publication that specializes in independent bookstores. Another version went to one that is for old renovated movie theaters. Then I cleaned it up again and sold it to the local rag that's about Detroit area businesses."

"Is that legal?" Suarez asked.

Jamie laughed out loud. "Of course it is. I live with a cop, Suarez. You don't think I'd be committing illegal activities do you?"

"Only questionable ones," Malone muttered.

She slapped his arm playfully. "It's perfectly legal. I did all the research. Each one of those publications specialized in different audiences. I retain the rights to the articles. It's not uncommon. The trick is to find the right markets and adjust the articles accordingly. Like I said, it's perfectly legal."

"So do you remember much about your interview with Morrissey?" I asked.

"Yes, quite a bit. Although I must admit that I reviewed my notes before you got here. I met with him several times over the course of a week." She glanced at Malone. He nodded and slid his hand over hers.

"Whatever information you have or impressions you might recall could be a big help to our investigation."

Jamie drew a deep breath and let it out slowly. "Morrissey may have been a sharp businessman, but he was no choirboy. Within an hour after meeting him, he started flirting with me. I was scheduled to be with him all day, every day, for a week. Sitting in on meetings, visiting his operations, talking to his associates, everything I could think of. I'd done hours of research on the guy and had already lined up articles with the different magazines I described. Fortunately, I hadn't committed to a specific agenda. I was able to ignore or downplay his comments and keep the interview going."

"What happened?" I asked.

"After the first day, I changed things up. I called some of his associates and made arrangements to interview them alone. When I had to meet with Morrissey again, I took Ernie with me. He's an old friend who is a photographer. Morrissey was subdued, but he still suggested getting together a few times after that."

"Flirting with a beautiful woman is hardly illegal," Suarez said.

Jamie batted her lashes at him. "Flirting was one thing. Morrissey didn't take the hint. He offered to buy me dinner, take me away for the weekend up to Mackinac Island, and a few other trips. This was after I'd interviewed his wife too."

"Sounds like he was a real hound," Malone said.

"No argument there. I kept my distance and got enough material to write the articles professionally."

"What about the colleagues you interviewed," I asked, "were any of them female?"

"Many of them were. They were all very attractive.

I asked a couple of them point blank if they ever had any problems with Morrissey. They avoided the question and commented about how much they liked their jobs."

I drank some coffee. Malone stared at me. He knew what I was thinking.

"This could be grounds for a sexual harassment lawsuit if he behaved this way with his employees. But that might not be serious enough for murder," Malone said.

"Maybe not. But if he continued to pursue someone who wasn't interested, maybe they reached their breaking point. It happens."

Jamie slid a thick envelope across the table to me. "These are copies of all my notes, the actual articles that were published, along with all the photos taken. I used a tape recorder for the interviews and downloaded the conversations there as well. You might pick up something from the way he answered questions."

A quick peek inside the envelope confirmed it was heavy with paperwork. "Thanks, Jamie."

"Will this cause you any trouble, you know, like the First Amendment or freedom of the press?" Suarez asked.

Jamie shook her head. "I was working on my own at the time. All that reference material, research and interview notes are my property. If anything in there can help you get a better sense of Morrissey and identify his killer, I want you to have it."

"Thank you, Ms. Richmond."

"You can call me Jamie."

We all stood from the table. I shook hands with Malone. Jamie stepped up and surprised me by draping her arms around my neck and giving me a lingering kiss on the lips. Over her shoulder I could see Suarez's eyes bulging. Malone gave his head a shake.

"I still owe you, Chene," she said quietly as she stepped away.

"Whatever you think you owe me was settled a long time ago."

She turned the intensity of those green eyes up a notch and locked them on mine. "Not to me. Not a thousand times over."

"See you around, Chene." Malone slipped an arm around her waist. "Nice to meet you, Suarez."

"Take care of her, Sarge," I said as we headed for the door.

"It's a challenge, but I do my best."

Back in the car I flipped through the pages of notes in the envelope. There was also a large stack of glossy photographs. Some of these were of the victim. Others were shots with several of the key people we'd met this morning. A couple were vaguely familiar. I glanced at Suarez.

"Pull up those photos from Morrissey's cell phone."

Vivid pictures began to fill the screen. Slowly he scrolled through them. I spread out the photos from Jamie's collection, tucking the shots of Morrissey back into the envelope. There was no match. A couple were possible but their faces were blurred in the cell phone photos. Jamie had noted the subject's names and roles on the back. Suarez muttered something in Spanish and put his phone back in his pocket.

"So what's it mean, boss?"

"It means that Morrissey liked to play house with

his employees. He could have ensured loyalty amongst his staff by paying them well. Or offering a piece of the company stock. But I'm beginning to think he used the business to stoke his extracurricular passions."

"And that could be a motive?"

"Depends on who knew it. Maybe Colleen got tired of it. Or maybe he hit on the wrong woman."

"So what do we do now?"

I considered our options. "We're not far from one of his theaters. Let's continue our interviews and see what shakes loose."

Chapter Seven

The Nostalgia Theater in downtown Farmington looked like something frozen in time. It occupied a large space four buildings down from the intersection of Grand River Avenue and Farmington Road. According to the plaque out front from the local historical society, it had been built in 1940. Originally the theater was also used for live entertainment. There was a small balcony that had been converted into a second theater when Morrissey purchased the building. The Art Deco sign out front could be seen from a mile away. I parked across the street and pulled Valerie Mann's list of employees from my pocket.

"Hey, boss. What was Jamie talking about, that she owes you?"

I considered brushing it off, but it wasn't really a secret. The rest of the squad knew about it. And Cantrell had recruited him.

"It was a little more than a year ago. A friend of hers got kidnapped. Nobody could find her anywhere. Jamie figured it out, but got in over her head. Malone got worried and pinged her phone. She was on an island out by Lake St. Clair. I was closer, so one of the other detectives and I went to check her out. We pulled Jamie and her friend from the water and got them transported to a hospital."

"Did you take down the kidnapper?"

"No. Jamie did. She shot him. Twice."

He rocked back against his seat. "Damn! She looked so sweet and innocent."

"You ought to know by now, looks can be deceiving."

"That's one fierce redhead."

"Which is also something to keep in mind. Let's go."

According to the list, Alexis Buford was the manager of the Farmington Theater. There was a matinee showing of a couple of Disney flicks. The lobby was jumping with moms, babysitters and youngsters. We approached the ticket booth. The teenage girl behind the glass eyed us suspiciously.

I held up my identification. "I'm looking for Alexis Buford."

"Yeah, I didn't think you were here to watch the Muppets." She gave me a quick smile and disappeared. She returned a minute later. "Alex is up in the balcony. She'll meet you there."

We ducked inside and found a staircase just beyond the small lobby. Apparently the balcony feature was already underway. Standing by the door to the seats was an attractive, curvy brunette, wearing khakis and a red golf shirt with the theater logo above the heart. She was about five feet eight inches tall, which put her only a couple of inches shorter than me. She towered over Suarez. Her hair was clipped short with some auburn highlights. Introductions were made.

"Is there someplace we can talk?" I asked.

"The office here is the size of a broom closet. This show started twenty minutes ago and the one on the main floor is ready to begin. I'm not really comfortable having this conversation in the lobby."

"I'm open to suggestions."

She fidgeted. "This is not easy for me. I really liked Kyle."

"Seems to me there's a coffee shop down the block with some outdoor tables. How about if we talk there?"

She relaxed a little. "That would be great."

"Detective Suarez will walk down and get us a table."

"You got it, boss."

I followed Alexis Buford as she checked the balcony to make sure everything was in order. She trotted down the narrow stairs and ducked into the main floor auditorium. I leaned against the wall, looking at the crowd of kids and chaperones. There were over a hundred getting settled into their seats as the lights began to dim. She stayed beside me as the music came up and the film got underway. Once she was satisfied that everything was in order, Alexis nodded toward the door. In the lobby she spoke briefly to an older woman behind the concession stand.

She was quiet as we walked down the block. The girl from the box office had retrieved Alex's purse, which dangled from her right shoulder. A pair of large oval sunglasses hid her eyes. At the coffee shop I was pleased to see that Suarez had procured a wrought iron outdoor table away from anyone else. Three cardboard cups sat in a disposable tray on the table.

"Two black and one with cream and sugar."

"I'd prefer a French Vanilla latte," Alexis said quietly.

Suarez cut his eyes to me. I nodded. He went inside to get it.

I suspected that Suarez had checked his phone to see if Alexis Buford was one of Morrissey's pinup girls. While I hadn't studied each photo closely, I didn't think she was in the mix.

"Tell me about working for Kyle Morrissey."

She drew a deep breath to steady herself. "He was a good guy. Very smart. He seemed to know what people wanted. He understood how to make money but he wasn't interested in taking over the world."

"Just his little corner of it?"

"Something like that. The summer matinee was his idea. Parents or adults pay one dollar and kids are free. We never expect to draw much on the box office, but we do good numbers on the concession stands."

Suarez came back with her coffee. "Here you go, Ms. Buford."

"Call me Alex or Alexis, please."

"Okay, Alex, you worked for Morrissey for eight years. Tell us about that."

"I grew up near the theater in Royal Oak. As a kid, we were always going there. When I went to college, I studied history, with a minor in art. I had no idea what I was going to do with that, but it's what I was interested in. The summer between my junior and senior year, I hired at the Nostalgia in Royal Oak."

"What happened after graduation?" Suarez asked.

"I received a card from Kyle with a check in it and a note, offering me a job. We'd talked a couple of times during the summer when I was working. My interest in history made sense when I started looking at older movies. So a month after graduation, I was working full time in Royal Oak."

"Did he start you in management?"

She laughed lightly. "Hardly. I worked everything. Box office, concession stands, sweeping up popcorn and mopping the floors. It was hardly glamorous, but it was fun."

"You ever have any problems with Kyle Morrissey?"

"Nothing I couldn't handle." She took a deep pull on the latte and sat straighter in her chair.

"What did you handle?"

She gave her head a slow shake but didn't respond.

I stepped into the conversation. "Alex, we're investigating his murder. We need to understand everything about Kyle. Tell us what you handled."

She studied me for a moment then huffed out a breath in frustration. "In the beginning he didn't pay any special attention to me. I was just another employee, which was fine. But after a couple of years, he would make a point to talk to me whenever he was in Royal Oak. He asked me about the history of a movie. Testing me. Told me he was always interested in the backstory. You know, the behind the scenes details that most people never know about."

"Go on."

"So one day he told me that I could use the computer in the office and do some research. I could do that on the clock. Find a few films that people hadn't seen in twenty years or more. Get some juicy background. If I could find six that were worthwhile, he'd run them. It was a challenge." Alexis gave her shoulders a little shrug. "I'm competitive. I did it."

"What happened?" Suarez asked.

"I found him six classics. Plenty of background, gossip columns, news stories, things from the archives.

Wrote a report that was ten pages long. Included some of the original promotional posters and box office numbers." She flashed a smile at the memory. Alex was turning her coffee cup in slow circles on the table. "Kyle loved it. He made arrangements to show each film. I got promoted to assistant manager."

"That doesn't sound like a problem," I said.

"That part wasn't. But a few months later, he came by. Wanted me to keep going with the research. Do some more digging, find more films that people have forgotten about. Play up the golden age of movies. I could even design some of the promotional material. It was a great assignment."

"So what happened?"

"He came by a few nights later. Kyle knew I was the manager on duty. He waited until the film was running, claimed he was just checking the house. Stopped by my little office to say hello. I think he'd been drinking." Alex paused, her coffee cup clenched in her hand now.

"What did he do?" I asked quietly.

She shuddered at the memory. "He put his hands on me. I was looking in a file cabinet for some notes, sort of bent at the waist. Before I could straighten up, he was pressed against me from behind. And he put his hands on my breasts. Not gently, but very rough."

"How did you react to that?"

Alexis pulled off her sunglasses and dropped them on the table. She massaged the bridge of her nose with her thumb and forefinger. "I slammed him. Snapped my head back and smashed it into his face. Then I stomped on his instep as hard as I could. Nobody touches me like that. And then..."

There was a pause so long I had to prompt her. "Then what?"

"Then I turned around and kicked him in the balls."

Suarez flinched in his chair. "Served him right."

"I'm surprised you still work for him," I said.

Alexis blew out a breath. "We came to an understanding. There was an opening in Farmington. It was a step up. I wrote down everything that happened that night and everything leading up to it. My roommate witnessed it and it's in my safety deposit box. If he ever tried anything like that again, I'd sue him. If he tried to fire me, I'd bring that out. I love my job. I'm very good at it."

We sat there, drinking our coffee. Alexis picked up her sunglasses and slid them back in place.

"Have the women who work for you here mentioned any problems with Kyle Morrissey?" Suarez asked.

"No. That was part of our deal. My theater is off limits. I don't know if he plays grab ass anywhere else. I can't worry about everyone. But I can damn well make sure my theater is a safe place for people to work."

The three of us sat there quietly for a moment. "We appreciate your time, Alexis." I slid her one of my business cards. "If you think of anything else that might be helpful, give me a call."

She finished her coffee and got to her feet. Both Suarez and I got a firm handshake and we watched as she strode back to the theater.

"Guess we can cross that one off the list, boss."

"I'm not so sure about that. If she was strong enough to deflect Morrissey's attention, he might have considered that a challenge. He was competitive too."

****

We parked in front of the bookstore. There was an early afternoon crowd wandering through the aisles of the Bloomfield Hills location, checking out the racks of paperbacks, posters and paraphernalia. As we entered, I saw what looked like a guy in a NASA spacesuit moving slowly up the aisle, taking exaggerated steps. Suarez raised his eyebrows at me, then stepped over to the cashier's area and flashed his badge. I watched the astronaut reach the end of the aisle, bending at the waist to shake hands with a wide-eyed six-year-old. The guy turned and moved to the rear of the store.

"The boss will be right out," Suarez said.

We were about to take bets on her hair color when a pretty brunette emerged from the rear of the store. She playfully grappled with the spaceman, then headed our way. A wide smile crossed her lips as she extended her hand. She was casually dressed in navy slacks, a white blouse and brown leather sandals. Her hair was in a ponytail that dangled to the middle of her back. She was shorter but more athletic than the other women we'd met today. Good muscle tone. Small breasts, waist and hips. You could sense the energy within.

"I'm Chelsea Coles." The smile wavered on her lips for a moment as she inspected us. "You're really the cops?"

We showed her our badges. She motioned us toward one of the cozy areas with upholstered chairs over by the shop windows. Chelsea and I sat facing each other. Suarez took a chair on the edge, with his back to the store.

"How can I help you?"

I relayed our standard conversation, about how we were looking into everyone who dealt with Morrissey on a regular basis. Suarez and I took turns asking questions.

Chelsea rolled her head slowly, as if she were worrying out a knot of tension. "I've known Kyle about a year and a half. I was working for one of the big chain bookstores. He used to come in periodically to check out our activity. We got to talking about books and magazines. When he mentioned his plans to open the Imagination Stations, I was hooked. It was an opportunity to have more control over the inventory, get creative with promotions and the daily operation."

"Morrissey give you a free hand with the business?" Suarez asked.

"To a degree. Each store has a limited budget to spend any way they see fit on promotional or decorating schemes. Managers treat the store as if it were their own, so we tend to put more effort into it."

"What type of promos have you done?" I asked.

"Regular bookworm things. Convinced a couple of local authors to come in for discussions and autographs. Had a wine and cheese party one night. Staged a Halloween party for people to dress up. We've even posted short stories on our website that are written by locals. We're always trying something unusual. It's what sets us apart from the big guys."

"How did you get along with Morrissey?"

She squirmed in her chair. "Good."

Suarez looked at me. I gave my head a little shake and turned my gaze toward the displays of books. The silent treatment might work on this one. I watched the spaceman work his way slowly up the aisle.

Chelsea kept flicking her gaze from me to Suarez. Neither one of us spoke. Several minutes passed without a comment. She caved in first.

"If you have no other questions—" she started to move from her seat.

Ramon waved her back into her chair. "We're just getting warmed up. Suppose you tell us the real version of your association with Morrissey."

She shifted nervously. Down the aisle, the guy in the spacesuit paused to ruffle the head of a teenager in the mystery section across from our spot.

"I'd rather not discuss it."

"But we'd rather you did," Suarez countered.

"Then you'll just have to arrest me, or whatever it is you guys do with an uncooperative person. Right now, I've got work to do." She stood up so quickly that her chair tipped over backward.

Suarez rose and flicked a hand out to catch her by the wrist. Chelsea let out a small cry of surprise and that's when everything went crazy. One moment we were having a quiet conversation and the next, it looked like something out of a bad Hollywood movie.

Suarez was no longer standing. The spaceman had him pinned against the window, at least six inches off the floor. Whoever was inside that suit was no weakling, as he sent me flying ass backward over my chair with a simple backhand slap across the chest. Chelsea was tugging at the guy's left arm, trying to persuade him to release Suarez. She was having no effect on the situation.

"Put him down." I stepped around her to face the guy.

Chelsea turned to me. "Don't hurt him! He doesn't

mean any harm. He's just looking out for me. Please."

Suarez continued to struggle, trying to break free. No such luck. This was not a situation to draw a weapon. I hesitated, trying to come up with a solution.

"Who's in the suit?"

"My brother, Zack. He's just trying to help me." Chelsea continued to tug at his arm. "Please, don't hurt him."

I gently pulled her back. "Follow my lead."

She hesitated for half a second, then nodded. I moved her to the window, beside Suarez. Calmly, she stood beside me, then she took my hand and beamed a smile at her brother.

"Zack. Please, put him down. He wasn't trying to hurt me. See. Everything's okay. These men are from the police. They're just asking me some questions. Please, Zack."

Ever so slightly the helmet rotated toward us. Suarez had both hands wrapped around Zack's wrist, still trying to break his hold. I watched the head bob slowly, then the pressure eased on Suarez's throat as he gently slid to the floor.

Suarez drew in several deep breaths and began massaging his neck where the gloved hands had pinned him. Chelsea latched onto Zack's arm and moved him toward the rear of the store.

"You hurt?"

"Just my pride. That dude has power. Reminds me of taking on the Motor City Warlords." He looked warily at the spaceman. "Think I'll walk it off. You cool here?"

"Yeah. I'll meet you outside." I followed Chelsea and her brother. They went into a storeroom in the back, where cases of stock were neatly arranged on shelves. He was sitting on a heavy wooden stool. Chelsea was unclasping the space suit, lifting off the helmet as I entered the room.

"Everything okay back here?"

She nodded. "How's your partner?"

"He'll be fine. More surprised than anything is my guess. I'd still like to talk to you. And Zack. I'll make it brief."

Zack rose from the stool and began unzipping the suit. He'd pulled off the heavy gloves while my attention was on Chelsea. I watched him strip down to a T shirt and khaki shorts. Zack hung the suit neatly on a hook by the door and pulled on a pair of sneakers. He reminded me of Kozlowski, only smaller. Probably six two, two twenty- five, and rock solid. But the face gave it away.

"You're not going to hurt him are you?" Chelsea whispered beside me.

"Doubt that I could without a cannon."

She nodded. "Physically, he's twenty. Mentally and emotionally, probably ten or eleven. He helps out around the store, dresses in the costumes we get, and it gives us a chance to be together. He's been living with me since our mother died."

"So he was just protecting you when Suarez grabbed your arm."

"Sure. Zack jumps to conclusions sometimes." She hesitated a beat. "But I guess we all do." She watched him take a vacuum cleaner from a closet filled with cleaning supplies and head out to the front of the store. A minute later we could hear its motor through the wall. Chelsea checked her watch again. "I really should get back to work."

I raised a hand. "Tell me about Morrissey."

She slowly exhaled. "Will you leave us alone if I do?"

"No guarantees. We're trying to find out who killed him."

"Okay. He made a pass at me. Shortly after we opened. Kyle came in early, wanted to check things out. Gave me this friendly hug. Then another one. Tried to kiss me. I didn't know what he had in mind, but I wasn't interested in that kind of relationship with my boss. So I pushed him away. Told him that wasn't my style, and that if it was a job requirement, I was out of here."

"Then what happened?"

"He laughed it off. Said he was just carried away with the excitement over another new enterprise. Kyle kept telling me that he had big plans for the store and the whole business. He envisioned having as many bookstores as he has theaters. Or more."

"That's it?"

She nodded.

"Then why didn't you tell us before?"

"I don't like remembering it. Sometimes I wonder if he hired me for my experience and potential or if he thought my panties would be a nice little trophy."

I bit back a smile, but not before she saw it. "Anyone else know about this incident?"

Chelsea shook her head. "It was early. About an hour before we opened for the day. I was the only one here. I think he planned it that way."

"How did he treat you afterward?"

She considered it. "Same as before. He still showed

interest and enthusiasm for my ideas. We've made a profit after the first eight weeks in operation. That's damn good."

"He ever give you any grief about Zack working here?"

Another shake of the head. "No. I've got free rein when it comes to hiring. Besides, Zack's a good worker. He handles all the heavy cases, keeps the place neat and doesn't bother anyone."

"Except the occasional cop."

A quick flash of red tinged her cheeks. "He thought I was in trouble. We look out for each other. You're not going to do anything to him, are you? Zack didn't really hurt your friend."

"He's not my friend. He's just another detective working this case." For some ridiculous reason, Ted's face floated in front of my mind, and I could hear his stupid question. 'Name six'.

"Does that mean Zack's okay?"

I hesitated, turning it over in my mind. "Sure. Did he ever talk to Morrissey?"

"Usually when he stopped in, Kyle would chat with Zack for a minute. Like I said, he was always friendly. Everybody liked Kyle." Her eyes flicked to the storeroom door. "I really should get out front. The afternoon can be busy."

I gave her one of my cards. "Anything unusual comes to mind, give me a call. And don't worry about Zack."

She walked away.

I didn't bother to state the obvious. Somebody out there didn't like Kyle Morrissey. They didn't like him so much they killed him.

Chapter Eight

Exiting the store, I could see Suarez leaning against the Pontiac. As I crossed the lot, a silver Bentley sedan rolled slowly down the aisle. When I slowed my pace to allow it to pass, the car silently eased to a stop.

"What's shaking, Chene?" A gravelly voice with an asthmatic wheeze asked.

I bent slightly and checked the driver's profile. It wasn't really necessary. I'd already placed the spiffy wheels, not to mention the distinctive voice.

"Been a long time, Max. You checking out the books or stocking up on wine?"

"Looking for you, actually. Mr. Agonasti would like to see you."

I leaned a palm against the roof of the Bentley. There was no grit to the surface. The wax was so smooth, my hand almost slid off. "How is Leo?"

"Doing well. But he'd rather tell you himself."

Movement caught my eye. Suarez had been watching my conversation and was now stepping over to become a part of it. Max rolled his head toward Suarez. "Fresh meat, Chene?"

I tried to give him a disgusted look, but I'm not sure how successful it was. I waited until Suarez came alongside me to introduce him.

"Detective Ramon Suarez, meet Maximo Aurelio. Also known as Maxie A."

They shook hands. I noticed how Ramon's fingers disappeared inside Max's grip. They exchanged a brief nod and Max resumed his conversation.

"You want to hop in and I'll drive you over?"

"Nothing personal, Max, but I'll take my own car."

Max patted the plush leather interior. "Don't know what you're missing, Chene. It's like floating on a cloud on a summer's day. If I didn't know better, I'd swear you had no taste."

"Just keeping the conflicts to a minimum. Where's he at?"

"The marina. I'll lead ya over."

"Fair enough."

Max rolled the luxury sedan to the end of the aisle and waited for us to enter the Pontiac. I could feel Suarez's eyes on me the whole time we exited the lot and started south. "What?"

"Do you know who that guy is?"

"I introduced you, remember."

"You going to tell me how you know a reputed gunner for one of Motown's most notorious crime bosses?"

"Alleged crime boss. And Max has never been charged with any crime. Neither has his associate. They are very careful about any involvement in criminal activity."

"Boss, you keep coming up with surprises."

I followed Max as he turned east. It would take over half an hour to reach the lake. There was plenty of time to fill Suarez in.

"Back when I was in uniform, I was patrolling a park area one night. Found a car on the side of the road. Young couple inside, getting frisky. Only she wasn't willing to play. Guy had been pushing the booze on her, trying to get her loose and compliant. She told me her name. I cuffed the guy to his car, radioed for another unit to pick him up, and took her home."

Ahead of me Max entered the freeway and hit the gas. I dropped in behind him, cruising steadily at eighty. Suarez gestured with his hand to hurry me along with the story. "And she was…"

"The daughter of Leo Agonasti. He was very appreciative of what I did. Offered me a large reward for the name of the kid involved. I refused. Offered me a job. Refused that too. Told him the system would take care of this creep. He didn't want to accept that. Kept pressing a reward at me. I finally told him I'd take no money, but would consider it a reward if he gave his word that no harm would come to the kid if Agonasti ever learned who did it. Reluctantly, he agreed."

"Christ, you've got brass balls."

I shrugged. "Anyway, Agonasti keeps an ear to the ground. Always knows what cases we're involved in. Once in a while, I'll get a message to come see him. Like now. Usually, he's got information that will help the investigation."

Suarez was slowly shaking his head in disbelief. "Does Pappy Cantrell know about this arrangement?"

"Sure. He knows how it works with Agonasti. It's strictly professional."

At the marina, we rolled to a stop on a freshly paved strip beside the yachts. The smallest vessel there was probably forty feet in length. It was a dazzling display of varnished mahogany and teak, polished chrome sparkling and pennants snapping in the summer breeze. Max led us to a sixty-footer near the far end of the pier.

Leo Agonasti liked to say he was a student of life. He had a love of history, particularly anything to do with the Detroit area since the city was settled by the French. But he was most knowledgeable about the twentieth century. If it happened in Motown, he knew about it. From crooked labor unions to shady politicians, Leo could tell you stories. He was leaning against the cabin door, watching our approach. Max must have called him as we were on the way. Agonasti was not the type to sit placidly waiting for anyone's arrival. He looked fit, with the solid upper body of someone who had done his share of manual labor. He squeezed my hand firmly and looked me straight in the eye.

"It's been too long, Jeff. Far too long."

"Nice to see you, Mr. Agonasti. You're looking well."

He clapped me on the shoulder. "When are you going to call me Leo? After all these years, there's no need for formalities."

"Old habits die hard."

Agonasti waved me into the salon on the rear of the yacht. Max followed. I hesitated, watching Suarez step aboard. Agonasti was about to have some fun.

"You must be Ramon Suarez. Welcome aboard, Detective. You had a good track record with the Detroit P.D. How do you like working with the State?"

"It has its moments," Suarez said. Instinctively he grabbed the door frame for support. I wondered if this was the first time Suarez had been on a boat of any kind.

"Come, sit down. How about a drink?" Agonasti

gestured at Max, who was bringing a pitcher of iced tea out of a small refrigerator. "Unless you'd like a beer, Ramon?"

"Tea's cool. I'll pretend its tequila."

"Quite a yacht, Leo," I said. "This one new?"

Max handed me a glass. "We picked it up a few weeks back. Haven't had the chance to really break it in yet. The captain I hired isn't very reliable."

"A damn shame," Agonasti said. "It's a perfect day for a ride." He hesitated briefly. "What do you say, Jeff? Want to take it for a shakedown cruise?"

"Why not?"

I moved to the wheelhouse and checked the switches. After activating the blower to air out the engine room, I kicked in the twin diesels and the generator. Max quickly walked to the bow and unhooked the connector to the shore power. Once he'd secured it to a wooden piling, he released to bow line from a shiny chrome cleat. He draped this over the same spot, making it easy to reattach upon our return. A glance over my shoulder confirmed Agonasti had done the same thing with the stern line. Max released the spring line, which secured the boat at its midpoint.

Suarez appeared at my elbow, looking a bit green. "You have any idea what the hell you're doing?"

"Trust me."

"Last time somebody said 'trust me', I found out it means 'fuck you' in Yiddish. And I got shot in the ass."

I eased the engines into reverse. Once clear of the dock, I spun the boat on its heel by putting the right engine, known as the starboard side, into forward and leaving the left or port engine in reverse. When I had the right angle, I flipped the left engine into forward and we pulled out of the marina and headed toward the lake. Beyond the marina's break wall, I gave the throttles a little more power and pointed her out toward the middle of the lake.

"Care to try it from the bridge?" Agonasti jerked his thumb above us.

"It would be a shame not to."

I stepped aside and Max took the wheel. Agonasti led me to a chrome ladder at the rear of the salon that took us up to the fly-bridge. From there we had an unobstructed view of the lake. We settled into a pair of captain's chairs behind an identical set of controls. Agonasti tapped the horn once. I felt the wheel wiggle beneath my hands, a signal that Max was relinquishing the controls. I nudged the throttles and felt the wind tug at my clothes. This far out on the lake, no remote microphones would be effective. Although he was retired, I was sure Agonasti was still under the surveillance of some kind of a task force.

"What do you think, Jeff?"

"Hell of a ride. Why don't you run it?"

He shrugged his thick shoulders. "Never learned how. Figured it was easier to have someone else who feels comfortable at the helm. I wouldn't have been able to back her out of the dock."

"Just takes practice."

"It wouldn't be right if I had trouble handling it. May give people the wrong impression. And I certainly don't want that."

I thought about that. Pity the fool who joked about Agonasti's inability to dock a boat. If the old rumors were true, he'd find a dozen painful ways to make the person regret their comments.

"So how's the homicide investigation coming?" Agonasti had carried the tea up with him and was twirling his glass slowly, watching the ice cubes roll around the rim.

"Typical. Chasing down leads, talking to his contacts. Same old song and dance." I shifted my eyes from the water to him. "You ever meet?"

Agonasti merely shook his head.

"Then why the interest?"

"I'm interested in many things, especially when someone is brutally murdered. A family man, too."

"Are you referring to that in the traditional sense?"

His face split into a wide grin. "That's what I like about you, Jeff. Always straight to the point. No pulling punches."

"You didn't answer my question."

Again the grin. "See what I mean. No, Morrissey was not connected with any organized crime syndicate."

"So there must be some reason his death piques your interest?"

"I like old movies. Kick it up a notch."

I increased the throttles to three-quarter speed. He'd tell me what was on his mind when he was ready. I leaned back in the chair and sipped my tea, one hand loosely on the wheel. I wondered how Suarez was fairing down below. A glance over my shoulder proved we were alone. Max was probably watching him get his sea legs.

We continued running northeast, across Lake St. Clair in the general direction of Port Huron. Agonasti gestured toward the right and I fell into the wake of an ore freighter that was headed in the same direction.

"Morrissey's murder appeared to be an execution," Leo said. "It made me curious. I've asked around. No one had any dealings with him. Whoever killed him might have been attempting to steer the investigation away and focus it on the family."

I shrugged. "Makes sense. Shot at close range. Not as messy as through the ear, but just as effective."

"Killers today don't have the stomach for a signature hit. They don't want to get their Guccis dirty. Most hits nowadays are as subtle as a drive-by shooting."

"So you wanted to make sure we don't waste our time searching for any organized crime connections?"

Agonasti's head bobbed slowly on his shoulders. "Trail's getting cold, Jeff. Whoever did this to Morrissey shouldn't get away with it. Guy was a straight arrow. Wife and kids and all that jazz."

My phone buzzed in my jacket. Agonasti raised an eyebrow while I dug it out and pressed the button.

"Chene."

"Where the hell you at?" Kozlowski grumbled in my ear. "You guys are an hour late checking in."

"We're in the middle of Lake St. Clair, conducting an interview and enjoying a cruise on a million-dollar yacht."

He paused, uncertain whether to believe me or not. "You got the kid with you?"

"Unless he fell overboard."

"I picked up the autopsy report from Fen. Something odd caught my eye."

"Such as?"

"Didn't you tell me that Morrissey was a fitness freak?"

I took a moment to replay yesterday's conversation with the victim's family. "Yeah, he was a runner, played tennis, did some sports with his kids. Why?"

"Fen found traces of nicotine in his system."

"What about the car?"

"Nah, I double checked it. No cigars, cigarettes or chewing tobacco."

We were both silent for a moment, considering options. "Maybe he went for the occasional stogie to celebrate a big deal or a conquest."

"Doesn't feel right," Kozlowski said.

"Yeah, I know what you mean."

"We'll figure it out. You going to make it for the squad meeting?"

"We'll be there in an hour." I broke the connection and pocketed the phone. Agonasti met my eyes. "Gotta head back to the marina."

"Damn shame, Jeff. I was enjoying the ride."

Easing the boat into a wide turn, I swung it back in the general direction of the shore. We didn't speak during the remainder of the cruise. I spotted a landmark when we pulled out from the marina, so had no difficulty finding the entrance from the lake. Agonasti dozed, letting the sun warm his face while the wind ruffled his gray hair.

Cutting the throttles, I eased the yacht into the canal for the marina. Max moved along the starboard side of the boat, until he was crouched low on the bow. I reduced the speed, then put one engine in reverse and kept the other in forward and swung the yacht around. When it was lined up with the slip, I crept forward until Max grabbed a line and secured it. A short pulse in reverse gently rocked the boat back far enough to attach the other lines. Once the yacht was in place, he reconnected the power cord as well.

From below, Max cut the engines and the generator. The sudden silence was short lived. A burly man wearing a tank top and stained khaki pants appeared at the bow. He had a large paper bag in the crook of his right arm. A baseball cap was perched at an awkward angle atop his head.

"What's the big idea?" he yelled in my direction.

Agonasti straightened in his chair, a disgusted expression on his face. "I was hoping to avoid any unpleasantness today."

"You know this guy?"

"Name's Thompson. He was sent by the agent who runs the marina when I requested a captain. The man may know how to run a boat, but he's an ignorant slob. And he smokes."

Agonasti considered smokers to be a lower life form. From the dock Thompson was attempting to carry on a conversation with either Max or Suarez. He was rapidly becoming louder. How this man remained employed would be a mystery of its own.

"We've got to get back to the squad." I paused to shake Agonasti's hand. "Thanks for the tea and the cruise."

"You handle it well, Jeff. Come back anytime." Agonasti looked beyond me, his eyes taking in Thompson. There was a flash of anger, but it faded quickly.

Suarez stepped onto the dock. "I can't wait to get back to terra firma."

Max and I nodded briefly at each other as I moved to the dock. Suarez had started for the mainland, only to find his way blocked by Thompson. Suarez hesitated when I approached.

"What do you think you were doing? No one's supposed to run this barge but me!" Thompson pointed a dirty finger in my direction. Up close I could see the tank top was stretched to the breaking point over a stomach gone to seed long ago.

"Step aside."

"No way. I don't like strangers running my boat!"

"I believe the yacht you are referring to belongs to Mr. Agonasti."

"When I run it, it's my boat." Again Thompson jabbed his finger at me. From above me I could hear the snort of muffled laughter. Max must have come forward to watch the show.

"I'm only going to tell you once more. Step aside."

Thompson surged forward, his finger thrust out before him like a miniature lance. "I'm not stepping—"

I grabbed the finger and bent it backward, twisting it enough to snap it, but turning with it to spin him around. With two strides, I ran him face first into the large wooden piling that held the lines for the yacht. I could hear the crunch of bone as his nose broke. Thompson howled in pain and tried to break free. I gave his arm a shake, then snatched the cap from his head and got a handful of greasy black hair. I thumped his head once more on the piling for good measure.

"Listen up, asshole. Number one, your presence on this yacht is no longer required. Number two, you just tried to assault a police officer. That's a chargeable offense. Number three, if you bother my friends there in any way, shape or form, I'll come back and finish this. And believe me, you won't look any prettier when I get done."

I released his hair and wiped my hand on the back of his shirt, then let go of his arm. Stepping back, I prepared for the inevitable retaliation. I wasn't disappointed. Thompson spun, blood dripping down his face and charged. The walkway was only three feet across. I had to time it well. As he launched himself at me, I spun to the right and dragged my left foot, hooking his ankle as he went by. Lacing my hands together, I swung around, completing the spin and driving both hands into his back like a hammer. Thompson flew beyond the edge of the walkway and dropped into the canal.

A roar of laughter floated down from above. Agonasti had joined Max at the rail. Apparently they enjoyed how the confrontation played out. Agonasti sketched a brief salute in my direction as Suarez and I headed for the parking lot.

"Where the hell did you learn how to do that?"

"You think you're the only one who ever rumbled with gangs?"

"Ain't no gangbanger I've ever seen move like that."

I shrugged. "Sometimes, you improvise."

Chapter Nine

We gathered in the conference room. Cantrell wasted no time firing up a fresh cigarette. Once a cloud of smoke was circling overhead, he nodded in my direction. I gave the others an update of our efforts, describing the interviews at the company offices, the meeting with Malone and Jamie Richmond and the interviews with the two site managers. Cantrell was about to move on when I held up my hand.

"I was also contacted by Leo Agonasti."

Despite my earlier comment to Suarez, Cantrell was less than pleased with this knowledge. "Fuck me hard."

"It's worthwhile."

"Al Capone gonna confess?" he snapped.

I ignored the dig. "He wanted to save us some time. The way Morrissey was killed could have looked like a hit. Agonasti checked it out. There was no connection between Morrissey and OC. Nobody had a reason to order an assassin."

The tip of Cantrell's cigarette glowed bright red. He huffed out more smoke but said nothing else.

"You think it's solid?" Kozlowski asked.

"No reason to doubt him. He gains nothing by steering us in the wrong direction."

Cantrell thrust two gnarled fingers at me. "Y'all better keep that out of the reports. Damn governor be havin' a coronary he reads that."

"I'll cover it."

"Git to it." He turned toward Laura. "Whatcha got, girlie?"

Laura recapped the day at the Grosse Pointe Hunt Club, interviewing staff and members to learn more about Morrissey. They had also been able to confirm the alibi for Nicholas Trent. Laura was thorough. She talked to employees who had been there for a long time and learned about the Morrissey family dynamics.

"Kyle Morrissey was very competitive. He played a lot of tennis, mostly singles and took lessons with a pro to keep his game sharp. He occasionally would have a set with Trent but he easily destroyed him."

"The guy had ten years on Trent, but twice the talent," Donna said.

"He hit on any of the female employees?" Kozlowski asked.

"Not that we could learn. The tennis pro he trained with is a guy. And we checked the photos Koz found, but didn't run across anyone we recognized."

"What about the wife? Colleen Morrissey spend much time there?" I asked.

Donna nodded. "She does. Everyone we talked with spoke very highly of her. She's worked on different committees, fundraising events, summer festivals and programs for the kids. As a matter of fact, we bumped into her there."

She pulled a small envelope from her notebook and passed it to Cantrell.

"The hell is this?" He peered inside cautiously.

"Two tickets to the Glamour Train. It's the big fundraiser that the victim was working on. Mrs.

Morrissey insisted I take them. Her treat. I don't know if it's ethical or not, but I didn't want to hurt her feelings."

Cantrell tapped the envelope against table. You couldn't help but notice that his nails were ragged and uneven and in desperate need of trimming. He flicked his gaze around the room and brought it back to me.

"Whatcha think, Chene?"

"Not exactly the type of function I'd fit into, but Spears and Atwater would. If the only one who knows they are on the job is Mrs. Morrissey, they might learn a bit more about the victim."

Cantrell glanced at Kozlowski. He nodded in agreement. Pappy flipped the tickets back to Donna. "Y'all do it right. Dress up like yer supposed to be there."

Donna slid one ticket from the envelope and passed it to Laura. Suarez peeked over her shoulder.

"Maybe they need a chaperone, Pappy. Somebody to keep them out of trouble, in case the bad guys are on the train."

Cantrell ignored him and nodded at Kozlowski. He described the briefing with Naughton and the crew from Squad Five. Three team members conducted the interviews with the employees from the manufacturing shop. As part of their efforts, they had also downloaded all photos and video from the warriors' phones that related to Saturday's games. It turned out that most of the shots were of the employees in various gear and splotches of paint. No one paid much attention to the other gamers.

"But just in case, Naughton is having all video and photos sent to the cyber squad. We'll put a name to every face we can. Naughton and one of his guys started tracking down the other players. I'll coordinate with his squad in the morning for updates. It will take time, but we knew that going in."

Cantrell grunted and nodded. Kozlowski raised a massive hand.

"Copies of the autopsy have been entered into the files. Morrissey was shot three times, in the forehead, the chest, and in the crotch. Sort of a straight line. Slugs look like .22 caliber. Since no brass was found at the scene, it sounds like he used a revolver. With the widow and the governor pressing, the body was released this afternoon. But we may have something here. Morrissey was into fitness."

"Whatcha gettin' at?"

"The autopsy found nicotine in his system." Koz looked at me.

"The widow confirmed that Morrissey didn't smoke. Not even a stogie with the boys on poker night."

"So how's he get nicotine in his system?" Suarez asked. "And what does that mean, anyway? We all probably have some in our bodies."

Cantrell puffed out a cloud. We watched it dissipate across the ceiling and slip through a crack in the casement window.

"Nicotine is poisonous," I said, "the right concentration can be deadly."

"Whatcha sayin'?"

Everyone was looking to me to elaborate. I kept my eyes on Pappy. "You take a jar and place three or four cigarettes in some water. Let it sit overnight. Strain the mixture. Pour the liquid into something with a strong taste, such as scotch, and serve. Death normally occurs within an hour, if the dosage is high. Or mix it with a skin lotion and let the victim absorb the poison that way. Even faster."

Cantrell withdrew his smoldering cigarette and studied it. Then he stuck it back in the corner of his mouth, chuckled and shook his head. "Y'all one sick bastard, Chene."

"You already knew that. But the nicotine in his system complicates matters."

"How so?" Donna asked.

"Because we may have two different people trying to kill him. One tried to poison him and the other took a more direct approach and shot him three times."

****

Back at the house, I dumped the contents of the envelope from Jamie Richmond on the desk in the small bedroom I use as an office. I loaded the flash drive on the computer and started playing the audio files. Kyle Morrissey had the voice of an average guy, nothing distinctive or out of the ordinary. Jamie's voice was clear and direct as she asked questions. I noticed Morrissey tended to give long, elaborate answers. You could hear the level of flirtation rising as he became more comfortable with her.

I was restless. We were only two days into this complex case, yet I wanted to be farther along. With so many factors and potential players involved, we knew this was going to take time. But I wanted to do something. I needed to clear my head. After dragging a lightweight leather jacket from the closet, I locked the house and took off.

Ted lived in an older part of Grosse Pointe, not far from the lake. His brick bungalow was sedate by comparison to some of his neighbors with their three-story castles reaching for the sky. A life-long bachelor, Ted never fussed over his house. It was the garage that he lived for. The original plans had a two car detached garage at the back of the lot, with a long cement driveway. Ted lived there barely a year when he made the only renovations to the property. He had another garage built directly in front of the first, an extension that gave him room for four cars. As far as I knew, I was the only person he'd given a key to it.

Ted was a gearhead. There was no other way to put it. The entire back wall of the garage was lined with tools. While Ted's generosity often shined, he drew the line at his wheels. I parked on the street and let myself in the garage through the three locks on the side door. After disabling the alarm. By the right front corner of the garage was a small section relegated to me. I did a quick inspection of tires, fuel, oil and lights before rolling up the door and hitting the starter.

Ted's cravings all ran to the four-wheeled variety. I'd always been a sucker for motorcycles. A few years ago I'd stumbled onto a Harley Davidson Softtail at a police auction. A combination of luck and sweat had brought me enough parts to put it in solid running order. There was no fairing, or windshield, to deflect the bugs and the breeze. That's the way I liked it.

I powered out along the lake, enjoying the blast of fresh air on my face. In shadowy places, the pavement was slick, so I had to stay alert. The wind tugged at my clothes, gusting every so often with enough force to lift me from the saddle, if I dared to let go. Not a chance in hell.

I cruised out Jefferson, the roadway I was named

after, until the light at Metropolitan Parkway. Turning right would lead me to the beach. Left offered a further expanse of black-topped freedom. I swung left.

The Harley rumbled through the gears with a low, deep-throated roar, gliding effortlessly down the road. The Parkway changed names, becoming Sixteen Mile Road, then Big Beaver Road. I often wondered whose creativity was in play when they dreamed up these street names. The light at Woodward switched red as I was approaching. For the first time in an hour, my mind drifted back to the Morrissey homicide. One of his theaters was not far from here. I turned south along the avenue.

The sidewalk in front of the theater was jammed with patrons of all ages. Kids in the latest punk fashions mingled with graying parents and teenagers. The marquee listed "The Great Race," a comedy with Tony Curtis, Jack Lemmon, Natalie Wood and Peter Falk. I'd seen it many times. I rolled down the block and found a good place to park the bike in a neighboring strip mall on the west side of the street. Locking my helmet to the frame, I headed for the theater.

For once my timing was good. The eight o'clock showing had just gotten underway. There were two screens at this little theater, similar to the setup in Farmington. Another show wasn't scheduled to begin until nine. The teenagers behind the concession stands were bustling about, restocking cups and boxes of candy in preparation for the next wave of customers. The air was thick with the fragrant aroma of freshly made popcorn. As I waited for the manager, I had to fight off the urge to purchase a box.

"I'm Elizabeth Rains." Her voice was confident

and her handshake was firm. "Colleen said to answer any questions you might have."

"I'd appreciate that."

Her eyes flicked over my jeans, boots and motorcycle jacket. Apparently I didn't match her image of a police detective. "I expected an officer to come by earlier today."

I shrugged, the leather creaking on my shoulders. "We've got a lot of ground to cover. But I do appreciate your taking the time to talk with me now."

She beamed a wide smile at me. "Both screens are going and it's too early for a lineup for the second shows. C'mon, I'll show you around."

Elizabeth Rains led me up a wide staircase to the second floor. Colorful posters adorned the walls, tucked into ornate frames. I glanced quickly at the artwork but kept my attention on her.

Perhaps I was becoming jaded by the women Kyle Morrissey surrounded himself with. I was expecting Elizabeth Rains to be another attractive woman, a possible candidate for his personal photo gallery and some extracurricular activity. The smile and the confident attitude were charming, but she didn't fit the physical mold I'd seen throughout the day. Elizabeth was about five foot five with sandy brown hair that was cut short. She wore it a little longer on the sides and had a tendency to brush a stray lock behind her ear. Dark brown eyes were partially hidden behind a small pair of glasses. Her ears were adorned with multiple piercings. She wasn't heavy, but she was rounder than any of Morrissey's other female employees I'd met.

We paused outside the balcony doors. The movie was the old Hitchcock classic "North by Northwest."

Elizabeth checked the crowd and nodded, a pleased look on her face. She guided me away from the doors.

"We can talk privately up here."

"Looks pretty busy for a Monday night."

"We usually draw a good crowd. It's a combination of old movies and reasonable prices. This location always does well."

"Is that a compliment to Morrissey's wisdom or your own skills?"

Elizabeth tipped her head toward me and smiled. "A bit of both. Kyle always thought this was his showcase. The building had been vacant for years before he renovated it. He was determined to make it successful. I bought into that goal."

"So how long have you worked for him?"

Elizabeth stroked her right earlobe. "Almost fifteen years now. I was one of his earliest hires. Back then Colleen and I worked together a lot. We knew each other in high school. Kyle was always hustling, trying everything he could think of to build the business."

"Fifteen years is a long time to work with one company nowadays."

"That's true. But I've got a pretty good gig here. My husband is a financial analyst with one of the big three. He makes excellent money. My income doesn't pay the bills, but it keeps me in wine and shoes and the occasional vacation with girlfriends, so I'm okay with that. It's a job that I'm very good at. That's more important to me than a six figure salary."

Her answers were straightforward and had the ring of honesty to them. I had a lot of experience reading people. Nothing about her demeanor or responses were sending up any signals or concerns.

"What about working with Kyle? Did you ever have any problems?"

She flashed me that smile again. "Everybody has issues with their boss at some stage. I'm sure you do as well."

"Yeah, but my boss didn't get murdered the other day."

"Good point."

"So tell me about the issues."

Elizabeth tugged at her earlobe again. "Kyle and I had a fling years ago. Nothing big. I was going through a rough patch with my marriage. Colleen was busy with the kids and wasn't around that much."

"How far back are we talking?"

"Nine, maybe ten years. We were here, going over reports before a meeting with the city council. There was some nonsense that we had to go through for a restoration project. It was late. We were both tense. The job, our personal lives, everything was in upheaval. It was like nothing was going right for either of us."

I nodded. "It happens."

"Yeah, and I started it. I never thought Kyle found me attractive. Always believed that was one of the reasons Colleen liked me working here. But when I pressed him up against the wall, it was like throwing a switch."

"How long did that last?"

Elizabeth's eyes went out of focus as she considered it. "About three weeks."

"Did you end it, or did he?"

She took a moment before answering. "It was mutual. Fun while it lasted but we both knew there were too many people involved who could get hurt. So we turned our attention to other things."

"No hard feelings?"

She gave her head a brief shake. "We kept it friendly. It was just sex. Neither one of us were looking for true love. Just wanted to blow off a little steam, get rid of the tension that was building up."

"Did any of your employees ever have a problem with Morrissey?"

"No, Kyle knew better than to play around here. Besides, I make it a practice to hire a lot of kids, both male and female. Turnover is normal given the industry. I have two assistant managers and both are older females. Older than me. Rounder too." She said this last part with another grin. "No sense tempting the old fool."

"Did you have any concerns about the business continuing here? Any rumors about plans changing, the company going in a new direction?"

Elizabeth shook her head. "Birmingham loves us now. We are an integral part of a thriving downtown community. It says so right in their literature. Kyle knew that. It's not just about the movies. It's entertainment. It's a commitment."

We headed down the stairs. "Do you have any thoughts as to who would want to harm Morrissey?"

"The business is solid. And he and Colleen seem pretty happy with life in general. Maybe it was a random thing."

Maybe it was. But I had my doubts. I left Elizabeth Rains in the lobby and headed for the Harley. Another interview down and so much more to think about. I rolled south on Woodward, trying to make some sense of it all. At Twelve Mile Road, I realized that Simone's apartment was only a few miles away to the west. I could stop by and surprise her. But I needed to focus on the case. Indecision set in. When the light went green, I roughly twisted the throttle and launched the bike farther south. Maybe I'd see her tomorrow. Or maybe not.

Chapter Ten

Before the meeting ended yesterday, I'd dealt out the assignments. Koz would follow up with Naughton and Squad Five on the interviews. He would check in with the Cyber Squad to see if anything had come up with the videos and photos from the warriors' phones. Koz even suggested Suarez ride along. They would also take a number of the remaining participants from the war games and conduct their own interviews.

Yesterday Cantrell met with a local judge and obtained search warrants for all of Morrissey's properties and vehicles. He'd also gotten a warrant for all financial records, bank accounts and legal files. Laura was going to call on his banks and meet with his accountant to review both personal and professional accounts.

Donna was with me. We were planning to visit the rest of the bookstores and theaters. I got to the post early and updated my report to include last night's conversation with Elizabeth Rains and my thoughts about the material Jamie had given me. While waiting for Donna to arrive, I checked the local newscasts for any other comments on Morrissey. There wasn't much, beyond the fact no memorial service had been scheduled as yet. With the big fundraising event set for Wednesday, I couldn't imagine Colleen Morrissey focusing on anything else.

There was a profile on Morrissey on the Free Press website. Most of the material was a rehash of earlier articles and what I knew from Jamie's research. But the column hinted at more information about recent projects he had been considering. I printed out the article and tucked it in my notes. It may be nothing, but then again, it may be something. It was too early in the investigation to rule anything out.

"Hey, boss."

I glanced up to see Donna sitting at the desk directly across from me. For years that had been Megan McDonald's spot. She'd transferred to a training position at the academy after we'd wrapped up the serial killer case. I was still getting used to Donna working there.

"You ready?"

She nodded. Her eyes flicked around the empty squad room.

"Nervous?"

"Yeah. But I won't let you down."

"I know."

"Any sage words of wisdom before we hit the street?"

I thought back to Suarez and his reluctance yesterday at the company headquarters. "Identify yourself. Make sure you put the recorder on a table or hold it close to the interviewee. Get their names right. Spell them out if you're not sure. And participate. Ask questions. Watch their body language. Watch their eyes and expressions. Don't let them get away with one word answers."

She beamed a smile. "In other words, do what you do."

"Yeah, that will work."

The two remaining bookstores were in Grosse Pointe Woods and Warren. The other theaters were in Royal Oak, St. Clair Shores, Mount Clemens and Grosse Pointe Woods. The last was only a block from the bookstore. It hadn't been my intention yesterday but we'd covered the locations furthest away.

Geographically, we made a circuit, saving the two Grosse Pointe locations for last. Each visit was a reflection of Monday's activity. The only surprise came at the Royal Oak theater, where the manager was a guy named Pete Gentry. He and Morrissey had connected over sports and movies when he was in high school. Pete was in his early thirties and with the company for five years. He'd been an athlete in college. He and Morrissey played tennis once a week until Pete blew out his knee.

"Did you notice anything odd about that guy?" Donna asked me.

"Seemed a little intense when he was talking to you."

Pete had a focused way of looking at you when answering your questions that could be unnerving, as if no one else in the universe existed. I wondered what she made of that.

"He's an average looking guy, but I'll bet he reminded Morrissey of himself. Like there wasn't a woman alive who wouldn't let him do whatever he wanted with her if he amped up that smile a little."

"He get to you?"

She winked at me as we were getting into the car. "I let him think he did. Gave him the impression that he was in control."

We hit the Grosse Pointe theater next. I parked on Mack Avenue, the tree-lined street that gave way to upscale stores. The sidewalks were clean and free from any litter. The cars at the curb were not the kind you'd find ten miles down the road in Detroit. Mercedes, Volvos, BMW's, Cadillacs, Lexus and Porsches all gleamed wax and spoke of brilliant paint jobs. Dented fenders, missing hubcaps and chipped paint were not allowed here. The rain had stopped, but the overcast sky couldn't dim the shine. Donna chuckled as she got out of the car.

"They might tow away your Pontiac for lack of value."

"Or because it needs a wash."

The theater was on the end of the block. From the front, it looked like a boutique, with old movie posters set in the display windows. The four doors in the center were narrow, but outfitted with brass hardware and beveled glass. To the right was the ticket window. Above the counter was a list of the movies scheduled for today and the show times. There was only one screen here. I glanced at the schedule. "City Slickers" a great comedy with Billy Crystal and Jack Palance. The booth was vacant. We had just missed the start of the first show.

Donna tried the doors. Number four was unlocked and we stepped in as a crash of thunder announced another downpour.

Two teen-age girls were restocking the snack counter. A couple of straggling customers were gathering up popcorn and drinks. From behind the theater doors, the music was already announcing the film. The girl on the right, who had at least six earrings dangling from each ear, glanced up at our approach.

"Movie just started. If you hurry, you won't miss much."

Donna had her badge out. "State Police. We need to speak to the manager." She kept her voice low and confidential. I turned my eyes to the posters on the wall that featured coming attractions.

She appeared at my elbow with a small box of popcorn. "The smell was getting to me. I love this stuff." Donna offered the box and I shook some out into my hand. It was still warm, a generous mix of white and yellow kernels with a healthy dose of salt. Morrissey's team learned not to skimp on the essentials.

The earring girl came out from the behind the counter and led us to a small office behind the ticket booth. Inside, a chubby woman with jet black hair was in the middle of an animated phone conversation. She rolled her eyes toward the ceiling, waved us into the vacant chairs across from her and tried several times to end the call. Each effort was interrupted by the party on the other end. Her gaze narrowed as she listened. At length she took control of the situation.

"Listen to me, Charlie. You are not the only supplier in town. If you're not going to make it right, then you can kiss my big Italian ass, right in the middle of Mack Avenue at rush hour. You've got until five o'clock to get me replacement tanks, or I'll switch to another brand." She banged the phone onto its base and puffed out her cheeks. "Wiseass bastard. Thinks because I'm a woman I don't know jack-shit about my business." She shook her head as if to clear her thoughts. "Sorry, guys. I'm not normally so touchy."

"Having a bad day?" Donna asked.

"It's been bad ever since I heard about Kyle. I spent most of yesterday in tears. Damned if I'll do that again." She pulled a tissue from the box on her desk and blotted her eyes. "You guys working his case?"

"We are. Along with several others. I'm Chene. This is Spears. State Police. And you are?"

"Margaret Witter."

"Tell us about the operation here, Margaret. How long you've worked for Morrissey. The programs. The works."

She described what had become the protocol for all of Morrissey's key employees. Friendly, fair, businesslike. He encouraged ideas and comments from everything to the soft drinks used to promotions for one house or the whole chain. According to Margaret, Morrissey once spent five grand to install a new sound system, then ripped it out two weeks later because the quality didn't match the films. He wasn't a perfectionist, but was damn close to it.

"How about the staff here? Concession stand, ticket sales, projectionist. Anybody have a problem with Morrissey, or vice versa?" Donna asked.

Margaret shook her head slowly. "The two kids on the counter are summer help. Just started a couple of weeks ago. There's ten others on board, mostly for the summer. All of them got along well with Kyle when they met him. He was friendly."

"Most of your crew kids?" I asked.

"I get a lot of high schoolers. It's normal for this business. Word spreads through friends. It's not strenuous work and I'm flexible when it comes to the schedule, what with summer vacations and graduation parties and the usual teenage stuff. I tend to hire some new ones in late August to replace those going off to college. That way they're trained and ready to go when we hit the holidays and summer vacation."

"Any vendors Morrissey didn't get along with?"

Margaret shook her head. "Most of the theaters are working with the same suppliers. Whenever someone wanted to try another source for something, we'd get samples sent to each location. All the managers got to vote on it. If Kyle liked it and we all hated it, he'd stand by our decision. There's been more than a few attempts at getting a cheaper brand of popcorn or candy. It may not sound like much, but quality snacks keep some people coming back." Her eyes flicked to the popcorn container in Donna's hand. She smiled briefly. "Need I say more?"

Donna returned the smile. "I'm a sucker for fresh popcorn. You can't compare this to the microwave crap."

I steered the conversation back to the investigation. "No problems with the customers? Any irate fans who can't get the shows they want to see? Anyone who visits frequently and does nothing but complain?"

"No, we have a very genteel crowd. Even with a lot of regulars, we draw plenty of families with the type of movies we run. Kyle loved comedies and adventure movies. Not so graphic as a lot of today's movies, which may explain the calmer crowds."

"How about your relationship with Morrissey?" I asked.

She hesitated for a heartbeat before answering. "Kyle was a great guy. Knew when to lighten things up with a joke or a flirtatious comment, and when to concentrate on business."

"He ever hit on you?"

Margaret sighed deeply. She rested her forearms on the desk, cupping her elbows in her palms. "Honey, I wish to Christ he had. I'm the kind of girl who would have taken him up on it in a New York minute." Her eyes flicked briefly to Donna. "But he never did. With a beautiful wife like Colleen, why would he even look twice at me?"

Donna asked about upcoming movies. My eyes did a quick inventory of the little office. Phones, computer, copier, file cabinet and a safe. Nothing unusual. No unnecessary decor. Margaret offered to let us question the other employees who were present, but I declined. For the moment, anyway.

Back outside, Donna and I dashed through the raindrops for the comfort of the Pontiac. It was going to be one of those Michigan monsoons, with heavy rain all day.

"She didn't exactly fit the mold," Donna said.

"According to the employee list, she's been with Morrissey for a long time. Maybe Colleen had more input about hiring back then. Or Morrissey didn't start opting for fringe benefits until the business grew and he was more successful."

She gave her head a shake. "But wouldn't that put him at more risk?"

"Legal fees, lawsuits, settlements and court costs would certainly play a factor. He may have had the urges in the beginning, but didn't act on them."

The Grosse Pointe bookstore was our last stop. Samantha Griggs was the manager and she was carved from the Morrissey playbook. Young, smart and attractive. She also flashed a large diamond engagement ring.

"Kyle was very supportive of local authors. He was always talking about ways to bring more of them in, to encourage their efforts," Samantha said. She had a soft voice that made me think of a Southern Belle. There was just a hint of an accent.

"How long have you worked here?" Donna asked.

"Six months now. I moved to the area with my husband. We're from South Carolina. He's doing research and development with General Motors."

"Did you work in bookstores before?"

"I was in retail. Mostly clothing. There was a notice in the store when I came in, so I applied and was hired right away. After a month I was made assistant manager. Then the manager went out on maternity leave and decided not to come back. I got the promotion, and here I am." She said this last bit with a dazzling smile and a raised an arm toward a rack of books, like one of the models at the auto show, trying to redirect wandering eyes back to the product.

Samantha was polite and professional. She'd had no problems with Morrissey and was saddened by his death. There was a moment of confusion when we'd asked about her relationship with him. Maybe dealing with lecherous bosses didn't happen in the sunny south. Donna was quiet as we rushed back out to the car.

"What's next, boss?"

I realized it was almost two o'clock. We'd been going at it steadily without a break. Popcorn can only last so long.

"Let's grab some food."

"Thank God. I was about to fade away from lack of nourishment."

Everyone is a smart ass.

****

Since we were close, I headed over to Sharkey's. The lunch rush was long over but there were still about a dozen people in the saloon. I caught Ted's eye as we moved toward a large booth in the far corner. A waitress stopped by and filled two mugs of coffee before hurrying away. Donna sat back and wrapped her hands around the mug.

"No menus?" she asked curiously.

"No need. Anything you allergic to or don't like to eat?"

"I'm not big on sea urchin, but other than that, I'm pretty flexible."

The daily specials were listed on the board by the main door. I'd already checked it out on the way. Ted circled around from the back of the bar and shot me a look with his eyebrows raised. I held up two fingers in a peace sign, then pointed them at Donna and back to myself. He nodded once and disappeared into the kitchen.

"Why do I get the feeling that you're a regular customer?"

It dawned on me this was the first time I'd brought Donna here. Kozlowski and my old partner McDonald knew about this place, as did Cantrell. But I hadn't brought the rookies over yet. Before I could fill her in, Ted appeared beside the table.

"About damn time, Chene. I was beginning to think you're ashamed of me."

"After all these years, you know that's true."

As I made the introductions, Ted slid into the booth beside Donna. Before conversation got started, the

137

waitress returned. On her tray were two steaming bowls of jambalaya and a basket of sourdough rolls. She hustled away, returning with a fresh pot of coffee and a mug for Ted. He sat there quietly for a moment while we dug in. Then Ted tried to work his charm on Donna. I ignored him and focused on lunch.

After the meal Ted diplomatically tried to pry into the investigation. Donna almost slipped, but was quick to recover.

"The boss doesn't like it when we discuss details outside of the squad."

"He won't ever know. You must have some little tidbit you can share with me. I am a pillar of discretion."

Donna shook her head. "Of course he'll know."

"I won't tell him."

I stepped in. "You know the routine. When we get it wrapped up, I'll fill you in. Otherwise, you get your information from Channel 4."

"You're no fun, Chene."

"I get that a lot."

Chapter Eleven

Wednesday morning, I swung by the Cyber Squad to meet with Yekovich. His office was cluttered with reports and parts from several computer components. There was a worktable that filled the back wall of the room. Yekovich was staring at a monitor, his expression dull and lifeless.

"Whatcha watching?"

"Cat videos. Somebody filled a hard drive with hours of stupid cat videos. That's what it looks like at first glance."

"And with a closer look?"

He shifted his gaze to me and raised his coffee mug. "Surveillance videos. Somebody was staking out their home. This ain't your regular security system."

Yekovich explained that a woman had suspected her husband was being unfaithful. She'd hired someone to place hidden cameras throughout their house. Strangely, she avoided the bedrooms. The cameras were wired to motion detectors. Actual footage was laid behind the cat videos. Yekovich was helping one of the smaller local departments by checking the details. Apparently the husband had his own suspicions about the wife. Turns out each one was having multiple affairs. A confrontation ensued that led to her fatally stabbing him while he was choking her. It was unclear if charges were going to be filed.

"Guessing you want an update on Morrissey," Yekovich said.

"If you can tear yourself away from cat videos."

He shrugged. "Lots of soft porn hidden beneath that. But for you, Chene, I'll make an exception."

Yekovich led me down the hall to where his team of technicians were working. He stopped beside a skinny young woman whose platinum blonde hair was cut in ragged lengths and dyed several different colors. Her fingers were dancing across the keyboard like a concert pianist. I noticed a rainbow of colors on her nails. The cubicle was decorated with action figures and drawings of comic book heroes.

"Pinky, this is Chene. He's the lead on the Morrissey case."

The fingers stopped their dance and she swiveled around to face me. "I heard of you. Nice to finally meet."

"Thanks. I'm hoping you've uncovered some secrets."

She thumped a silver polished nail on the counter. "Most of the files in the system are strictly business. Proposals, spreadsheets, income statements, that kind of stuff. I'm almost done with the first pass. Then I'll go through it again, looking for anything that was recently deleted, rough drafts of documents, internet history and all that."

"Anything worthwhile?"

Pinky shrugged. "It's all good background. Financial figures reflect a profitable operation. Lots of promotional events with some video and still photos. No ghosts or shadows that look suspicious. But we have a long way to go. There are drives that were shared throughout the company and a couple of ones only Morrissey had access to. I'm going to focus on those today."

"Was the system backed up internally on a server?"

Pinky flashed a quick smile. "Pretty good, Sarge. No, it was cloud based. I've already hacked his password. That's on my list as well."

Yekovich chimed in. "Anything on that email Kozlowski flagged?"

She shifted her eyes to him. "The numbers for the senders account appear to be a random jumble. But that could mean something to whoever created it. This looks like it was only used to send that one message."

"Aren't most email accounts linked to a phone number?" I asked.

"Yes, but chances are this one was tied to a disposable phone. It's not active. Whatever details I can pull will be in the report."

"What time was the message sent?"

Pinky swung back to her keyboard and clicked away. "It showed up in his email account at exactly nine in the morning."

No other questions came to mind. I thanked Pinky and let her get back to work. Yekovich walked me outside.

"Don't let appearances fool you, Chene. She's one of the sharpest people I've got. Some kind of computer wizard."

"How's that?"

"Pinky taught herself how to write code when she was twelve. Started a business at fourteen designing websites. Got her degree in computer science from Lawrence Tech at sixteen and a Master's degree by the time she hit eighteen. Like I said, she's sharp."

"So how did you land her? With that type of talent, she could name her price and work anywhere."

Yekovich grinned. "Turns out she's a mystery junkie. Loves the idea of using her computer skills to fight crime."

"Yeah, I noticed the action figure theme."

"A couple of the guys call her Batgirl. I think she encourages it."

I drummed my fingers on the roof of the car. "Ask her to focus on that email account. There's got to be something tangible in that message."

"Will do. Good hunting, Chene."

****

It was six o'clock Wednesday evening. Donna and Laura were going out on the Glamour Train, Morrissey's fundraising event. Cantrell had been updated. He kicked the rest of us loose. We were working it hard, but sometimes inspiration materialized when we took a break. I dug out my phone and made the call.

"Hello, stranger."

"Hi. I know this is short notice, but are you free for dinner?"

Simone laughed lightly. "That's not short notice. That's no notice."

"It happens. So is that yes or no?"

"When and where?"

"Now. I'm on the east side but can be in Royal Oak is fifteen minutes."

"Fifteen minutes!"

"I'm stopping at Little Tree. It's been a while since I've had sushi."

She made a derogatory noise. "I'll meet you there." She clicked off without another word.

I didn't know if she was angry or not. But it wasn't long before I'd find out. I swung off the I-696 freeway at Woodward Avenue and worked my way over to Main Street. My luck held as I found a parking spot in the lot behind the restaurant. The place was three quarters full as I was guided to a small table near the windows. I sat with my back to the wall and was glancing at the menu when Simone came in. Getting to my feet, I tried to get a read on her. She pushed her sunglasses up into her hair and gave her head a gentle shake as she got close. Simone leaned in and gave me a brief kiss. She was tense.

"You okay?"

"Fine." Her mannerisms said otherwise.

I said nothing. She tried for a stern expression but couldn't hold it.

"You really don't get it, do you?"

Simone propped her left elbow on the table and cupped her chin in the palm of her hand. The waitress appeared. I ordered a glass of wine for each of us.

"What don't I get?" I asked when we were alone.

"You call a woman about dinner, but you give her no time to get ready. You invite her to the same restaurant where you had your first date. And you don't even think it's a big deal."

"You don't need time to get ready. You're beautiful."

She waved away the compliment with her free hand. "Is that so?"

"Yes, it is so. And if you needed more time to get ready, you could have told me. It's just that this place was close by for both of us and I'm hungry. It's been a long time since breakfast."

"Really. So it was just convenient?"

I nodded. "I haven't seen you since Sunday night. It's tough when we're in the middle of a complicated case. I just thought it would be nice to have dinner."

"So you're saying you missed me?"

This was unfamiliar territory for me. But I sensed there was only one right answer. "Yes. I miss you."

She relaxed a bit and rolled her eyes. "That's nice to hear. But would it have killed you to call me earlier?"

The waitress returned with our wine. Simone took a quick glance at the menu, then closed it and looked at me. I ordered sushi dinners for both of us.

"That's what we had last time," she said quietly.

"I remember. And for the record, I didn't think that was a date."

She shook her head and gave a little laugh. "You bought me a nice dinner and a glass of wine. We sat over on the other side of the room. We talked for a while. I learned about your background, you learned about mine. That was a date."

"Okay. It was a date."

"Our first date. You being a detective and all, I thought you'd remember."

I took a sip of wine. "I do remember. It was late March. I remember the conversation, the wine and the meal. You were wearing a yellow blouse with a gray wool skirt and a gray leather jacket."

She smiled. "So observant. But you gave me more than fifteen minutes to get ready that night."

"You could have said no tonight."

"Chene, for such a smart guy, you can be kind of dumb when it comes to women and dating."

"So I've been told. What exactly did I do wrong?"

She laughed and shook her head again. After another sip of wine, she put her chin back in her palm and stared at me. Her eyes were glowing now. Apparently I was about to be forgiven for whatever gaffe I'd made.

"What am I wearing? Look me in the eyes, Mr. Detective, and just tell me what I'm wearing."

I complied with her request. "Black high heels with open toes. Navy blue slacks, tailored to fit your shape. A white linen blouse with very fine blue and red stripes. One thin gold necklace and a pair of gold earrings that dangle. Another pair of diamond stud earrings. No watch, no rings, no bracelets."

"Impressive. So what do you think?"

"I think I'm still confused as to why you're upset."

I was saved from further humiliation by the arrival of dinner. Simone graciously changed the subject. We talked about her work and the Morrissey case. I told her about the recent interviews and the goldmine of photos and notes from Jamie Richmond, Malone's lady friend. We worked our way through dinner and another glass of wine and kept the conversation light. It was only as we walked out that I had a chance. Recently, when we walked together, I'd taken to sliding an arm around her waist. That's how we were as we stopped beside her car.

"Have you figured it out yet, Jeff?"

"Not a clue."

She stepped away from me and put her hands on her hips. "When was the last time I wore slacks when we went out? Not jeans, but slacks."

I thought about that. "I can't recall you ever wearing slacks before."

"Exactly. Do you know why I'm wearing slacks?"

"Not a clue," I repeated.

She huffed out a breath in frustration. "Because I haven't shaved my legs in a few days and wasn't expecting to see you tonight."

"So if I'd given you more than fifteen-minutes notice…"

"…I would have shaved my legs and worn a skirt."

Simone was struggling to keep a disgusted look on her face. It wasn't working. I took her hands and pulled her close.

"Next time, I'll give you more notice."

"Promise?"

"Yeah."

She hugged me. "You're still kind of dumb about women, Chene."

"I know. But there is one thing you should keep in mind."

Simone leaned back. "What's that?"

"I would pay to shave those legs."

She burst out laughing. Pushing me away, she got in her car and started it up. I watched her pull out of the parking space and start to exit the lot. Then she stopped, backed up alongside me and lowered the window. Her eyes were dancing as she took a moment to look at me.

"One question."

"What's that?"

"How much?"

****

It was after midnight and I was slowly driving

home. I'd given Simone a five- minute head start, then gone to her apartment. She greeted me with a warm smile. We kissed. I took her hand and led her to the bathroom. As the tub filled I took my time undressing her. Then I very carefully shaved her legs. Afterward we moved onto other things. I knew sleep wouldn't happen for me, so I opted to head home. Replaying the scene in the parking lot got me thinking about her last words. "How much?"

Money. Sometimes, it all comes down to money. In more than one situation, Cantrell would rub his thumb against his forefinger in a circular motion and grumble 'Y'all gotta follow 'em dollars' or words to that effect.

So now I was trying to figure out how Kyle Morrissey, a kid who barely made it out of college, with no funding from his dysfunctional family or friends, could suddenly put together a bankroll to buy the first theater. Not only to make the purchase, but to have enough capital to renovate it. This wasn't a case where you picked up a couple of gallons of Benjamin Moore semi-gloss and slapped it on the walls. From Laura's research, it was evident that a great deal of effort went into the old Shores Madrid.

So, where did the money come from?

There had to be an easy answer. But I was damned if I could figure it out. I needed more information. There were too many gaps.

****

Early Thursday morning I decided to recruit some help. Someone who was comfortable with research, who was used to digging deeper, who had a fresh set of eyes and a different perspective. So I made the call.

"Malone." His voice was thick with sleep.

"It's Chene. I've got a few more questions for Jamie. Is she around?"

There was a deep chuckle. "Yes, but she's not coherent. You have any idea how early it is?"

"Sun's been up for a couple of hours."

"She'll call you." The phone went silent.

I remembered now that Malone worked afternoons, finishing his shift around midnight. No wonder I woke him up.

It was an hour before Jamie called back.

"Sorry, Chene, but I'm adjusted to Malone's schedule. Neither one of us is functioning before nine. And even then it requires massive doses of caffeine."

"No problem. I wanted to thank you again for your notes on Morrissey."

"I hope they were helpful."

"Indeed. But that leads me to a question. Do you know how he put together the money to buy the Shores Madrid?"

Dead silence followed for so long I thought the connection broke. I was about to check and see if there was still a signal when Jamie cursed.

"I don't know. But that's something I should have looked into when researching him. Damn it! How did I miss it?"

"You're not the only one. Everything I can find seems to look like he just appeared on the scene at a city council meeting, with a proposal to buy the property for the amount of taxes due. Somewhere along the way, the theater had been foreclosed and the city ended up with it. They must have carried the previous owner's debt in the hopes that they'd be able to bring it back."

"But that doesn't explain where he got the money." There was a flicker of excitement in her voice. "I never saw anything about investors, silent or otherwise. There was nothing on the corporate records at the time beyond his wife and a couple of key people in management. I looked!"

"So you have any ideas about the money?"

"None." She paused, as if weighing the options. "But I can look into it. I still have a lot of contacts. I'll pull court records, public information, talk to a few friends and see what I can learn. This is important, isn't it?"

"It could be." I hesitated, weighing my options. "I can't ask you to do this, Jamie. I'll put one of the detectives on it."

There was another pause, followed by a loud, raucous laugh. "Bullshit, Chene. You called me hoping I'd jump in."

"No, I called you to ask about the money, not to draw you into part of an active police investigation." I managed to sound sincere.

"You're full of shit, Chene. And I'll let you know when I have some answers." Jamie was still laughing as she ended the call.

Donna looked up from her desk. "Do I want to know what that was about?"

"Not really. I'll let you know if it works out."

"Suarez called. He'll be here in five."

We were meeting this morning. Pappy Cantrell wanted an update from the Glamour Train event last night. I think he was also hoping that the rest of us may have had some form of inspiration. Knowing Laura and Donna had a late event, he had graciously pushed the meeting back until 8:30. That was gracious for Pappy.

Kozlowski was at his desk, staring intently at his computer. Laura wandered in with a dozen bagels and headed straight to the conference room. The rest of us followed.

Pappy was in his usual spot. Laura handed him the bag and a large cup of coffee. He winked at her.

"Y'all always was my favorite."

"Anybody bringing you coffee is your favorite," Koz said.

"True dat. But she also brung me breakfast." Cantrell rummaged in the bag and pulled out two bagels. Then he offered it to Laura and Donna before sliding it across the table. Suarez came in and dropped into his chair. Once the bagels had been divvied up, Cantrell turned his eyes on Laura. "Git on with it."

"There were about a hundred people on the train. It started out with drinks and appetizers. Waiters in tuxedos and gloves moving between the cars. Three railcars outfitted with different dining stations. People were encouraged to mingle about. Since that was the format, we worked opposite ends of the train. I think there were a dozen women modeling fashions." She passed last night's program around.

Donna chimed in. "Some of the patrons were also wearing designer outfits. Even the widow had on a dress that had to be worth a couple grand."

They went back and forth, describing the evening. Many people were taking pictures of the models. It was encouraged, with the hope that patrons would post the shots on social media and help promote the event and the designers. Once that was understood, both detectives worked their cameras. All photos were downloaded at the end of the night and sent to the cyber unit. The intent was to create one file. Donna made sure to capture all the waiters and staff as well as patrons.

"I talked to a lot of people who knew Kyle Morrissey," Laura said. "There were a few tears shed, mostly by the women. None of the men seemed to be overly upset by his murder. I caught more than a couple staring hungrily at Colleen."

"Any of 'em stakin' a claim?" Pappy asked.

"Not that I saw."

Cantrell turned his attention to me. "So what's it all mean?"

"Means we have a few more people to consider or eliminate." I nodded to Donna. "Take Laura with you. Cyber should be able to combine those pictures in short order. Meet up with the widow Morrissey and have her identify everyone."

"We got a copy of the invitation list last night. That might help too," Donna said.

"Yeah, but some people may have bought tickets then given them to someone else to use. Compare the photos against the guest list. Then check with the railroad. Get names of all the waiters and staff on that run."

"So we can compare them with the warriors," Laura said.

Morrissey's service was scheduled for Friday morning at Verheyden's Funeral Home in Grosse Pointe Park. Cantrell knew what I had in mind. He made a note to contact the Cyber Squad about video surveillance. It was understood that we would all be in attendance. Strange things have been known to occur at funerals and memorial services. On the off chance that the shooter attended, we may be able to match their photo with a facial recognition software.

Pappy nodded. "What else?"

I pointed at the program which had come to rest in from of Kozlowski. "Go to each store or designer that's listed. Talk to the owners, get details on the models. See what connection or interaction they had with Morrissey."

Koz gave me a single nod and placed a giant hand on the program, pulling it close. "It's a dirty job, but I'm up to the challenge."

"Take Suarez with you."

Cantrell raised his eyebrows at that but let it slide. "Whatcha gonna do?"

"I've got a meeting with a lawyer."

Chapter Twelve

There was plenty of time to make the drive to the law offices in Warren. I tried to see the attorney yesterday but he was tied up in court. His clerk assured me I'd get a solid fifteen minutes at ten o'clock. I'd start with fifteen and see where it went.

The office was located on the seventh floor of a new commercial building on Van Dyke, just a few miles up the road from the General Motors Tech Center. The firm was Garnett, Kiley and Cohen. My appointment was with Ben Cohen. The reception area was professionally decorated. There were portraits of the three founders, along with half a dozen associates. Arriving five minutes early, I was a little surprised that the attorney was immediately available.

Ben Cohen was an affable guy in his late thirties, a couple of inches shorter than me with a thick head of wavy brown hair and sharp brown eyes. He looked physically fit. I noticed a photo on the credenza behind him of several people on racing bicycles, all decked out in matching gear. Maybe riding a bike was a requirement to work there.

"What can I do for you, Sergeant Chene?" He waved me toward a small conversation area away from his desk. We settled into matching swivel rockers across a low coffee table.

"I need anything and everything you have on Kyle

Morrissey. Personal and professional paperwork. Whatever you've got."

Cohen grimaced. "I'm sure you're aware of client confidentiality."

"I am." Withdrawing the search warrant from my coat, I flipped it onto the table. The rocker was very comfortable. I waited while he reviewed it.

"This is rather unusual."

"So is homicide."

Cohen glanced up. "Point taken. We never did personal matters for Kyle. It's all corporate work. Each time he considered a new location or enterprise, we would draw up all the necessary documentation."

"Were you his primary contact?"

"I've only worked with him the last seven years. Martin Garnett, who founded the firm, was the original attorney of record. Martin suffered a debilitating stroke."

"That trigger the biker's gang?"

He grinned. "Actually, that was Marty's idea. We're a tightly knit group here. He heard several of us talking about how much fun it was to ride. Offered to sponsor a team in a local race. Once we got started it's hard to stop. The rides can be vigorous. We train a couple of times a week."

"How far do you ride?"

"Some races are a hundred miles. You should check it out."

I gave my head a negative shake. "Not without a motor. What can you tell me about Kyle Morrissey?"

Cohen hesitated before answering. "He was a smart businessman. But there were times when his actions confused me. I don't claim to understand his operations.

He would spend a great deal of time, energy and money on a project, then discard it if he couldn't make it fit with his mission."

"Any personnel related issues you have to deal with?"

A brief smile crossed his face. "Well, if you've been investigating Kyle, you probably stumbled upon an indiscretion or two."

"Let's say more than two. Anything go big? Like a sexual harassment claim?"

"Not quite. There were a few times when he would contact me and ask for an agreement to be drafted. Usually along the lines of a severance package, with a very generous payout."

I said nothing. Cohen rocked slightly in his chair, considering his next statement. He knew the game. I waited.

"A review of his files didn't reveal a pattern, more like the occasional indiscretion, going back more than ten years. After the second one I drafted for him, I offered Kyle some advice."

"Such as?"

"That perhaps it would be prudent for him to refrain from such extracurricular activities in lieu of his business and marriage and his net worth."

"You encouraged him to keep his dick in his pants."

Cohen chuckled. "That's a little blunt, but the message is the same."

"And his response?"

"He laughed. Kyle said if he couldn't have a little fun once in a while, what was the point of working so hard?"

"What was your reaction?"

"I made certain that none of our young female associates interacted with Mr. Morrissey. No reason to put our people at risk. He gave me the impression it was a challenge. I wondered if that was part of the attraction for him, as if it really was a harmless game."

"Maybe somebody didn't think it was harmless."

Cohen offered me the use of a conference room. I could review the files here and if there were some in particular that could be helpful, copies could be made. Rather than actual paper files, the conference room had a desktop computer with a large screen that would make it easy to read the documents. It didn't take Cohen long to get it set up. Perhaps he'd been expecting this.

"I have a client waiting. Is there anything else I can do for you, Sergeant Chene?"

"You have any idea where he got the money to start the business?"

Cohen shook his head. "He'd already been operational for several years before he came to the firm. Marty met him at some charity event and they hit it off. I'm not sure who handled his legal efforts before then. Honestly, I have no idea."

"You're not the only one." We shook hands and he guided me to the conference room.

I spent the next three hours poring over the corporate documents. Cohen's clerk was a young woman named Emma, a second year law student who was attending Wayne State University. She wore a somber black suit with low heels and an ivory blouse. Emma quickly showed me the computer system and the files and brought me a large cup of very good coffee in a heavy mug.

Most of the paperwork reflected the purchase or sale of properties, a partnership agreement, and the usual corporate registration documents for the state and the IRS. Cohen even included the settlement agreements. There were five of them. The oldest was a dozen years back, the most recent was three years ago. Maybe he was more selective now. Or maybe he just didn't bother paying someone off. Emma provided copies from those that contained the pertinent details. Now I had more information, but there were still a lot of questions. And very few answers. I needed answers.

****

On my way to Morrissey's office, my phone started ringing. Ted didn't even wait for me to speak.

"I need you to swing by here today."

"And hello to you too. I'm in the middle of a homicide case."

"I wouldn't ask if it wasn't important."

Ted could be many things, but he rarely asked for my help. "It will be tonight."

"Whenever. As long as it's today."

"Later, old man."

He hung up without another word. I didn't have time to wonder what that was about as I parked in front of Morrissey's building. The mood in the office was subdued. Valerie Mann was expecting me. Without delay she steered me to her office. I noticed that Colleen's office was dark. Valerie's expression was stern. She pointed me toward a visitor's chair as she took her seat behind the desk.

"Things are a little stressful, Detective. What do you need?"

"I was hoping to speak with Mrs. Morrissey."

"She's making the final arrangements for tomorrow's funeral. I don't expect her to be in the office again until next Monday."

"Which is why I'm hoping you can fill in some blanks for me."

Valerie laced her fingers as if she wanted me to admire her manicure. It still looked as polished as it had on Monday when we'd first met. I waited while she drew a breath and let it out slowly.

"I know you have a job to do. It's just a very difficult time for all of us."

"I understand. Are there any concerns about the business continuing?"

"Why no! Colleen has assured us that we will maintain operations, just as Kyle would have wanted. Each unit is profitable, although some more so than others. I doubt she would consider selling."

I wasn't convinced. "Are there potential buyers for the business?"

"There have been a few overtures the last couple of years. But nothing Kyle took seriously. The movies and the bookstores are like his children. He'd never sell."

"I met with the company's lawyers earlier. Do you know if Kyle and Colleen have a personal attorney?"

She hesitated. I watched her eyes flick away. Here it comes.

"I'm sure they must, but I have no idea who that might be."

"It's a bad idea to lie to a cop, Valerie. Sooner or later, the truth comes back to bite you in the ass."

Her body jolted as if I'd slapped her. "There may be something in Kyle's contact list. He didn't keep business cards. When someone gave him one, he'd put the details on his computer."

"And you have access to that file?"

"Yes. It's on the network."

"Let's take a look."

I could have had the Cyber Unit scan the files but there was a chance she'd give me more than just a name and a number. Valerie turned to the computer and pulled the chair closer to the desk as I came around beside her.

"Why did you lie to me?"

She shifted her head just enough to look me in the eye. "I don't like you."

"It's not a popularity contest. I'm trying to figure out who killed your boss."

"You're abrasive."

I shrugged. "If I have to be."

"Your mother must be so proud." Her voice was dripping with sarcasm.

"I wouldn't know. I never met her."

Valerie opened her mouth to say something, but no words came out. Her cheeks and throat flushed scarlet. She swallowed once and turned her attention to the computer. I watched as she scrolled through a list of files and brought up a folder labeled 'contacts'.

"So there must be some other reason you lied, other than not liking me."

"I just don't see how any of this could help you find his killer."

I pointed at the computer monitor. Slowly she ran through the list of names. Valerie stopped occasionally to jot down the details for several people listed as attorneys. It was tempting to see if there were any recent emails between them and Morrissey. I was about to ask but figured Yekovich and Pinky would be able to tell me. We finished with the list. Valerie switched off the computer.

"Want to tell me about the lie?"

She let out a ragged breath. "You're impossible."

I rested a hip on the desk. She remained in the big chair. Self-consciously she crossed her legs, then tugged the hem of her skirt down toward her knee. It didn't cover much. "I'm in no hurry."

"I thought you were trying to catch a killer."

"I am. But my boss gets pissed if I do a sloppy job and miss something."

Valerie folded her hands in her lap. "I have nothing more to say. Unless you have questions related to Mr. Morrissey's business dealings, I'm going to ask you to leave. We have a number of things to finish up before tomorrow's services."

I decided not to push it. She was obviously holding something back. Whether it was pertinent to the case was anyone's guess. Tucking the papers into my pocket, I pushed away from the desk. Valerie stayed in the chair.

"Good-bye, Sergeant."

"I'll see you around, Ms. Mann."

It obviously wasn't the response she was hoping for.

****

Everyone else was on assignment. I could have called in the details to one of the support staff, but Pappy always liked to keep things close. It was just as easy to swing by the office. At my desk, I punched in the information on the five settlement agreements. A search of the state's driving license records gave me current addresses on two. Credit checks came up with one new last name, which led to an address and phone numbers. I'd found three out of the five. You can find almost anything on the Internet. Of course, access to official databases doesn't hurt.

A series of phone calls and I was back out the door a little after two. My first stop was with Abigail Prentiss, who was managing a women's clothing store in Mt. Clemens. She waved me toward a small office in the back. I watched as she opted to lean against the desk in the center of the room. Abigail was about thirty, with a very short cut to her thick blonde hair. There was humor dancing in her blue eyes and she flashed me a toothy grin. She braced one hand behind her on the desk. The other hand slowly rubbed her distended stomach.

"I haven't thought of Kyle Morrissey in almost five years."

"First things first," I said. "When are you due?"

"Three weeks. But this kid is either going to be a dancer or a soccer player. She doesn't stop moving."

Glancing beyond her I saw a series of finger painted pictures taped to the wall. "Second one?"

"Yes. Already have a boy, so the girl will make the set."

"How old is he?"

"Two. And if you're thinking he might be Kyle's you're dead wrong. He never got into my panties, despite his repeated efforts."

My palms went up defensively. "I hadn't gotten that far yet. Tell me about it."

"I was engaged when Kyle made his first pass at

me. He had always been charming. Thought I couldn't resist him, but I'd seen all his antics before. I worked the Shores Madrid for a year in high school and came back after college as an assistant manager. I was in the job for about a month before he tried the first time."

"What happened?"

Abigail closed her eyes. At first I thought she was reflecting on the past, until she began to rub slow circles across her stomach. She drew a deep breath, held it for as long as she could, then let it out in a gasp. "Definitely a dancer."

"Are you okay?"

She nodded. "Relax, Detective. I'm not going into labor. I hope."

"Three more weeks, huh?"

"Unless my doctor miscalculated." Abigail gave a little shudder. "Morrissey. First pass wasn't much. He happened to be there when I came in to work the evening shift. I'd just gotten engaged. Nick surprised me the night before with a ring. All the kids were clamoring around, checking it out. Everyone was hugging me. Morrissey did too. But he clung a bit longer than was comfortable."

I glanced at her left hand. She wasn't wearing jewelry. Abigail caught my eyes and laughed a deep, throaty blast.

"I'm guessing you don't have children, Detective. My whole body is swollen, including my fingers. There's no way I can wear my rings."

"Add that to the growing list of things I don't know about women. So Morrissey made the most of that clinch?"

"He did. I'm a little rounder than most of the

women he hired for the theaters, but he still went for it."

"What happened next?"

"About two weeks later, he stopped by. Said he wanted to get my reactions to some new movies he was considering." She shrugged. "I was skeptical. He put his arm around my shoulders when we were in the office, looking at the listings. I started to pull away and his hand slid down my arm. That's when he cupped my breast."

"What did you do?"

"Told him I was going to file a harassment claim. I'd managed to speed dial my home number on my cell phone. The whole conversation was being recorded on my answering machine. I told Morrissey that and said the media would be my second call. His wife would be the first."

"What did he do?"

Abigail shook her head and gave me a wry smile. "Son of a bitch didn't let go. He just kept rolling his thumb against my nipple. Said he'd understand if I wanted to quit and he'd give me a generous payment to make it all go away. He named a number. I told him to double it." She shrugged again. "He did. An attorney showed up at my apartment the next afternoon with a document and a check. He assured me it was real and encouraged me to have another attorney look it over. That was the last I ever saw of Morrissey."

I knew how much the payment had been. That was more than a year's salary for an assistant manager at a theater.

"So you had no other contact with him or the theater?"

"I called the manager and said I wouldn't be back. Then I called each of the girls working there, said if he ever touched them to call the cops. I think he stopped."

"Maybe he did."

Abigail thought about it. "I doubt it."

****

It was after eleven Thursday night when I stopped by Sharkey's. Ted was on a stool at the corner of the bar, scoping out the dwindling action. A scowl crossed his features as I approached.

"Thanks for finally showing up," he grumbled.

"I told you it would be late."

He fluttered a hand back and forth in front of me. "Yeah, yeah, yeah. Let's walk and talk." To my surprise he headed for the exit, stopping briefly to explain something to one of the bartenders.

The air was thick and steamy. I was hoping a little breeze from the lake would make it more comfortable. For a short man, Ted has always been able to cover a lot of ground quickly. He makes the most of his stride. I stepped in alongside him as we moved into the marina. Boats of various sizes, shapes and colors bobbed in their docks.

"All right, we're walking. Tell me what this is about."

"I'm almost out of time. If you hadn't shown up by midnight, I didn't know what I was gonna do." He stopped and rested a hand on a dock piling.

"You ain't Cinderella. Midnight has never been a problem for you. Out with it."

He shot me another scowl. "I need a favor."

"A favor? I'm neck deep in a homicide investigation and you need a favor."

Ted raised his hands. "It's not really for me. It's for a friend. She needs our help. And I already promised it would be taken care of."

"Imagine my surprise that there's a woman involved."

"When did you become so sarcastic?"

"I learned it from you! Tell me what the hell is going on."

So he did.

Tied to the dock behind him was a sleek fiberglass boat. The hull and deck gleamed under the marina's lights. Turns out the boat belonged to a guy who had been enjoying a mid-life crisis when he suffered a fatal heart attack at the most inopportune moment. Since he'd never changed his will, the ex-wife was going to inherit the boat along with the rest of his estate. But everything was being delayed as his latest girlfriend was suing to get her share of the fortune. Meanwhile money was tight.

"What does this have to do with me?"

"The lady is a good friend of mine."

"Which translates to mean that you're playing house with the ex-wife." It was a statement, not a question.

He shrugged, neither confirming nor denying it. How convenient.

"So what do you need me for?"

"The marina will charge her another month's fees if the boat is still here after midnight. So I thought since you've got that house on a canal and there's a dock right there, maybe you could take it and keep it while all this is getting worked out."

"That's your emergency? You want to store your

current plaything's boat at my place?"

He shrugged again. "When you put it that way…"

Exasperation edged my voice. "What other way would you put it?"

"C'mon, Jeff. You can use it any time you want. The guy had it detailed at the start of the season. The bottom's been scrubbed, fresh wax all around and even the chrome's polished." Ted dug into his pocket and pulled out a set of keys.

I left him standing there and walked down the dock to take a closer look. The boat was gorgeous. The chrome twinkled. There were snaps and grommets around the cockpit area to accommodate a canvas cover. It was a short step from the pier to the deck. It took me less than a minute to familiarize myself with the equipment.

Ted whistled. I looked up and saw him toss the keys in my direction. I plucked them out of the air. He moved down the dock to track my movements.

"She's a twenty-eight-footer. The cabin is pretty cozy. He's got radar, a full communications and sound system. Everything below is like new. I don't think there are three hundred hours on the engine."

"I'm not buying this, old man."

"Nah, you're just gonna store it for me. A few weeks, a month at the outside and you get to use it whenever you want."

"What about paperwork? Last thing I need is to get stopped out on the lake and try to explain this fish story."

Ted pointed at a cupboard next to the wheel. Inside were the complete registration, insurance papers and the owner's manual. I locked it up.

"It shouldn't take you more than fifteen minutes to get to your place. I'll meet you there and bring you back for your car."

What the hell could I say? It was a gorgeous boat.

Chapter Thirteen

It wasn't raining Friday morning, but it was overcast and threatening. I got to St. Clare of Montefalco Church on Mack Avenue early and checked with the tech squad. They were ready and well positioned. I was wearing my charcoal suit with a burgundy tie. Just being in dress clothes made me uncomfortable. Using the side mirror on the surveillance van, I checked my reflection. After paying respects to the family at the funeral home across the street, I drifted toward the church. Now Morrissey's friends and family were arriving for the funeral Mass.

Blending into the crowd were the other four members of the squad. Donna was dressed in a black suit, with slacks. Ramon wore a dark blue vested suit and a somber expression. Maybe there was hope for him yet. I noticed he gently took Donna's elbow and steered her toward a pew on the right side.

Kozlowski was in a gray pin-striped suit that would have wrapped around me twice. Laura had chosen a knee length black knit dress that hugged her figure and offered the occasional flash of leg where the skirt was slit. Not exactly crime fighting attire, but I doubted she'd be giving chase to anyone today. The intent was to blend into the crowd and observe.

Most of the visitors were already inside the church, mumbling in deference to the huge chapel that could easily handle a thousand people. I was speaking to one of the uniformed officers who would be escorting the procession to the cemetery when I sensed someone approaching. Her footsteps were quick and determined on the old marble floors.

"Hello, Sergeant."

There was tension in her voice, as if she had been gearing up for a conflict. I nodded to the cop and turned around to face her. Valerie Mann was wearing a black suit with a short black skirt and a white blouse, open at the throat. A small gold chain twinkled in the dim light of the church. She had a tiny black bag dangling from her shoulder, big enough to hold a lipstick and maybe a small bottle of perfume.

"Ms. Mann. I expected you to be seated up front."

"That's for the family and close friends. There are a number of employees sitting over there. People who worked with Kyle for a long time." She paused and made a minor adjustment to her collar. "Why are you here?"

"It's part of the investigation. Police often attend a funeral."

Anger flashed in her eyes. "You'll embarrass the family."

"I doubt that. I'll stay in the background. No one will think twice about my being here, unless you call attention to it."

Above us the pipe organ music began. Where we stood by the main entrance, I could see the hearse bringing the casket from the funeral home across the street. I checked my watch and turned back toward the chapel. Valerie remained at my side.

"You shouldn't be here, Sergeant."

I took her by the arm and guided her toward a pew on the left side of the chapel, about where the others from the office were sitting. "That's not up to you. Now unless you want to make a scene, I'd suggest you join your colleagues and let me do my job."

Valerie bit back a response as the music continued. Yanking her arm from my hand, she slid into the pew beside Andreski, the marketing guy. I drifted back into the recesses of the enormous Catholic church.

She'd been ready for a fight, probably simmering all night long like a pot of five alarm chili. What I couldn't quite figure out was why. Did she want Morrissey's killer to get away with it? Or was there something else she was afraid our investigation would uncover? If that was the case, why take such an aggressive attitude toward me? At the back of the church, the pallbearers were starting to come forward. I glanced at Valerie and saw the confusion on her face as Morrissey's casket moved toward the altar.

The ceremony went faster than I anticipated. The priest was about Morrissey's age, and claimed to have known him well. Listening with half an ear to the sermon about death and being reborn, I scanned the faces in attendance. There were several people I had met during the investigation, along with some local dignitaries and low level celebrities. But no one seemed out of place to me. Most of the people were genuinely there to pay their respects to Morrissey or his family. As the group followed the casket out, Valerie fell into step beside me.

"Find the killer?"

"Not yet. Sometimes they show up to witness the ceremony."

"Isn't that kind of a cliché?"

Her comment reminded me of the conversation I'd had with the widow on Monday. I nodded in agreement. "Most homicides are committed by someone the victim knew. In this case, if it was someone he was close to, their absence at the funeral might be suspicious. And that's the last thing a killer wants to do, draw attention in their direction."

We were outside the church now and people were filing toward their cars for the procession to the cemetery. I saw Kozlowski's BMW about ten spaces back in the line and Suarez's car was near the end. My Pontiac was toward the middle. Valerie stayed beside me.

"You're going to the cemetery?"

"Yeah. Want to tag along?"

She nodded. At my car I opened the passenger door and she slid quickly into the seat. Reflexively my eyes flicked to her trim legs as she swept them into the car. I'm a guy. Who could blame me? I'm also a detective. We're trained to notice details.

We didn't speak for a few minutes when the procession got under way. It was a thirty-minute ride out to the cemetery in Mt. Clemens. My eyes were on the traffic, most of the time.

"I'm sorry." She said it so quietly I almost missed it.

"Forget it."

"No, I can't." Her voice remained subdued. "I know you have a job to do. Kyle being murdered has shaken me up more than I realized. It's surreal. And every time I see you, it's a reminder that not only is he dead, but that someone brutally murdered him."

171

"Lighten up, girlie."

She spun toward me, a momentary flash of anger. "Girlie?"

"No disrespect intended. That's a term my boss has been known to use."

"I still feel bad." Her voice returned to that quiet tone.

"You've been defensive around me since we met. These are trying circumstances. We all want the same thing."

"I hope you're right." She turned back toward the windshield. "You should wear a suit more often, Sergeant. Makes you look professional."

"I'll keep that in mind."

The priest did a quick summation at the grave. This could have been urged on by the storm clouds that gathered quickly on the horizon and the low rumble of thunder that accompanied them.

One of the directors from the funeral home made an announcement that the family would be hosting a luncheon at a nearby restaurant, and that all in attendance were welcome. Slowly the crowd began to disperse. Valerie and I remained just off to the side of the gravesite, watching the last of the mourners speak with the family. We moved back a few cars and the rest of the squad gathered around.

"This is Valerie Mann, from Mr. Morrissey's office. You've already met Detective Suarez." I introduced her to Kozlowski, Spears and Atwater.

"How you want to play it, Chene?" Koz asked.

"Let's go to the luncheon. Mingle and spread out." I turned to Valerie. "I'll give you a ride back to the church, unless you want to go to the wake."

"Colleen would expect me to be there. I'll go with you."

Kozlowski hesitated, then took Laura's arm. Suarez followed his lead and guided Donna away. The other mourners were already headed for their cars.

****

There were just too many possibilities. Too many options. And still we had no motive. Jealousy. Anger. Greed. Something had to trigger Morrissey's death. It's possible someone revealed a motive during the wake. A few people got up after the meal and shared old stories about Kyle Morrissey. Somehow as things broke up, I found myself with Valerie Mann still by my side. The anger that had been bubbling beneath the surface was gone. In a demure voice she asked if I could give her a ride back to the church for her car. We were almost there when my cell phone buzzed.

"Chene."

"Hi, Sergeant Chene. It's Dale Morrissey." He sounded young and nervous.

"Thought we were skipping formalities."

"I just wanted to thank you again for coming to the service today, Jeff."

"Everything okay?"

"I don't know if it's wrong or not, but I found something I think you should see. Can you swing by?"

"Sure. I'll be there in about ten minutes."

"Thanks. I'll meet you out front." There was a click and the line went dead. I slid the phone back in my pocket.

"Troubles?" Valerie asked.

"I dunno. That was Dale Morrissey. Said he found something he thinks I should see. I'll find out after I drop you off."

"Maybe I should go with you. I know Dale. He's a good kid. He's comfortable with me."

There was no reason I could think of to keep her out. So I shrugged and spun a quick left on Mack Avenue and headed toward the Morrissey home. Dale was wearing jeans and a green T shirt. He was leaning on the fender of an old Dodge sedan when I pulled to the curb. He recognized Valerie and nodded briefly. She stepped over and gave him a hug.

"Thanks for coming, Jeff."

"No trouble at all."

"Where's everyone else, Dale?" Valerie asked.

He jerked a thumb at the house. Judging by the cars lining the street and the noise coming from the open door, there were many people inside. "Some of Mom's friends and relatives are keeping her company. Mostly women. I was getting claustrophobic so I came outside."

"A little estrogen overdose?" Valerie asked with a quick grin.

"Something like that."

We walked up the drive to the garage. Dale had moved the Camaro out. The finish sparkled in the late afternoon sun. The morning's clouds had departed, leaving a clear sky and bright sunshine. He'd put the top down and snapped the vinyl cover in place. Even the leather seats gleamed.

"It's a beauty," Valerie remarked. "What year?"

"It's a '67. Dad and I kind of worked on it together. This was the time of day he always liked to go for a cruise out by the lake."

Valerie drummed her fingers on the hood. "You

should go for a ride."

"I don't have my graduated license. I can't drive by myself yet and there's no chance I could tear Mom away from the family. Besides, it wouldn't be right to take off."

I walked around the car, admiring the lines again. I noticed that the plates were current and the tires looked new. Valerie met my eyes across the hood. We'd both seen the wistful look on Dale's face. "Got your license with you?"

"Yeah."

I raised a hand and walked to the side door of the house. It took only a minute to have the conversation with Colleen Morrissey. Dale and Valerie watched me approach the passenger side. I opened the door and looked at her. "You coming along, or afraid the wind might mess your hair?"

A flash of tension crossed her features. "Was that a sexist remark?"

"No, that was a legitimate question. Dale and I are going for a ride. You're welcome to tag along, but it's too nice to put the top up."

She slipped past me and eased into the back seat. Dale was still standing by the driver's door as I got in.

"I can drive it?"

"Let's go."

He was behind the wheel in a heartbeat. But instead of revving the engine and roaring down the drive, he handled the car with respect. The kid took his time getting it down the street until he hit Lakeshore Drive. He hesitated briefly at the corner.

"Where should we go?"

"Wherever you want!" Valerie yelled from the

back.

He turned left and accelerated smoothly down the road. We rolled out beyond the border of Grosse Pointe, and headed up along the lake. After a while the view of the lake was blocked by marinas and stores, but you could still smell the water. It had a crisp, clean scent that tickled the back of my throat. I wasn't about to dip a cup in and drink it, but the image was appealing.

Dale rolled out past the marinas, where residential neighborhoods took over for a few miles. Instinctively, my eyes flicked to the right as we passed my street. I checked his actions behind the wheel. Hands in the nine and three positions. Eyes switching from the mirrors to the traffic around him. He was doing five under the speed limit. Morrissey taught him well.

We were almost to New Baltimore when Dale pulled off the road into a turnaround. I got the impression this was where his father would have headed back. Valerie leaned forward and whispered something in the kid's ear. His face split into a wide grin. I could see them lock eyes in the rearview mirror. Dale checked traffic, then gunned the engine and roared back onto the boulevard. The rear end of the Camaro came around quickly and I thought for a minute he overcompensated, but the kid brought it back under control. He stomped on the accelerator and pushed the needle above sixty. Behind me, Valerie let loose a squeal of glee.

"She made me do it!" Dale shouted over the wind.

I slid my sunglasses down my nose and looked over the lenses at him. "Don't bother explaining it to me."

Dale goosed the pedal once more, then let the

needle drop back down to a comfortable forty-five. He glanced at me then returned his attention to the road.

I twisted around in my seat and checked out Valerie Mann. The wind was blowing her hair straight back from her head. She was in the middle of the seat, with her arms stretched out across the back. I couldn't see her eyes because of her sunglasses, but the smile on her lips appeared to be pure pleasure.

As we came into St. Clair Shores, Dale brought the Camaro back down to forty. There was more traffic here. He kept to the right lane. The light at Eleven Mile Road caught him and he eased the car to a stop. From the corner of my eye, I watched him draw a deep breath, then ease it out slowly.

"Pull into Mastro's," I said.

Just south of the light was a small brick building. Mastro's offered a variety of ice cream and candy. It's a popular hangout for families and kids.

Dale and Valerie opted for ice cream cones. We sat at one of the outdoor tables, watching the customers come and go. Most of the guys checked out the Camaro and nodded approvingly at Dale. More than a few cast a quick glance at Valerie. "Can't remember the last time I had real ice cream," she said quietly. "I usually get frozen yogurt, or sorbet. Do you have any idea how much fat is in this stuff?"

"One cone won't kill you."

Dale finished his in record time. "It's impossible to eat ice cream and be angry. Or sad."

"Must have something to do with endorphins and sugar," Valerie suggested.

Dale was sitting with Valerie beside him.

"Thanks, Jeff."

"Anytime."

He brushed aside the response. "I wasn't just talking about the ice cream. I was referring to giving me a chance to blow off some steam."

"Like I said, anytime." I turned my gaze to Valerie. "What did you tell this young man when we were turning around?"

She pretended to be busy with the last of her cone. A sly smile crossed her lips. "Told him not to worry about getting stopped. No cop's going to ticket someone for speeding when there's another cop in the car."

"You hope."

Her windblown hair had settled back onto her shoulders. It was the first time I had seen her look so relaxed.

"Hey! I nearly forgot why I called you!" Dale was up and moving to the car. We followed him around to the trunk.

"Check this out, Jeff. I noticed it when I was putting the wax back in the bin."

There was a clear plastic storage container on the left side of the trunk. You could see bottles of polish, tar remover and wax, along with a chamois and some clean rags neatly folded inside. Unlike the modern cars that used temporary spare tires, this one had a full sized tire and wheel, perched on the shelf beneath the deck. The original Camaro and its sister the Firebird had a deep well for suitcases or groceries between the rear wheels. This one didn't. There was a level surface that ran across the gap. The whole trunk was covered in gray outdoor carpet. I noticed there were hooks set into the wall and a cord that ran across the bin to hold it in place. Dale snagged the gray carpet with his fingers and tugged it back. This revealed a smooth steel surface that ran the width and depth of the trunk.

I leaned over and rapped my knuckles against it. There was a barely audible thud in response.

"What is it?" Valerie asked.

Dale leaned closer. "It's not standard equipment. I looked at the owner's manual and checked it out online."

"This is a custom unit." I ran my hands across the surface, feeling for a hinge or latch. Nothing. I looked to Dale. "Let me see your car keys."

He handed over the ring. It was an old leather tag with the Camaro emblem stitched into it. There were four keys on the ring. Two were for the car. Dale identified the other two as a house and garage key. Nothing there to open the magic box.

"Could it be some kind of counterweight, for traction or stability?" he asked.

I shrugged. "Possible. But I'd be more inclined to think this is some kind of vault. Did your dad have a safe or lock box at home?"

"Not that I know of."

Valerie was tracing the edges of the carpet. "So what's your idea, Chene? How do you open it?"

Using my phone, I snapped pictures of the unit. Then I pulled the carpet back in place and closed the trunk. "Could be something bizarre, like voice activated. First, we need to figure out who built it."

"I can check with Mom, have her go through any papers Dad kept. He always got a receipt for any work done on the cars. Especially the Camaro."

"Good a place to start as any." I flipped Dale the

keys.

He extended them back in my direction. "Want to drive it, Jeff?"

"I appreciate it, but I may not have as much self-control as you."

Valerie stepped between us and took the offered keys. "Would you mind letting a woman drive this beauty?"

Dale shook his head. "Not at all. Just don't tell Mom. Dad never let her get behind the wheel."

He climbed in back while I took the shotgun seat. Valerie adjusted the mirrors and her own seat before firing up the engine. She drove confidently, cruising down Lakeshore Drive. Only twice did she stomp on the pedal to feel the power of the big Chevy motor. She passed the street where Morrissey's lived, then did a quick u-turn about a mile later and rolled it gently down the tree-lined lane to their house. Dale wasn't nearly as tense as we pulled up the driveway. Valerie parked the Camaro just outside the garage.

"Nice baby." She patted the steering wheel affectionately.

"Come back anytime you'd like to go for a ride," Dale said. "And I'll check into the papers on the Camaro."

She gave him another quick hug. This time I noticed a flash of color come to his cheeks. Couldn't blame him a bit. He turned toward me as she stepped back and we shook hands firmly.

"I'll try a few things on my end. Keep in touch."

Chapter Fourteen

Valerie was quiet while I drove to her car, still parked by the church from the morning's funeral. I couldn't tell if she was mad, disappointed, confused or just deep in thought. I was still thinking about the pleasant drive in the Camaro, a nice diversion from the homicide investigation. She broke the silence as we pulled into the lot.

"Pretty smooth, Sergeant Chene."

"How's that?" I parked and lowered the windows to let the summer air drift in. Valerie turned and put her back against the door. She crossed her arms and let a frown creep over her features. Suddenly we were right back at the earlier confrontation.

"The way you worked Dale. Pretty smooth."

"I didn't work him."

"But you saw a way to get what you wanted."

My euphoric mood faded in a blur. "I don't know what nonsense you're spouting, but you've got the wrong idea."

"I've been around enough cops to know how it works. What you did was just a variation of the good cop, bad cop routine. You cozied up to the kid to get him comfortable, then got what you wanted."

Half a dozen responses leapt to my mind. My tongue grabbed the first one. "Girlie, you are full of shit!"

Her reaction was just like yesterday when I caught her in the lie. She jerked back as if I'd physically assaulted her. I could see the argument brewing but cut in before she had a chance to say anything.

"For your information, I did not work the kid in any way, shape or form. He called me. I went. He was tense, upset and hurting. He'd spent the day burying his dad. No teenage boy should have to do that. Maybe he was looking for some male companionship. Maybe . . ."

"Or it could have been. . ."

"Shut up!" I waved a finger in her face. "This is my dime. You'll get your chance. As I was saying, maybe he just needed an outsider to talk to. You saw him drooling over that car. It was his main connection to his father. Letting him take those wheels for a ride may be the only form of closure Dale ever has. I'm no shrink, and I'm not going to try to give you the six million possible theories as to what was going on.

"But I believe he called for two reasons. To show me what he found, and to get away from the women in that house. I didn't push him, play him or force him to hand anything over. I let him take his time. When he was ready, he talked. There was no brow beating. No threats. Nothing that could be construed as intimidation. So if you think I was working that kid, then yes, girlie, you are full of shit."

I took my sunglasses off and flung them up on the dashboard. She had raised her left hand to her mouth and was slowly brushing her fingertips across her lips. We sat there in silence for a couple of minutes. At length she tentatively reached over to the dash and picked up my glasses.

"You broke them."

I shrugged.

"Do that often?" She twirled them by the earpiece.

I shook my head. "First time."

A smile attempted to quiver across her lips, but she wouldn't let it. "Well that wasn't very smart."

Another shrug.

She set the glasses back on the dash. "Don't call me girlie."

"Don't fall for stereotypes."

"Okay, maybe I was wrong."

"Ain't no maybes about it."

"So you meant what you said. About being around for Dale if he needs you?"

"Why not? The kid isn't exactly surrounded with any men he can confide in. His mom will help, but there will be times he's more comfortable talking to another guy."

"So how long will you be there for him?"

I shrugged again. It wasn't something I normally did, but arguing churned up a lot of energy in me, and it needed somewhere to go. "As long as he wants. Or needs me."

"So what happens when the case is over? Do you fade into the distance?"

"Depends. No two cases are exactly the same. Even no two homicides are identical. I'm not talking about victims and the killers. It's the families who get left behind. The survivors. How Dale and his sister adjust to life without their dad isn't something that's going to be determined by the end of the summer. It will affect the rest of their lives."

There was another failed attempt at a smile. "You're starting to sound psychological here."

"Just practical. And a few years' experience doesn't hurt either."

I climbed out and walked around to her side. She unlocked her car and stood there.

"There's more to you than meets the eye, Sergeant."

"That a personal opinion or a professional evaluation?"

Valerie bobbed her head slightly. "Yes."

"That was a two-part question."

"I know."

Neither of us spoke. I couldn't get a read on what she was thinking or her body language. She appeared guarded and open at the same time. Contradictory messages. I could feel a pulse of energy coming off her. She took a step closer and put her hand on my chest, right over my heart. The hum of traffic on Mack Avenue finally caught her attention. Quickly she stepped back. Then Valerie Mann opened the door and slid inside.

"Good night, Chene.

"Good night, girlie."

****

I never slept that night. My mind kept replaying the events of the day, trying to put it together. At one point I sprawled on the sofa in the living room and watched the eastern sky slowly welcome the dawn. Nothing clicked. I gave up and headed for the shower.

Saturday morning, I went through my files, trying to dredge up a memory from several years ago. Koz was working on his computer, reviewing notes on another case before a court appearance Monday. We had talked about my evening with Dale Morrissey and the strange box in the Camaro's trunk. I looked up when he snapped his fingers and grinned broadly.

"Something funny?"

He pointed at his computer screen. "I found him. Dude was a cat burglar. They called him T V. Got caught twice 'cause he was such a fancy dresser, never wore rubber soles even when he was pulling a job. Slipped both times on waxed floors and tripped the burglar alarms."

"Wasn't that the guy who broke into the old Hamburger Mansion out in Clarkston, trying to steal some painting?"

"That's the one."

The screen showed the profile on Thelonious Edgar Van Eagan. TEE VEE.

"What about him?"

"He got out about two years ago. Since he'd already been nailed twice, he decided to go straight, rather than face a permanent home in Jackson State Prison. He went to work with a security company as a consultant, until he got enough backing to open his own business."

Koz extended his left hand palm up and curled the fingers back and forth slowly, as if waiting for a tip to be paid. I smacked his hand aside.

"You're supposed to ask about his own operation."

"Okay, tell me about his operation."

"He's making customized safes."

****

Kozlowski drove to the address on file for Van Eagan. This guy either had some serious backers or knew the importance of identifying his market. He had a natty looking storefront just south of downtown

Birmingham, next door to a high class jewelry store. Koz parked in the lot and tried his best to suppress a know-it-all grin that kept crossing his face. I made a comment about simple minds and simple pleasures and headed inside.

There was no gaudy sign above the door, nothing to indicate what type of business it was. As we walked in, a fashion model type greeted us with a sunny smile. She wore a designer dress and jewelry that probably cost more than my Harley. She politely assured us that Mr. Van Eagan would join us momentarily and escorted us to a cozy grouping of leather chairs. After serving up gourmet coffee, she disappeared.

"Nice to see Tee Vee doing so well," Koz said. "Guy always talked like he was from some formal school, using ten dollar words instead of plain English."

"You think any of this comes from the proceeds of his ill-gotten gains?"

"Nah. You know crime don't pay."

"Truer words never spoken."

We drank the fancy coffee. Kozlowski was beginning to eye the little platter of designer pastries on the side table when Van Eagan approached.

"Good afternoon, gentlemen, how may I be…"

Kozlowski unfolded his extra-long frame from the leather chair and turned to face him. Van Eagan's voice died in mid-sentence.

"What say, Tee Vee."

Van Eagan momentarily lost his composure. Something in his eyes registered Kozlowski in less time than it took him to blink. He snapped his gaze quickly to me, then back to Koz.

"It has been many years since we've conversed,

Detective Kozlowski."

"No shit, Tee Vee. This here is Sergeant Chene." Koz rubbed the lapel of Van Eagan's suit between the massive thumb and forefinger of his right hand. "Business must be damned good to keep you in silk ties and fine wool suits."

I had to give him credit. He neither flinched nor pulled back at the touch of the Polish giant. He was definitely cool.

"Perhaps we should talk in my office."

A playful look spread across Koz's face. He always enjoyed making people uncomfortable. It was a talent that came to him easily. I intervened and had Van Eagan lead us out of the showroom.

"You ruinin' my fun, Chene."

"Timing, my brother. It's all in the timing."

He flashed a devilish grin. "So if he doesn't cooperate, you're gonna let me pick up where I left off."

"But of course."

Van Eagan's office was in the center of the building. One glass wall overlooked the showroom, where the leggy fashion model was checking the coffee set up and rearranging the pastries. Other than her desk there was a walnut stand filled with various brochures. Van Eagan's office was spacious. There was a polished oak desk, with two upholstered chairs facing it and an ergonomic swivel chair behind it. The only thing on the desk was a telephone, a titanium letter opener and a small stack of mail. Apparently Van Eagan had been going through his daily business routine. A small refrigerator hummed in the corner of the office.

I took a good look at Van Eagan. Tall and thin,

with a full head of thick black hair that was neatly styled. His nails looked manicured and there were no scrapes or rough skin on his hands or face. The fingers were long and delicate. For some reason, he made me think of a glass swizzle stick, like the ones used for martinis in the old movies.

"Now. What can I do for you, Detective Kozlowski?"

"We want to talk history, Tee Vee."

Van Eagan flicked his hands apart. "I would prefer to leave the past alone, Detective. My dues to society have been paid. I'm a legitimate businessman now. My company maintains pristine records. My investors would not have it any other way."

"I understand you sell specialty items. The unusual safes and vaults."

"That's correct. Our clientele prefers the unique arrangements to keep their possessions secure. Distinctive locations and locking mechanisms is part of our trademark. Client confidentiality is the foundation of our mission. Allow me to show you our production area."

Van Eagan led us through a rear door of his office into the shop area. Four men in jeans and T shirts were in the room. One was working with a cutting torch. Two more were assembling hinges on the door of a small safe. The other was at a computer console. Van Eagan nodded to each one and guided us to a far corner of the room.

"A significant component of our business is confidentiality. Our reputation for secrecy is impeccable. We do not share information about our customers."

I jumped in before Koz could get started again. "If you did the work we think you did, I can guarantee you that this particular client will never complain about any information you provide."

"I'm disinclined to confirm my clientele or any relevant details."

"Don't get your Armani in a twist," Koz said. "We're after information."

He calmly slid a palm over his tie. "Our clients are very secretive. Their privacy is paramount to our reputation."

"Do you represent other companies, or do you sell only those materials you design and build yourself?" I asked.

"The majority of our merchandise comes from two suppliers, one local, the other in California. Depending on the requirements of the order."

I described the box in the trunk of Morrissey's car, without mentioning the make or his name. Van Eagan allowed himself a knowing smile and a brief nod of the head.

"Of course. That would be the Camaro for the late Mr. Morrissey. So unfortunate, what happened to him."

Koz loomed forward and braced a massive palm on the wall beside Van Eagan's head. "You pretty quick with that response, Tee Vee."

He shook his head slightly. "Really, Detective, you must provide me with a little credit. That is a very high profile case. It is no secret that your department is heading up the investigation. Besides, Mr. Morrissey was a referral and a valued customer."

"Keep talking."

"Morrissey was referred by one of the city council

members. He ordered some customized vaults for the theaters and the bookstores. They had to be very compact, using both keys and a combination. There was also a special compartment that had a drop slot included, which had an additional locking device. We installed these at four of his locations and were scheduled to replace other units within the year."

"Sounds cozy," Koz said.

He and Van Eagan opted to stare at each other. I waved a couple of fingers between them to get Van Eagan's attention back on track.

"The Camaro."

"Yes, the car. Beautiful vehicle. He was very proud of it. Kyle Morrissey approached me back in March. He required a special vault for the trunk. Something solid. He had no concerns about the weight, but he wanted to be assured that it would be fireproof and pick proof as well.

"We worked out the dimensions and built it to his specifications. He also had the trunk area reinforced, to support the container. Even with today's scientific advancements, a vault of this nature would have substantial weight."

"So how do you open the damn thing?" Koz asked. "From the pictures Chene showed me, there's no opening for keys, or any kind of slot for a magnetic card. What's that leave, a remote device?"

Van Eagan's face split with a dazzling smile. "I am impressed, Detective Kozlowski. Actually, this unit calls for a combination."

"There was no place for a dial that I could see," I said.

"Not that type of combination, Sergeant. I am

referring to a combination of magnets and a radio signal."

Van Eagan was settling into the comfortable mode of an expert. He looked beyond us to the workers across the room. Two of them nodded in Van Eagan's direction. He returned the gesture. It was apparent that all four had stopped working and were watching our exchange. Bringing his gaze back around, his voice took on a reverent tone as he explained.

"Morrissey's request was somewhat unusual, but that is part of our specialty. I have actually sold three other vaults to fit in the confines of a vehicle. Most of the work we do here is the finishing touch. The heavy work is done at the factory where the original vault is designed and cast. We may do artwork on the door, or some certain special features."

"Like the Camaro," I prompted.

Van Eagan nodded slowly. "Yes. Mr. Morrissey had the vault set to react to a remote control device. It looked similar to the ones commonly used by automobile manufacturers."

"So what about the magnets, Tee Vee?" Kozlowski asked.

Van Eagan fiddled with the cuffs on his shirt. His eyes were locked on his wrists. Koz glanced at me. I could see his jaw clench. I raised two fingers.

"The magnets, Tee Vee," he prompted again.

Still no response. I was getting bored. All it took to change the situation was a slight inclination of the head. Koz never took his eyes off Van Eagan, but said quietly, "How long?"

"Sixty should do."

"Then I can hurt him?"

"Yassuh."

Van Eagan shifted uncomfortably. His attention now focused on Kozlowski and the close proximity of his hand by Van Eagan's shoulder. I turned my back to them and faced the crew of workers. Two of them started toward me. Both my gun and badge were visible but it didn't seem to slow them down. I held up a palm.

"That's close enough."

Behind me Van Eagan cleared his throat. "Back to work, guys." The lapse into common language wasn't lost on any of us. "Be cool."

Reluctantly the two men walked back to the center of the room. I shifted ninety degrees so I could watch them and Van Eagan. He was standing on his tiptoes. Kozlowski had a firm grip on the knot of his necktie and was lifting him off the floor. It reminded me of Suarez jammed against the bookstore window.

Van Eagan's nostrils flared "I suppose this is some variation of interrogation. Akin to good cop, bad cop?"

"More like bad cop, angry cop," I said. "We get impatient when people start jerking us around during a homicide investigation. Maybe you had something to do with Morrissey's killing."

Van Eagan struggled to maintain his composure. He was losing that battle. "Unequivocally not, Sergeant. The good detective will tell you, that was never part of my modus operandi. I abhor violence."

I had to give him credit for how quickly he resumed the ten-dollar word routine. "You may not have pulled the trigger, Tee Vee, but you could have set it up. Maybe business here isn't as rosy as you claim it is."

A sheen of sweat covered Van Eagan's face. "Kyle

Morrissey was a valued client. He never quibbled on an invoice. We had more projects to complete. I had absolutely no reason to wish him harm."

"Sure about that?"

There was a lengthy silence. Kozlowski was slowly increasing the pressure on the necktie, raising it just a little higher in the process. There was no expression on his face. His eyes were locked on Van Eagan's.

"Time," he whispered.

"Do it."

Van Eagan struggled valiantly and began talking fast, the words cascading from his mouth. "All right! All right! All right!"

Koz relaxed his grip and let Van Eagan's feet hit the floor. "We're listening."

"There are four magnets, about the size of a business card. In the center of the lid, fanned out to look like a compass. Then use the remote for his car. Not the Camaro. His regular car. I think it's a Lexus." Van Eagan had sweated through his shirt and his face was dripping. Tentatively, he used his left hand to wipe his face, then rubbed the moisture onto his slacks.

"What else?" I shifted my gaze back to the workers.

"Any of the magnets will work on the interior box that we installed in his theaters.

"He ever tell you what he wanted the vault in the Camaro for?"

He shook his head back and forth quickly. "I make it a policy never to ask. I'm marketing security. It could be money or stocks or trade secrets. I don't need to know." He swallowed hard. "I don't want to know."

There was a snort of laughter from Koz. "Nice to

know you got scruples."

"What about the homicide?" I said.

"I know nothing about that. I swear on my dear grandmother's grave I know nothing else."

Koz released him and stepped back. "For Granny's sake, that better be straight. Otherwise, you may want to join her. Obstruction of an officer in such a prominent investigation could easily lead to your return to Jackson."

I'd noticed an exit from the workshop to the parking lot. There was no need to go back through the office. We started to head in that direction. I took a last look at Van Eagan. He hadn't moved.

"We may be in touch, if we need help opening those vaults. You will cooperate, won't you?"

He took a long, deep breath and let it out slowly. "Of course."

"I figured you'd say that."

Chapter Fifteen

I settled into the passenger seat as Koz pulled out into traffic on Woodward. He punched up the volume on a jazz track, stopping at a light to adjust his sunglasses.

"Nice moves," I said, thinking back to how he handled Van Eagan.

"Dumb shit had to make it look good. Instead of just cooperating with us in the first place, he tries to play it cool so he can impress his crew."

"You recognize someone?"

"Tall, scrawny guy. Shaved skull. Parts of a tattoo visible on the neck. Name's Zocker. Did a couple of years in Jackson with Tee Vee."

"You think Van Eagan's still active, or maybe he's just helping out an old friend down on his luck?"

Koz's face split into a wide grin. "With Tee Vee, you never can tell."

We debated whether to go back to the squad or take a shot at the Camaro. I called Dale Morrissey and left a message for him to call. Then I called the duty officer at the post. Two sets of car keys had been part of the package. Van Egan was right. The other car was a Lexus coupe. All the property had been claimed by the widow the day before the funeral.

Staring out the window, I tried to remember seeing a Lexus at the house. There had been so many cars parked on the street last night, it was possible I'd driven right passed it. But I didn't think so. Mrs. Morrissey drove a bright red Jaguar. Koz stopped at a light and faced me.

"Impound yard?"

"Why not. I don't think the widow's picked it up yet."

"So what do you think is in the trunk?"

"I dunno. But maybe it will give us a lead."

The light changed and Koz rocketed down the highway. "God knows we could use one right now. Something that would narrow down that suspect pool would be nice."

"With this case, that would be welcome change."

It took three calls to locate the Lexus. Chesterfield Township police had originally towed the vehicle to their facility on the day of the shooting. Then it had been transferred to one of the state lots when we took over the case. Under normal circumstances, the vehicle would not have been moved until it was released and claimed by the family. But a large auto theft ring had been cracked three nights ago, and all of the vehicles recovered had been taken to the primary lot. Units impounded from other events were dispatched to satellite lots, so the detectives and insurance investigators working the case would have all the vehicles at one site.

We found the Lexus, parked with several other expensive cars. The entire row was barricaded in by two dump trucks that looked like they hadn't moved of their own accord in years. The manager of the lot gave us a crooked grin and gestured at his own security measures. Someone would be hard pressed to steal anything from his facility.

A crime scene investigator had checked the contents of the vehicle. The keys had been left with the manager. Koz slid behind the wheel and fired it up. The big engine purred quietly. He found the interior release for the hood and the trunk and began going through the paperwork in the glove box. I started in the engine compartment after he turned off the motor. There was nothing out of the ordinary that I could see. It didn't make sense that Morrissey would hide anything there that would require him crawling beneath the car. It would have to be someplace with easy access.

I went to the trunk. Inside was a gym duffel bag, filled with the type of gear used for playing tennis. There were two expensive racquets, a couple of cans of tennis balls, shorts, shoes and polo shirts. Sweat bands. A battered Timex watch with scratches on the crystal. There were no spare pockets or hidden compartments in the gym bag. Tucked into a web sling was a bottle from a national brand of flavored tea.

I set it on the ground and ran my fingers around the carpet in the trunk. There was a hole near the latch, where the carpet lifted up to reveal the spare tire. I removed the tire and the jack assembly. The trunk was empty. I was about to put things back when Koz appeared beside me.

"Nothing up front. I checked with Rudy, to see if his crew had taken anything out. The forensic sweep didn't turn up anything out of the ordinary. They're checking the hair and fibers. Probably match everything to Morrissey and his old lady. Here's an inventory of the contents."

Kozlowski handed over his phone. I swiped at the

screen and read the list. Owner's manual, two flashlights, a half-empty bottle of tea in a cup holder and forty-five cents in the ashtray. I passed it back to him.

"You pop the seat cushions?"

Koz gave me an insulted look, as if he had never tossed a car before. "Yeah, front and back. This ride's in good shape. I'd bet Morrissey had it detailed not long ago. And you know Fen's techs would do a thorough job."

He watched me return the jack and the spare to the storage area and reset the carpet. I was bending over to pick up the duffel bag when something caught my eye. On the inside of the trunk lid was a small black square. He saw me hesitate and followed my gaze at the trunk.

"You see what I see?"

"Looks like you found the keys."

It took both hands to pry the magnets loose from the underside of the trunk lid. They were so small and inconspicuous if you didn't know what you were looking for, you wouldn't pay any attention to them. Morrissey was pretty smooth. He always had the Lexus with him, so he always had the magic keys. If these worked the secret compartments on the vaults Van Eagan had installed, he could have hiding spots at each of his locations. Koz opened his hatch and we transferred the magnets to his car. I closed Morrissey's trunk and leaned against it. He settled beside me.

"Now what?"

I ran my hand along the car's sleek deck. "We're still considering the possibility of two killers. One with the gun, one with poison."

"Yeah, but we've yet to figure out a delivery

system for the nicotine."

"Let me see that list again."

Koz handed back his phone. I scrolled down, pausing near the end. He stared at the screen. "Fuck me hard."

"Definitely a possibility."

Kozlowski recovered his phone and made the call. "What's next?"

"Let's go see what's behind door number one."

****

No one answered the bell. From the street, I could see the garage door was closed where the Camaro was parked. The red Jaguar was visible in the driveway. Koz cocked his head, leaning it toward the rear of the house.

"Mozart. One of the early pieces. Piano, maybe cello."

The surprise must have been evident on my face.

"What? You think all I listen to is rock and jazz?"

"I had no idea you enjoyed classical music."

"I know Mozart. I dated a pianist for a while. She practiced the damn thing three hours every day."

We headed toward the back yard. "So you like Mozart."

"Can't stand it. But I can recognize it."

Colleen Morrissey was sitting in one of the padded deck chairs, a glass of dark liquid in one hand. Her eyes were hidden behind large oval sunglasses. A small stereo was on the table beside her. She didn't move at our approach, until I called her name.

We exchanged hellos and I introduced Kozlowski. It always impresses me how the Polish giant can switch so easily from intimidating to sincerity. He expressed his condolences on the loss of her husband and gently squeezed her hand.

"I was just enjoying the quiet. The kids are out and the onslaught of relatives seems to be subsiding."

"How are you holding up?" Koz asked.

"The kids are doing better. They're slowly getting back into their normal summer routine. Running with friends, going to the lake. Probably looking for short-lived passionate romances."

He leaned forward. "I asked about you. It's got to be difficult trying to keep things together for the children. Maintaining a semblance of order is no easy trick, following the events of the last week."

Colleen turned her full attention on Kozlowski. She removed her sunglasses. There was a tremor brewing just beneath the surface. Her eyes were hard as she stared at him. Her gaze flicked to me, then back to Koz.

"I have to be strong. My children are depending on me. They are my first priority. My family has always been my first priority. Then comes the business. There is no room in my life for weakness now."

"That's understandable."

"And I'm still looking for answers. Hopefully from you."

Kozlowski nodded. "Right now, we keep coming up with questions. But we're thinking you might be able to help us find the answers."

Colleen got to her feet. Her bare legs were tanned a deep shade. She was wearing white shorts with a red tank top. Her arms were as tan as her legs.

"It's Saturday. Yesterday I buried my husband and was surrounded by too many nosy people prying into my situation with false concerns. You'll forgive me if

I'm not in the mood to give you any answers."

I raised a hand to calm her. "We just want to look at the Camaro."

"Whatever for?"

"Did your husband ever talk to you about a vault?" I asked. "Something custom-made?"

"No. He had a safe installed at each of the theaters. And he would have one in each of the bookstores. But that's just a standard business practice. We didn't discuss those matters. Kyle would only tell me about the special events or things that he wanted me involved with."

"We have reason to believe that he had one installed in the Camaro. With your permission, we'd like to open it."

She hesitated. "Why?"

"Because it's possible the vault may contain something that will aid our investigation."

Another hesitation. "In what way?"

"Whatever's in the vault could turn out to be the motive that pushed the killer over the edge. We need his keys to the Lexus to open the vault."

Colleen drew in a deep breath and let it out slowly. Her expression turned to one of pure determination. "I want you to find whoever is responsible for his death. I want him to pay for what he did to my husband. For what he did to my children. I want my family to feel safe." She paused to focus on me. "I want my life back," she snapped.

Koz and I could only look at each other in silence. At length, she marched past us and went into the house. She returned a moment later with several key rings in her hand. We followed her to the garage. Colleen uncovered a keypad on the side of the building and entered a number. The door behind the Camaro rolled smoothly out of sight. She handed me the bundle of keys. I unlocked the trunk, then pulled the carpeting out of the way. Kozlowski and Colleen peeked over the lip of the trunk.

"Pretty slick," Koz said.

"Let's see if Tee Vee was honest." When we arrived I'd recovered the magnets from Kozlowski's trunk. Now I pressed them on the lid in the design Van Eagan had described.

Stepping back, I flipped through the jumble of keys Colleen had given me. There were several different rings, all intertwined into a watchman's nightmare. Dangling from two different sections were remote units for cars. I selected one and pressed the button marked for unlocking the doors. We heard a clicking noise behind us.

"That's for my car." Colleen smiled and pointed at the Jag.

Taking the other remote, I aimed it at the Camaro and pressed the button. This time the clicking noise was much softer. Koz leaned forward and prodded the lid of the vault. It was open an inch or two. There was an interior hinge, set back near the shelf for the spare tire. With only the slight pressure of his finger, the lid eased up, exposing its secrets.

Colleen started to pull back, but curiosity got the better of her. We watched her reach into the safe and withdraw a small leather bag that fit neatly in her palm. Then another. And another. Soon she had six of them, lined up in a row on the hood of the Jaguar. There were several brown manila envelopes in the bottom of the vault. She put the envelopes on the windshield, then peered at the empty safe.

"Kyle was always clever. He loved gadgets," she said with a sigh. "How did you know it was here?"

"Dale found it. He called yesterday and wanted to show it to me. But he didn't know how to open it." I could see the confusion on her face, so I kept going. "We traced the box back to the company that sold it to your husband. Specialized units like this aren't available at the local hardware store. The manager told us how to open it."

"Now what?"

"Why don't we take these inside and see what was worth hiding," Koz said.

Colleen weighed that, then figured it could do no harm. She gathered up four of the leather bags and headed for the deck. Koz hefted one of the bags and looked over his sunglasses at me.

"You taking any bets?"

"Nope. But I'm sure these aren't his marble collection." I picked up the manila envelopes and followed the widow.

Colleen was seated at the kitchen table with her hands folded in her lap. She nervously chewed on her bottom lip.

"I'm afraid to look inside." She turned to Kozlowski. "Would you?"

"Of course."

Gently, he loosened the cord around one of the bags he had brought in. Then he poked a thick finger into the neck, opening it wide. His eyes flicked to the bag, then to me, then back to the bag. Cautiously, he laid it on the table in front of the window and let the contents slide out.

Green stones poured onto the wooden surface. The smallest was the size of my thumb. The largest, the size of an egg.

"Oh, my," Colleen gasped. "Are they real?"

"I'm no expert, but I think those are emeralds," he said.

In quick succession, she opened the other five bags. Three held different types of gems: diamonds, rubies and sapphires. There were more emeralds in the fourth one. The last one was filled with a jewel I didn't recognize.

"I had no idea," Colleen whispered, letting the precious gems sift through her fingers. "Why would he hide all of this?"

"Any number of reasons," I said. "He could have started buying them as a whim, something that he knew would always increase in value. Kyle could sell them if he needed cash quickly. Maybe it was intended for retirement. Maybe it was his plan to pay for the kids' college funds."

"What's all this worth?"

"Hard to say. But I know how you can find out."

I got the number from the website and called Jared Devonshire. For years his family has owned and operated the premiere upscale jewelry store in the Grosse Pointes. Jared worked there even while in high school. If anyone could put a price on these goodies, he could. A quick explanation was all it took. He arrived ten minutes later. I introduced him to Colleen Morrissey.

Devonshire's Italian suit probably cost more than three grand. The creases were razor sharp, his shoes gleaming, nails perfectly trimmed. With a full head of dark hair and pearly white teeth, he could have been a model. Except for his nose. It had been broken a couple of times over the years, once in a hockey game, once playing football. He spoke quietly to the widow, expressing his condolences. Then he turned to Kozlowski.

"Hello, Giant."

"Hey, diamond boy. You bring your loupe?"

"No self-respecting jeweler travels without one." Devonshire withdrew it from the pocket of his coat. He turned toward Colleen. "Sergeant Chene said you found a few uncut stones."

She motioned toward the table. "More than a few."

Jared paused, staring at the piles of gems Colleen had gathered beside each leather pouch. Tentatively, he picked up one of the emeralds, rolling it between his fingers before looking at it through the loupe. He didn't say a word, but repeated the process with one from each of the piles.

"What's that one?" Kozlowski asked, hooking a thumb at the gem we hadn't been able to identify.

"Imperial Topaz. It can be very expensive." Finished, he gingerly placed the diamond on the pile, then dropped the loupe back in his pocket.

"Well?" Colleen asked anxiously.

"Well, they are real. Some very, very good quality. There are some little imperfections. I could only speculate on their value without having an opportunity to thoroughly appraise them."

"How about a guess?" I asked.

Devonshire raised his manicured hands slightly. It must have been the Grosse Pointe version of a shrug. "I don't guess in matters such as these. It could be very misleading to Mrs. Morrissey."

Koz scowled and folded his arms. Devonshire ignored him.

"C'mon, Jared. I'm sure the lady won't hold it against you if your estimation is off the mark."

Colleen nodded anxiously in agreement, a curious expression on her face.

"Could be a quarter. Could even be as much as a half."

Koz let out a low whistle. Devonshire turned and walked out to his car to collect his briefcase. Colleen Morrissey watched him go, then shifted to us.

"I'm a bit confused."

"With your permission. Mr. Devonshire will take these items to his place of business. There, he will measure, weigh and evaluate each precious gem. Once that process is complete, he will give you an itemized list along with their current value. While we're here, he'll give you a detailed receipt for the number of items of each type he is taking."

Her voice had a nervous quake to it. "But what did he mean, a quarter or a half?"

Kozlowski reassuringly placed a hand on her shoulder. "Dollars. A quarter to a half million dollars."

Chapter Sixteen

Jared did a complete inventory and gave Colleen Morrissey a receipt, then Koz and I escorted him back to his store on Mack Avenue. Neither one of us spoke about the possibility that the stones were a motive for the killing. Chances were few people knew Morrissey had a stash like that. If he was as clever as I believed, he'd probably bought them from different merchants and had been collecting them for years.

The manila envelopes from the Camaro's vault were on the back seat. One envelope had contained receipts from gem dealers. I'd given that to Devonshire for comparison with the stones. Colleen had taken a quick peek at the contents of the others, then handed them over. She said they were proposals for another location. It may be nothing. Yet Morrissey had considered them important enough to lock in the secret vault. That got my attention.

This case was filled with more twists and turns than a crooked politician's bank accounts. Morrissey was well liked. A womanizer, but accepted even by the women he employed and pursued. Good family. Strong ties with both kids and the wife. Successful business, but not something any corporation would consider for a takeover. Money. Deep pockets for the jewels and traditional savings, probably to take care of the family in case a problem arose. But nothing that would be common knowledge. Yet somebody had brutally executed him. And it was entirely possible someone else had tried as well. I reclined the seat and propped my boots on the dash while Koz headed back to the office.

He nudged me when we were in the parking lot at the post. The vehicle was off. We sat in silence while I got my bearings. I was surprised to see that it was past six. Some days go by in a blur. This was one of them.

"You gonna analyze that paperwork tonight?"

I shook my head. "I'm just going to check with Cantrell and call it a day. You?"

"Got a date. Should have just enough time to change. Grab some dinner and then go to the concert out at Meadowbrook."

"Pavillion or lawn?"

"Lawn. Those seats were made for runts like you. I prefer a large blanket, some wine and a soft woman."

I popped the door, reaching back to gather up the manila folders. "Be cool."

"Always. Get some rest, Chene. You look like shit."

I watched him pull away, then headed into the station. Cantrell was at his desk, fingers laced behind his head. There was no paperwork on the surface. He preferred oral reports or the computer screen. Paperwork meant bureaucracy and Cantrell was determined to fight it every single step of the way.

After giving him a quick summary of the day, he waved me out like a pesky fly. I took the hint, locked the manila folders in my desk and headed for the door.

****

Simone was waiting when I got home. She met me

in the kitchen, a glass of wine in her hand. The sun was still out, blasting down with a high intensity on the world. It had been like this all day. But I had an escape in mind.

"You looked tired." She stepped close for a kiss.

"You look fantastic." It was true. She wore a sleeveless cream colored top and a pair of navy shorts. Her hair was swept back. Large sunglasses were perched on the crown of her head.

"You're very sweet. How is the case going?"

"It's a mess. I've got more suspects than I know what to do with. But let's forget about that for a while."

Her eyes sparkled. "What did you have in mind?"

"Dinner and a surprise, although not necessarily in that order."

Simone grabbed her purse from the counter. "I like surprises."

"That's good to know."

As I locked the house she turned toward the street. Only when she realized I wasn't following did she look back.

"Do you like staring at my ass?"

"Absolutely. You have a beautiful ass. Probably the nicest one I've ever seen."

"Probably?"

The laughter was building in my chest. "Well, it's the best one I've ever seen naked. Does that help?"

She flashed a brilliant smile. "It does." She started to turn back toward the street.

"You're going the wrong way." I jerked a thumb over my shoulder.

Puzzled, she walked back to me. Only now did she see the boat tied up at the dock. She stood by the edge of the garage as I removed the canvas cover and stowed it below deck.

"Where did this yacht come from?"

I fired up the blower to clear the engine compartment of fumes and began to untie the stern. "This is a boat. It's not big enough to be considered a yacht." I dropped the line on the deck and held out my hand.

Reluctantly she took it and made the step from dry land. I keyed the engine and let it warm up. In a minute I'd removed the bow and spring lines from the dock and was ready to go. Simone was still standing in the center of the deck, looking uncertain.

"You didn't answer my question."

I guided her over to the large seat behind the controls on the starboard side. As I put the craft in gear and idled toward the lake, I told her about Ted's favor. Simone knew a little about the old saloonkeeper and our relationship. When I reached the lake I pointed at a button on the dash.

"Press that and count to three."

Grinning like a schoolgirl, Simone thumbed the horn. She settled back on the comfortable seat, pulled her sunglasses on and shook out her hair. "Let's see what this baby can do."

"Yes ma'am." I gave it some throttle and headed out across the lake.

"How did you learn to drive a boat?" Simone's voice had a trace of awe. She knew about my background, being abandoned at birth and raised in the orphanage by Catholic nuns. That didn't sound like the beginning of life on the water. I was tempted to shrug it off, but knew she wouldn't let it go.

"The summer I was fourteen, I had my days free. As long as I was back to the orphanage in time for dinner, they trusted me to behave. Mostly they thought I just walked to the library every day. I liked books.

"What I was really doing was sneaking into restaurants, doing the 'dine and dash' like a wily criminal."

"Dine and dash? What in the world is that?"

I shook my head in mock dismay. "Clearly you've led a sheltered life. Dine and dash is when you sneak out of the restaurant without paying the bill. It's quite daring for a teenager."

"You didn't!"

"I did. And more than once too. I was getting pretty good at it. Anyway, I rode the bus out to the Nautical Mile in St. Clair Shores. Boats interested me. I just walked up and down the docks, looking at all these beautiful rigs. One day I ducked into Sharkey's for lunch. As I was skipping out, Ted caught me."

"You're kidding!"

"Nope. He gave me the choice of paying up or working it off. So I scrubbed dishes for a couple of hours and he called it even. When I came back, he gave me a job."

Her eyes dazzling with delight, Simone shook her head. "But that doesn't explain how you learned about boats?"

The more I hung out at the bar, the more Ted trusted me. One afternoon he borrowed a friend's cabin cruiser and took me for a ride on the lake. Along the way he showed me how to operate it. He taught me the rules of the water, how to approach other boats and who had the right of way. Pretty soon we were going out on

211

the lake once a week. Eventually I grew comfortable on the water, even when the weather was rough.

"So your life of crime ended up being a good thing. Are there any more nefarious tales I should know about?"

"Define nefarious."

"Let's call it wicked or slightly illegal behavior."

I paused. Just being out on the water with her on this summer night was enjoyable. I cut the throttles, slowing the boat as we glided back in the general direction of the house. The breeze ruffled her hair. Simone closed her eyes and tilted her head back, drinking in the fresh air.

"Well, it wasn't illegal but it could have been slightly wicked."

She turned and bumped a shoulder against my chest. "Tell me."

"Understand that the statute of limitations has long passed."

"You just said it wasn't illegal."

"It wasn't."

Simone reached past me and pulled the throttle back, slowing the boat even more. "Tell me."

So I did. I was sixteen when it happened. One of the benefactors for the orphanage took all the nuns out to his cottage at the end of the school year for a day's picnic. There were a handful of kids from the orphanage who were brought along as well. That year it was cold and rainy, a miserable day. Everyone was crowded inside. The nuns were in their full black and white habits, the kids in jeans and T shirts.

"There was one nun, a real taskmaster. Her name was Sister Columbus. She was small but the toughest person I've ever known."

Simone nodded and made a 'get on with it' gesture.

Turns out this benefactor had a couple of boats at the dock there. Sister Columbus had a brief chat with him, then came over and thumped me on the arm.

"Let's go for a boat ride."

"It's raining out, Sister."

"God doesn't mind a little rain, Jefferson, and neither do I. Our friend says you can drive that little speedboat."

When I looked beyond her there stood the benefactor nodding his approval. I recognized him from Sharkey's. Apparently he'd seen me there and out on the lake with Ted. Five minutes later we were outfitted with windbreakers and life jackets.

The little speedboat turned out to be a ten-foot-long hydroplane with a fiberglass hull and a fifty horsepower outboard motor. The benefactor gave me a sixty second lesson in the controls, cast off the lines and threw me a salute. I motored out away from the dock and as we hit the open water, a large yacht roared past.

I paused in telling my story and turned the boat away from shore and headed south on the lake toward the Grosse Pointes. Simone rocked against me as I nudged the throttles for more speed.

"You'd better keep talking, Chene, if you expect any romance tonight." She unsuccessfully tried to say this with a straight face.

Up ahead another boat raced toward us. I shifted, letting him pass about twenty feet off the port bow. As it went by, I guided the speedboat gently through the other vessel's wake, rocking the boat back and forth. Simone turned, resting her hip against my leg. I dropped one hand from the wheel and wrapped it around her waist, drawing her even closer.

"The waves we just went through is a boat's wake. Depending on the size of the boat and the speed, they can be quite large. It's usually a series of six waves, three on each side. An experienced sailor knows the proper way to take them, easing his craft over the rolling water."

She nodded in understanding. The hint of a smile was in her eyes, tugging at the corners of her mouth. But she said nothing.

"So I knew the right way to cross that yacht's wake. Instead, I jammed the throttle open and raced that hydroplane over the first roller, through the middle of the second wave and then over the third one, fast enough to put the boat airborne."

An incredulous look crossed Simone's face. "You didn't!"

"I did. Sister Columbus was screaming bloody murder as a hundred gallons of water flooded the cockpit where we sat. As we crashed back onto the surface, I did the same thing on the other side, racing over the first wave, through the second and getting airborne on the third." I gave the wheel a spin and headed farther away from shore.

"She must have been furious. What happened?"

I shrugged. "The last thing I expected. As we came through the final wave, she jabbed me with an elbow. I figured this was when I would be doomed to hell, no matter what else I did with my life."

"What did she say?"

"Sister Columbus merely pointed at the stern of the yacht and yelled three words I will never forget."

"What did she say?" Simone repeated.

"Do it again!"

The feisty little nun was having the ride of her life. At her urging, we chased that yacht for about a mile, jumping through its wake from one side to the other. Eventually we turned around and headed back to the benefactor's place. When we pulled into the dock he was standing there, waiting to secure the boat. He guided Sister Columbus back to the house, where several nuns helped her out of the sodden habit and into a heavy robe. A towel became an improvised turban. The benefactor found a sweatshirt and an old pair of jeans for me. All the clothes got tossed in the dryer.

"So she wasn't mad?"

"Nope. It was the most fun she'd ever had. Later on at dinner, she sat across the table from me, still wearing this goofy turban. I got a big smile and a wink from her."

"I can't believe you really tried to drown a nun."

"Told you it was nefarious."

We cruised down the waterway, far enough from the shore that we didn't have to worry about any other boats entering the lake. Soon we passed the Grosse Pointe Yacht Club where the sparkle of chrome still twinkled in the fading sunlight. Simone was perched on the captain's bench, her head tilted back, enjoying the sun and the breeze on her face. From my peripheral vision, I could see her smile widen.

"How much money does a boat like this cost?"

"I don't know exactly. Probably depends on how old or new it is and how many features are on it."

"If I had the money, I'd buy one for you."

That response made me chuckle. "That's very

sweet."

"It's only money, Jeff."

The laugh died in my throat. "It's always about the money." Maybe money was at the root of Morrissey's murder.

Simone sensed the change in my mood. "So how fast will this boat go?"

"Only one way to find out." I looked over my shoulder to make sure no one else was close by. Then I spun the wheel, taking us out north on the lake. Gradually I pushed the throttle down. The fiberglass beauty leapt from the water and felt like it was sprouting wings. Beside me Simone screamed in delight. We raced across the water, leaving our cares and thoughts of homicide behind us.

****

It was just after midnight when my phone buzzed. Simone was sleeping peacefully. I snagged the device from the bedside table and walked out to the screened in porch at the back of the house before answering on the third ring.

"Chene."

"Hey, it's Jamie." There was a brief pause. "Hope I didn't wake you." In the background I could hear a bark of laughter.

"I get the impression you expected to wake me."

She laughed warmly in my ear. "Hey, turnabout is fair play."

"Sorry to disappoint you."

"No big deal. I got some details for you. Malone suggested I wait until morning, but I figured, what the hell, it might be important."

"You get a lot of information at midnight?"

"Sometimes, Chene, that's the way it works. A few of my old contacts gave me a lead, which pointed me in a different direction. This may be a fishing expedition, but that's what research often resembles."

I dropped onto the rattan sofa. The cushions were cool against my skin. Outside there was just enough starlight to see the boat bobbing gently at the dock. "So what did you learn?"

"Not so fast, cowboy. Some of this cost me more than just a few favors."

Before I could respond Simone appeared in the doorway. She didn't say a word, just moved to the sofa and settled on my lap. Her arms went around my neck and she rested her head on my shoulder.

"If you've got something solid, you can name your price."

"I'm not talking a few dollars here. I put a lot of effort into this."

"And I appreciate that." Simone started kissing my neck. "You gonna name your price, Jamie?"

"Maybe you should hear what I've got first." Again I could hear laughter in the background. Malone was obviously enjoying this.

"Fine. I'll be at your place at ten. We'll continue these negotiations then."

"Deal!"

"Tell Malone to have the coffee ready."

"Night, Chene."

"Good night, Jamie."

Simone shifted on my lap. Somehow I managed to end the call.

"I didn't like it when you were gone. And here I find you sitting in the dark, talking to another woman."

"It's about the case."

"Mmm hmm."

I explained that Jamie had been looking for the source of Morrissey's money. Simone drew one hand from my neck and began to lightly dig her nails into my chest.

"Do you really want to talk now?" she whispered in my ear.

"No."

"You could come back to bed and try to sleep."

"We could do that."

She breathed softly on my ear. "I've got some ideas how to relax you."

"I'll bet you do."

Chapter Seventeen

Sunday morning marked one week that we had officially been assigned the Morrissey homicide. Kozlowski and Laura were following up on an idea. Suarez was camped out at the post, updating his notes from the last couple of days. I gave him the folders we found in the Camaro's trunk. One was a proposal for a theater out near Rochester. The other was about a used bookstore that was up for sale in Pontiac. He was going to review the material and do some research on the properties.

Donna jumped at the chance to tag along with me to meet Jamie Richmond. I filled her in on the way across town. Jamie greeted us at the front door and led us out to the backyard. Donna gave me a curious look as we followed the slender redhead.

Malone was at a picnic table. Parts of the Sunday Free Press were scattered about. He raised his coffee in a salute. I made the introductions. Malone pointed at the thermal carafe and some empty mugs.

"Hope you're hungry, Chene. Help yourself."

Jamie came out bringing a large casserole dish. A basket on the table held plates and silverware.

"Fresh from the oven," she said with a smile. "It's an epicurean explosion."

Donna leaned forward and peeked inside. "Do I want to know?"

"Relax, Malone does the cooking. I just carried it."

We all looked at him. Malone shrugged. "Eggs, chorizo sausage, bacon, two kinds of peppers, onions, cheese and a few bits of smoked chicken."

"So it's whatever was in the refrigerator," I said.

"Pretty much," Jamie agreed. She served out generous portions to each of us.

Malone steered the conversation toward general topics as we enjoyed the meal. There was nothing but crumbs left in the bottom of the dish. Jamie disappeared into the house, returning with the carafe refilled and a brown accordion folder. Malone piled the dirty dishes together and moved them to the far end of the table.

"You're familiar with this case?" Donna asked him.

He nodded. "There's been a fair amount of attention in the media. Sounds like Morrissey was a popular guy. One of those 'rags-to-riches' kind of stories. A dedicated family man. A good guy. At least that's the spin the papers and television are putting on it. But I get the sense that's a bit down the road from the truth."

"Around the corner would be more like it," Donna remarked.

The others looked at me. "Jamie's instincts were right. Kyle Morrissey was no saint. He dallied with more than one employee and made passes at several others."

"Has that given you a lead on any suspects?" Malone asked.

"It hasn't helped us narrow down the pool." I shifted my gaze to Jamie, who was perched beside Malone. She was toying with the file. "You gonna share that information or keep us in suspense?"

A dazzling smile was my reward. "I'm got some bits and pieces. Put that together with a little conjecture and it might give you an idea or two."

"She loves being the center of attention," Malone muttered.

Jamie ignored him. "There is absolutely nothing in the public records that shows where Morrissey's capital came from. There was no family money to invest in anything beyond a late night run to Burger King. Maybe he found a pot of gold beside a leprechaun. He worked a number of jobs during high school and college, mostly manual labor. That helped pay for his classes. He did earn a couple of small scholarships. But there was nothing to equal what he needed to take ownership of the Shores Madrid. Unless he had money from the mob…"

"He didn't," I interjected.

"…because that might have been a possibility." Jamie's gaze locked on me. "You were pretty quick to shoot down the mob connection. Morrissey wouldn't be the first guy or the last one to get funding for a clean operation from a dirty source."

"Laundering money for the mob is a big business," Donna stated.

All three of them waited while I refilled my mug. "I have it on good authority that Morrissey had no connections with organized crime."

Jamie started to fidget across from me. Malone shook his head and slipped an arm around her waist. "Chene's got his own sources, Jamie. What else did you find?"

She drew a steadying breath and let it out with a

hiss. "Morrissey did his homework. Before he showed up at the city council meeting, he knew exactly how much tax money was owed on that theater. He knew what condition it was in. He knew what kind of work was needed to get it operational. He knew! The city showed those meetings on the local cable access channels, so the good citizens who couldn't attend in person could still see what was going on."

"You watched those tapes." Donna said. It wasn't a question, just a confirmation.

Jamie nodded. "You bet your sweet ass I did. And I watched the last couple before he made his pitch. And a couple after. Morrissey was there. Taking all kinds of notes. At one point following the last meeting before he got on the agenda, he was seen chatting with a couple of council members."

"He would have inspected the theater to know what kind of work it needed. Maybe some contractors as well," Malone suggested. He nodded in my direction.

"I'm sure he did. Nobody goes into a project like that blind."

Jamie drummed her fingers on the folder. I noticed the bright red polish on her nails, a shade or two darker than her hair. Her mouth twisted slightly, as if she were debating what to say. "I still can't find an answer, Chene. And it pisses me off. It's there, just lurking in the shadows. But I can't find it."

"Maybe you did find it, but just don't recognize it for what it is," I said.

"Don't patronize me!"

Malone burst out laughing. I ignored him and kept my gaze on Jamie. "What's in the file? I'm guessing it ain't recipes?"

Jamie roughly pushed Malone away. "What the hell. Here's what I found. Video copies of the meetings, press releases for the first theater, media clips on anything that had Kyle Morrissey's name attached to it. He looked like he was sixteen years old in the beginning, but that was just because he was surrounded by those geriatric politicians."

Jamie withdrew everything out of the file and spread it across the table. She had downloaded every scrap of information she could find, then printed it out. On the back of each sheet was a date of release or publication and the source of the material. There was a lot there from the Freep, along with bits from the Grosse Pointe News and the Macomb Daily. Malone gathered up the dirty dishes and headed inside. Donna and I slowly went through the documents. Jamie offered a running commentary.

"So it was like three months after he finished college that he made the bid to buy the theater," Jamie said. "He was on the agenda in September. I put a copy of the transcript in there as well. The city was so excited that he was going to take it over, they agreed to forego any property taxes for ten years, as an incentive for Kyle Morrissey to take his shot."

"If he crashed and burned, would the city get the property back?" Donna asked.

"When he made his pitch, Morrissey had managed to get a line of credit from a new local bank." Jamie tapped a red nail on a single sheet of paper. It was some type of tax form that indicated Morrissey's basic information and the name of the bank he was working with. "I tried, but my sources couldn't crack the bank records."

I spun the paper to me. This was a different company than the ones Morrissey currently used for the business or his personal accounts. Donna looked over my shoulder. She hadn't picked up on it. I knew this bank continued to operate. It made me wonder if Morrissey still had any ties there.

Malone returned with fresh coffee. "Taking over the world?" he asked with a grin.

"With every little step," Jamie answered.

As I was looking through the stack of papers, something tugged at my memory. I leaned back and let my gaze wander across the neat backyard. A large board privacy fence surrounded the property. Two old trees were at the outer edge of the lawn, just far enough apart to accommodate a hammock. It had all the makings of an idyllic spot. My eyes flicked to Jamie. She stared at me, ignoring the conversation between Donna and Malone. It was obvious the lack of a clear answer to Morrissey's money irritated her.

"I can't put a finger on it, Chene."

"You ain't the only one."

Malone cleared his throat. "You do remember how stubborn she can be."

Jamie sat straighter. "Stubbornness is one of my redeeming qualities. There has got to be an answer. Morrissey's money had to come from somewhere."

"Where did he work during college?" Donna asked.

"Lots of manual labor. Landscaping, snow removal, that kind of thing. Just before he finished school, he started working with a real estate developer. He was helping get some property ready for a new subdivision." Jamie reached into the stack of paper and rummaged around. "This was dumb luck. There was an article in the Pointe newspaper. Morrissey wasn't mentioned. But they ran a photo with the article and it named the guys in the crew."

I'd been gazing at the back fence, watching two cardinals. Her comment drew me back into the conversation. "The power of the internet?"

"Damn straight." Jamie passed over the copy. It wasn't very sharp, but it showed five guys in jeans and T-shirts leaning on shovels.

I read the article that was attached. The guys in the picture were all young. Several were grinning but a couple had sullen expressions. That flicker of an idea returned a little stronger. I looked up to see Jamie watching me intently.

"Can we take all this research?"

"Of course. But on one condition."

"Name it."

"You figure out where the money came from, you tell me. And…"

"That's more than one condition."

Malone snickered. Donna sat silently, watching our exchange.

"…and when you solve this case, I want to hear everything. Not just the sound bites you'll give to the media. I want everything."

There was no humor in her expression now. She held her gaze on mine. Her jaw clenched. Jamie was a picture of determination.

"You got it. But whatever I share with you, stays between us. This doesn't become fodder for another book."

She flashed me that dazzling smile. "Fodder?

Chene, you're such a sweet talker."

"Deal?"

"Deal!" With that she began to gather the various documents from the table. I watched as she squared the edges and returned them to the folder. When everything was inside she handed it to Donna.

Malone and Jamie escorted us out front. Donna stared wide eyed as the slender redhead once again rewarded me with a kiss as we were leaving.

"Better keep an eye on her, Malone."

He nodded and drew her close. "I usually do. Good luck, Chene."

"Thanks. And thanks for breakfast. I owe you one."

"Something tells me you'll be paying up soon." Malone's expression indicated he'd picked up on the clue about the same time I did.

"Later, Sarge."

****

Donna called Suarez and gave him the details as we drove east. Within ten minutes he was back on the line with some information. She clicked off the call and relayed the address. I wasn't getting my hopes up for much on a Sunday afternoon at the end of June, but it was worth a try.

Bonder Developments was located in Royal Oak, one of the suburbs in Oakland County. Their offices were not far from the Detroit Zoo, which was doing a thriving business that afternoon. I didn't expect Bonder's office to be open. There were no cars in the lot and the lights were off. Sometimes you got lucky. And we had to go right past it to get to Franklin Bonder's residence anyway. Donna was quiet on the drive. I didn't know if she was puzzling over the case or what we'd learned from Jamie. If she had questions, I expected her to ask them.

Franklin Bonder lived in Bloomfield Hills. I found my way through the series of twisting streets and ended on a cul-de-sac deep in the subdivision. There were four cars in the driveway. We parked on the street.

"What's the plan, boss?"

I shrugged. "Same as always. Ask the questions. Watch the responses. See if anything catches our attention."

"Do you think this guy even remembers Morrissey?"

"Only one way we're going to find out."

We were met at the door by a teenage girl in a bright yellow bikini. The idea of talking with cops appeared to bore her. She left us on the porch and closed the door. A minute later it was opened by a young woman in her early thirties. She was wearing a modest turquoise one-piece bathing suit with what looked like a man's unbuttoned white dress shirt over it. Coal black hair dusted the top of her shoulders. Her eyes were hidden behind a pair of sunglasses with large oval lenses.

"Seriously? Cops on a Sunday?"

"We're always working," I said. "We just have a few questions for Franklin Bonder if he's available."

She gave her head a slow shake. "He's available. Probably not coherent, but he's available. C'mon in."

We followed her through the house and out to a patio in the backyard. Seems like everyone was enjoying the great outdoors today. There was a large in-ground swimming pool, fitted out with a diving board and a slide at the deep end. There were four older teenage boys in the pool and lounging around the perimeter with two younger girls. In a corner close to the house, underneath a large umbrella was a cluster of chairs. Sprawled in one was an overweight guy in his late fifties or early sixties. His head was tilted back. As we got closer I realized he was snoring. I nudged his ankle with the toe of my boot. He shifted and snored some more. The woman started to chuckle.

"Sorry guys, but he's out for the count. Frankie usually gets hammered Saturday nights and doesn't return to humanity until sometime Monday morning."

Donna pushed her sunglasses up into her hair. "Maybe we could talk to his wife."

"You are talking to her."

I gestured toward the chairs. "Mind if we sit and talk for a few minutes, Mrs. Bonder?"

A quick smile crossed her face. "I'm still getting used to that. Call me Natalie."

"Chene and this is Spears." We moved away from the snoring man and settled into the upholstered patio chairs.

"I'm Frankie's latest. Wife number three. He outlived the first one, divorced the second one ten years after he married her. A month later he met me."

"Swept you off your feet?" Donna asked.

Natalie chuckled. "Hardly. It's a marriage of convenience. We both knew that from the beginning." Her gaze shifted to the kids at the pool. While the conversations continued, all eyes were on us. "The one in the yellow is my daughter. Just old enough to get into trouble, but not sharp enough to avoid it."

"Single parent?"

Natalie looked back to me. "Yeah. Almost seven

years. Barely made enough to keep us in food and an apartment, let alone clothes."

"How long have you and Mr. Bonder been together?" Donna said.

"About a year. Got my kid in a good school. Money is not an object anymore, but I don't know how long it will last. Frankie hits sixty next year. I'll be surprised if he lives to sixty-five." She removed her glasses and set them on the table. "I try to take care of him, but he's pretty set in his ways. So what's this all about anyway?"

I explained about the Morrissey investigation. Natalie waited until I was done before asking the question. "You don't really think Frankie had anything to do with it? The guy gets winded climbing the steps to the front porch. I can't picture him running around playing war."

"We think Morrissey worked for your husband about fifteen years ago. There's a chance that Franklin might remember him or that they kept in touch."

"You'd have a better chance talking to him at the office in the morning."

"Yeah, we'll do that."

Natalie started to rise. Donna touched her arm. "Those boys look a bit older than your daughter."

"She's fourteen. These are all new friends she's made since we moved in here. The boys come from money. They're very popular."

"Give me a minute, boss."

"Sure."

I sat back with Natalie and watched Donna approach the kids. Neither one of us was wearing a jacket. I wore my badge and gun on my hip. Donna had her badge dangling from a chain around her neck. She walked to the kids and squatted down easily on her haunches. Her expression remained calm and she spoke quietly. Within a minute all four boys were nodding eagerly. She straightened up, turned and walked back. My gaze remained on the group. The guys were all staring with wide eyes.

"Ready, boss?"

"Yeah. Thanks for your time, Natalie."

Donna handed her a business card. "Any time you have a problem or a question, just give me a call. Any time."

We walked out. Donna didn't say anything until we were headed down the block.

"What was that all about?"

"Just making sure they understood the ground rules. Girls that young are liable to do anything for a popular guy. Told them I knew their names and faces. And if one of those girls got so much as a hickey before she turned nineteen, I would know about it. And so would all the convicts they would be housed with in prison."

"Get their attention?"

"Damn straight."

****

We were spinning our wheels. Cantrell knew it. I was in his office. The others were in the bullpen, reading reports, updating the computer files. He thumbed the wheel on his lighter and sparked an ever-present cigarette to life.

"Y'all drillin' a dry hole. Give 'er up."

"We're chasing leads, Pappy."

"Chasin' yer tails more like it."

"It's a summer Sunday. The lab's shorthanded, so we can't get the toxicology reports until tomorrow at the earliest. Kozlowski and Laura struck out trying to connect with Morrissey's doctor. I've got some new research to review, that might give me an idea or two."

"How about that jeweler?"

Pappy knew about the uncut stones we'd found in the Camaro's trunk. That was another surprising twist that had to be followed. "He won't rush through that evaluation. Chances are he might even get the opinion from another expert to appraise those goodies as well."

"So y'all give it up. Take some time. Send the others out and start fresh in the mornin'."

It made sense, but this was unusual for Pappy. Weekends were just another day to work. Cantrell recognized that we weren't making any progress. So I followed his lead and cut the others loose. There were no complaints. Plans were made to pick up at the post in the morning.

It was mid-afternoon. Simone was spending the day with friends. I needed a distraction. Without intentionally planning it, I drove to Ted's house. I grabbed a lightweight leather jacket from the Pontiac's backseat. The Harley was resting just inside the door. Five minutes later, I was on the open road.

Chuck Berry said it best. There was no particular place to go. I just wanted to feel the wind in my face, see the road flashing by beneath my wheels. You can't ride a bike safely at high speeds without giving it your full attention. It's not just your skills and reflexes, but those of other drivers and vehicles you have to watch. I've seen too many accidents with bikes caused by someone in a nearby car unaware of the motorcycle cruising beside them.

I wound my way out to Telegraph Road, a major north-south thoroughfare. A mental coin flip led me south. The road was thick with bikers. I joined the flow, roaring past the mile roads until I hit Michigan Avenue. A swing to the east led me toward downtown Detroit. I zigzagged my way to Woodward and saw the crowd at Comerica Park where the Tigers were playing. At Jefferson Avenue I turned away from downtown, heading for the Grosse Pointes.

With the Detroit River on my right, I realized that Belle Isle was just ahead. The state had turned this nearly thousand-acre island property into an official park a few years ago. There were races for Indy cars and hydroplanes during the summer. A lot of money had renovated some of the facilities, including the zoo and the aquarium. I took the bridge across the river and began to slowly circle the island.

Not far from the entrance to the aquarium was a food truck. I rolled to a stop and put the bike on the stand. From here I could watch a steady stream of vehicles as they cruised the roads. There were bicyclists, joggers and dog walkers as well. When there was no line I went to the truck for a bottle of water and a bag of popcorn.

"How's business?" I asked the stocky guy behind the counter.

"Fantastic. Days like this were meant to be spent outdoors." He counted out my change then leaned an elbow on the rail. "Gotta love those renovations. More guys come out when things look good, rather than run down and beat to shit. Even those old buildings draw people in."

The popcorn was warm with a thin drizzle of melted butter. Not flavored oil, but real butter. "The old buildings?"

"You know, the casino, the conservatory, even the museum. Somebody said they were designed by a famous builder or architect or something like that."

"Huh. You sure about that?"

He tipped me a wink. "Hey man, I don't know shit. But if the tourists like it, they buy more food. You want a dog?"

"Pass. But thanks." I tucked a ten in his tip jar. There was a bench just beyond the parking area. It was facing the conservatory. I sat there, eating the popcorn and letting my mind wander. Some people love old buildings. They get a lot out of the history, of reliving the way things used to be. Maybe that extended to old theaters too.

Could there be a connection? Could it be that easy?

I pulled my phone and called the duty sergeant with a request. Five minutes later, he called back. I tossed the last of the popcorn to a few ducks passing by, got back on the Harley and hit the road.

****

Twenty minutes later I rolled to a stop in front of a small two story brick structure on Kercheval Avenue in Grosse Pointe Farms. After hooking my helmet to the bike's frame I turned and found myself face-to-face with an older, slight woman. She had dark brown hair shot through with blonde highlights. A playful smirk tugged at her lips.

"You're the cop?"

I showed her my creds. "And you are?"

"Izzy. I'm one of the directors at the Historical

Society. You've got the luck of the Irish, Sergeant."

"I look Irish to you?"

The smirk evolved into a full grin. "Sweetheart, everybody's something. Besides, you never heard of the Black Irish?"

"You got me there."

She leaned back and sized me up. "You may be black, but you're not a thoroughbred." Her eyes danced with merriment. "You're more like a White Russian. You know, vodka, Kahlua, and cream. No offense."

"None taken."

"So what can I help you with?"

I explained the puzzle of Kyle Morrissey's money. She stood there, hands on her rounded hips, the smirk returning briefly.

"I don't know if the money is a factor in his death or not. But the uncertainty is curious. And while identifying the source may not lead directly to the killer, it may give us a direction we're not exploring yet."

"You always work Sundays, Sergeant?"

"With a homicide, we work every day."

Izzy considered that. At length she crooked one finger at me. I followed her inside the corner building, which was the society's office. Large photographs decorated the walls of different events in the area, dating back to the early twentieth century. A couple of the photos seemed familiar. Large crowds gathered around a group of automobiles.

"I looked up Kyle Morrissey when we heard about his death." Izzy settled behind an old wooden desk. "He had been an occasional supporter of the society, but not what we would consider generous. Maybe history wasn't a big deal for him."

"Morrissey made his money capitalizing on old movie theaters, renovating them and showing Hollywood classics. Sounds like history would be right up his alley."

She cocked an eyebrow in a quizzical expression. "Or he could have used others love of history and classics to make his fortune."

"Damn, that's cynical."

Izzy flashed that smirk again. "One of my traits. Or maybe a curse."

"How long have you been interested in the historical side of the Pointes?"

"Just about all my life. Back in the day, there were huge estates in different parts of the Grosse Pointes. There were some terrific fortunes here. Going back to the days when Henry Ford got his start and was practically printing his own money. But what makes you think this area has anything to do with Kyle Morrissey?"

"It's a hunch. Morrissey was working manual labor while he was in college. There was no family money. Yet four months after graduation, he had enough of a bankroll to buy the Shores Madrid theater."

"Maybe he won the lottery?"

I shook my head. "No record of any sizeable winning. We checked."

"So what is it you're hoping to find here, Irish, on a Sunday afternoon?"

"Inspiration." I dropped into a chair on the other side of her desk. "Was there ever any scandals, any improprieties that were big in the Pointes?"

A bellow of laughter greeted this question.

"Sergeant, scandals make the world go around. The more money involved, the juicier the stories. Why, I could tell you tales that would make you blush."

I got the sense this was not exaggeration. Izzy probably had access to diaries and letters from some of society's greatest families. To prove the point, she climbed out of her chair and began to show me around. She knew the background of every photograph, every artifact that was on display. I let her go until she ran out of steam.

"Is any of this helpful?"

"Background information. From what I know, Kyle Morrissey was born and raised in St. Clair Shores, just across the city line. His widow said he often rode his bike down here as a kid and wandered around. He wanted the fame and fortune that was associated with the Pointes."

"Which might explain why he moved here," Izzy said.

"True. But that gives me an idea. Fifteen years ago Morrissey was doing labor for a developer. Is there any way to know if there was anything special about that project? There was an article and photo in the local paper about it."

Izzy went back to the desk and booted up the computer. I dropped back into the visitor chair and waited. My eyes continued to wander around the room, taking in all the old photographs.

"How's your historical knowledge of the local area, Irish?"

"Grosse Pointes mean money. The farther away from Alter Road and the Detroit city limits, the pricier the real estate. That's about the extent of it."

Izzy propped her elbows on the desk and laced her fingers together. Then she rested her chin on top of her stacked hands and fluttered her lashes at me. Obviously she was relishing the opportunity to share her knowledge with a captive audience.

"It's been almost a hundred years since Prohibition took place. And before you ask, I was not around when it happened."

"I didn't think so."

"The Grosse Pointes had several advantages to those who wanted to still enjoy the occasional alcoholic beverage. After all, it's but a short boat ride across the river to Canada. And many of the Pointers had waterfront property. Including the founding families of Detroit's automotive empires."

Izzy described some of the antics that followed during Prohibition. In addition to boat rides to Windsor and other ports for alcohol, some daring souls even attempted to drive across the ice in the middle of winter. There were rumors of rum runners from every ilk. Supposedly there was an old party store not far from where we sat that had a history of always having booze available for the discriminating clientele.

"Sounds colorful. But I don't know that it helps my case."

"Irish, you just never know what someone might stumble upon. A lot of those with fortunes were extravagant. There were artwork worth millions. Some bought fancy yachts, or fleets of cars. I've learned that there were private collections that had so many rare first editions that it would put public libraries to shame. If there was a price tag on anything, you'd find somebody in the Pointes holding onto it." She gave a little shake of her head. "The rich often color outside the lines."

"How's that?"

"Even today, the Pointes still attract people with money. But they also generate scandals. There were the four high school seniors who got caught up having sex with underage girls. Then there was the real estate guy who used houses from his listing as places to have illicit sex with his female clients." She gave me a broad wink. "Scandal doesn't stop at the Detroit city limits."

"Yeah, scandals don't have boundaries. Just like some people."

Izzy laughed at that. "Truer words have never been spoken, Irish."

"And what you're describing is fairly recent."

"Yes. In the last thirty years, many of those old lakefront estates were sold. Today's generations have no interest or funds to maintain the family mausoleum. A number of those properties were subdivided into modern mansions. Local celebrities bought up a handful. Newscasters, athletes, top chefs, just to name a few. Who knows what might have been discovered during the demolition?"

On the opposite wall was an artist rendering of one of the old estates. Something about it was vaguely familiar. I'd seen that picture before. Izzy caught my gaze.

"That's one of them. Perched right on the edge of the lake for years. Prime real estate that the family no longer wanted. All the heirs moved away, swanky places like Boulder, San Francisco, Austin and Longboat Key. Nobody wants to live in Michigan. They just want the money their ancestors made here."

I'd run out of questions. At least, for now. Izzy walked me outside. I thanked her for her time and information. She watched, hands on her hips as I pulled on the helmet and straddled the Harley. The smirk had returned to her face. Something told me it was perpetual. I hit the starter and rolled away.

And the glimmer of an idea began.

Chapter Eighteen

Monday morning's sunrise brought no answers. I'd managed a few hours of sleep and spent most of the evening relaxing on the sofa, listening to the water rock the boat in the canal. There were numerous points to follow up on. A scalding hot shower chased the cobwebs from my brain. Before I got to the post my phone buzzed. Cantrell. I swung into the lot beside Lil Nino's and found him at a booth in the corner.

"Y'all want some grits?" He actually said this with a straight face.

"Think I'll get an omelet." As if by magic, an attractive waitress appeared with a fresh pot of coffee. She topped off his mug and filled mine.

While waiting for the food, I filled Pappy in on my conversation yesterday with Izzy from the historical society. He leaned back and didn't comment until I was done. Our food arrived at that point and we dug in.

"Y'all thinkin' Morrissey found something at one of them jobs."

"Yeah. It would have to be something significant. Maybe a trunk of old stock certificates or a piano stuffed with gold coins. There's all kind of stories that come to light about ways people hid their fortunes because they didn't trust the banks. Especially during the Depression. And those estates were built back in the boom days."

Pappy considered it while working on his grits. "Rich people wanna keep dere treasures close. Betcha there was secret rooms and passages, just like in the movies." He paused to drain the remainder of his coffee. The waitress appeared with a fresh pot and topped off our mugs. I noticed she rested a hand on Cantrell's shoulder. She winked at him as she walked away.

"No wonder you like this restaurant."

"Grits is good."

"Customer service is better."

Finishing our meal, I laid out my plans for the day. Cantrell nodded and made a couple of suggestions. We were waiting for the check when my phone lit up. Yekovich from the Cyber Squad. And it wasn't even seven o'clock.

"Chene, you need to stop by. We may have found something."

"You're there now?"

"Fifteen minutes."

Pappy hooked a thumb at the door. I dropped some cash on the table. "I'll meet you there."

Yekovich was waiting in the parking lot. He had a cardboard tray with four giant size Styrofoam cups. He nodded as I approached and used his security pass to unlock the outer door.

"Tell me you haven't been sitting on information all weekend long."

"Hardly. And don't get me started about overtime."

"What are you talking about?"

He pointed down the hall past his office. "Most of my crew prefer to work nights. Less distractions. They're locked in a windowless room, so they can't tell if it's night or day anyway. I give them the flexibility to set their own schedule, as long as we get results."

"Makes sense."

"So Pinky gives me a call and said to drag you in. She wouldn't bother me if it wasn't something worthwhile."

He led me back to the workstations in the rear of the building. Pinky was standing on a thick mat, stretched out in a warrior pose from a yoga exercise. She ignored us for a moment then drew a slow, deep breath and held it for about a minute. I started to speak but Yekovich held up his hand. Apparently he'd seen this before. At length Pinky exhaled slowly and let her arms fall to her sides.

"Hey, Sarge."

"How's it going?"

She shook her hands out at the wrists as if she had just washed them. Without acknowledging him, Pinky took one of the jumbo coffee cups from Yekovich and peeled off the lid. Only then did she wiggle her eyebrows up and down at him. We waited until she took a healthy slug of coffee.

"Espresso. There's nothing quite like it," Yekovich said.

"Who needs Red Bull?" Pinky countered.

Before I could respond she waved the back of her hand toward her computer. I caught the sparkle of colors in the overhead lights. It looked like her manicure was fresh with some new pastels. Pinky perched on a stool and nudged the mouse with her elbow. There were two large monitors on her desk. On the right was a jumble of code. The left was a video that was set to play.

"It took me a lot longer than it should have. Tracking down this email address was a royal pain in the ass."

"But you did crack it," Yekovich said.

"Of course. But I don't think you'll like me much when you hear the rest." Pinky shifted her gaze in my direction.

"Try me."

"The email account was used only once, to send that message to your victim. In order to activate the account, they require a phone number."

"Which you got," Yekovich acknowledged.

Pinky flashed a quick grin. "Of course. But the number was a burner phone, like you'd expect. Used once to acknowledge the email account and once to send the message. I traced it back to where it was purchased." She pointed at the left hand monitor. "Here's the store video."

"You hacked the security system?" I asked.

She wiggled her fingers at me. "Tomato, toe-ma-toe." Then she tapped the keyboard and started the video.

We watched in silence. There was no audio. I recognized the banners and displays. This wasn't one of the big providers. It was a chain that specialized in cheaper model phones. They offered pay-as-you-go plans for people who had credit issues. The store must have just opened, as two sales people were moving around, turning on lights, restocking brochures. The security footage showed two separate shots. One was the entrance, the other the display area and check-out stand. The shop was a small one, tucked into the middle of a strip mall.

As we watched, the door opened and a guy entered. He was wearing jeans and a Red Wings T-shirt, with a Tigers baseball cap and sunglasses. He chatted briefly with one of the clerks, picked out a basic smart phone and pulled out his wallet. Cash was exchanged. The purchase was tucked into a plastic bag with the store's logo on it. Total time was about ten minutes. We waited in silence while the guy exited the store.

"That's all I got."

I grinned at her. "You got a lot. General description, height, size, and date of purchase."

Yekovich glanced at me. "You get all that from the video?"

I pointed at the monitor. On the frame around the door was one of those decals that indicate the height of a person. "We'll interview the store clerks and see if they remember anything else. And we can compare their size to the customer. It's a solid lead."

"I done good?" Pinky asked.

"Damn good."

She preened a little on the stool.

"But that means more work for you," I said.

"Like what?"

"I want you to compare this guy's details against all the videos from the war games. See if anyone matching his size shows up."

Yekovich groaned. "You're talking hundreds of hours of video."

"I'll get right on it, Sarge," Pinky said, her enthusiasm showing.

I nodded at Yekovich. "Get her some help. Cantrell's impatient."

"So there's one more thing. I think the guy used a

time delay feature to send his message," Pinky said.

"Say what?"

"Time delay. This video was from Thursday, almost 48 hours before Morrissey was shot. The phone was used within an hour of the purchase."

I glanced at Yekovich. "What was the time stamp on the Morrissey's phone with the email?"

"Saturday morning at nine."

Pinky was wiggling on the stool. "Like I said, time delay. You go into your email account. Write a message, go to the settings and you can schedule it to be sent at a later date and time. It's just that easy."

"I never knew that."

She shrugged. "Most techies know how to do it. Your average user doesn't look at all the options, they just want to send and receive stuff right away."

"So the guy has tech skills."

"He may not know how to write code, but he knows his way around."

Yekovich looked from me to Pinky. "Anything else you learned?"

"Not yet. But I'm not done. There's something hinky about that email address. I get the sense it's not just a jumble of numbers." She handed me a scrap of paper with the name and address for the phone store. "I copied this and sent it to your phone, along with a couple of close shots of the guy."

"Keep at it. That's great work, Pinky. Thanks."

She wiggled her eyebrows. "You got it, Sarge."

I turned to Yekovich. "Better keep the espresso coming."

He pointed at the cardboard tray. "You kidding? All four of those are for her."

****

Donna was ready when I got to the post. It didn't take long to fill her in. We got to the phone store just as they opened. Both people working had been there on Thursday morning a week ago. Unfortunately, there was nothing remarkable about the transaction. Turns out that was a pretty common event, when someone comes in, buys a cheap phone for cash and heads out. They didn't remember anything distinctive about the customer. No tattoos, scars or funny accents.

"So what now, boss?" Donna slumped in the passenger seat.

"We pick up where we left off yesterday. Let's go visit Franklin Bonder."

"Maybe he's sobered up."

"One can only hope."

Bonder's office was open for business. The receptionist tracked him down to a project site out in Farmington Hills, about twenty minutes west. He was inside a trailer that doubled as a portable office, going over blueprints with two workers. He waved them outside and pointed at a couple of camp chairs by the wall.

Bonder's voice was deep and gravelly, like someone with a perpetual cough. "Natalie told me you guys stopped by yesterday. Must really be important for a home visit on a Sunday."

"Homicide important enough for you?" Donna asked brusquely.

"I haven't killed anyone!"

I held up a hand. "We're getting off on the wrong foot. We're digging into the background on the victim. Kyle Morrissey. I know it's ancient history, but we think he worked for you about fifteen years ago."

"Ya kidding me? Fifteen years? I don't remember people who worked for me last year."

"How far back do you keep payroll records?"

Bonder propped his elbow on the draft table and scratched his cheek. "Well, that's a different story. My accountant and attorney are real sticklers for that shit. They nag me more than my first wife."

"How long?"

"Twenty years."

"So if Morrissey worked for you, it would still be on record."

He nodded. I pointed at the telephone that was propped on the edge of the table. Bonder took the hint and called his office. On the wall opposite the camp chairs was a diagram of the current project. It was a short street that dead ended in a small circle with lots for three houses. Five other lots lined each side of the street coming into the property. The legend Shadow Lane was across the top of the page. Bonder hung up and noticed where my attention was.

"Our latest effort. Thirteen of the nicest little homes, only minutes away from the main roads. Good schools, lots of city services, and plenty of personal touches to make each one unique. You in the market?"

"No, I'm good. So how do you find properties like this?"

Bonder rolled his eyes and grinned. "Lots of contacts. Lots of schmoozing with city planners, working with real estate agents, driving around looking at what's where. I started out buying crappy farmland that was close to the cities. As the population grew and people wanted to get out of Detroit, I kept going. The hard part is staying ahead of the demand."

"Thought the housing market went down the tubes a couple of years ago," Donna said.

"It slowed down, but it never went away. A few guys didn't pay attention to the warning signs, kept churning stuff out. Unrealistic prices with unrealistic mortgages. That's no way to run a business."

Before he could say anything else Bonder's phone rang. He listened for a minute, then pointed over his shoulder at a computer monitor on another desk. The three of us gathered around it.

"Morrissey did work for me. And it was fifteen years ago, January to early July. He was general labor. Back then it mostly muscle work. Clearing landscape and small trees, getting things ready for the heavy equipment. Then working alongside the machine operators as support."

"What's that like?" I asked.

Bonder clicked on a couple of files. Pictures of a large three story building filled the screen. He scrolled through it, showing different rooms from several angles.

"I remember this job. It was an estate right off Lakeshore in the Grosse Pointes. Gigantic old house with a separate garage up by the road. Even had a pool house, which is weird, since the pool was about fifteen feet from the lake. But I guess high society people needed a place to change from their tuxedos before they got wet."

"What's the story?"

Bonder pointed at the screen. "The estate went up for bid. We landed it. I took a crew inside in late March, started tearing out the fixtures. There was some really pricey shit inside. Glass doorknobs, crystal chandeliers, brass plates on the light switches, copper plumbing and more. We took it slow. Gutted each room. Filled up a couple of trucks with stuff that we could sell at auctions or to antique dealers. Even took the doors and the hardware from the kitchen cabinets.

"Once we had the house cleared, I turned the guys loose and let them do the demolition. That's the fun part. All the power, gas and water was cut off. So it's time to break out the sledge hammers and tear everything down. We knock out the walls, then throw it into dumpsters. There was good hardwood floors in there that we salvaged. I think we used some of that for a couple of the new places that we built."

"Then the heavy equipment?" Donna asked.

"Yeah, a couple of cranes and bulldozers. We tore off the roof in sections, then knocked down the exterior walls in stages, hauled away the crap. It was a hell of a job. That was one of the biggest we've ever done."

"So you tore down all three structures and subdivided the property?"

Bonder glanced at me and nodded. "Yeah, I worked with an architect who designed the new homes. He had the floor plans ready while we were doing demo and sold a dozen lots before we had it cleared."

"This your only project while Morrissey was working for you?"

"Hell yeah. Something this big demands all my attention."

I pointed at the monitor. "Can you show me the exterior shots of the old estate? As many angles as you have."

"Sure."

Bonder clicked through a series of photos. The last one must have been taken from the edge of the property, just before the lake. There was a large sprawling lawn, leading up to the front of the mansion. Recognition flashed through my mind.

"Fuck me hard."

****

All three of us were on the phones simultaneously. Bonder's interest had been triggered. He reached out to the Grosse Pointe Farms city offices and requested the original architectural drawings for the estate. He also called his office and had his assistant look into all of his contacts for that area. Donna contacted the historical society, trying to track down Izzy for more details. I called Olivia Sholtis, a reporter with Channel Four and asked her to check the station's archives for anything they may have on the original property owners. Realizing it was well after ten, I called Jamie Richmond.

"Chene, it's a good thing Malone isn't the jealous type," she said as a form of greeting. "Tell me you're onto something."

"It may not solve the murder, but it's a lead on the money. Your research gave me some direction."

I could hear the excitement building in her voice. "Don't keep me in suspense. What did you find?"

I laid it out for her. In the background I could hear the clacking of a computer keyboard. She was determined to be right in the thick of it. Quickly I explained the efforts of the others and my expectations.

"I'm not sitting on the sidelines, Chene. You wouldn't have this without me. There's gotta be something I can do."

It was a long shot, but there was a chance she could deliver. "See if you can find any of the remaining family. I think they're scattered across the country. But they might remember the old place. And there could be stories."

She hesitated. "Why dump this on me?"

"I'm not dumping. You're a successful author. People would be more willing to talk with you if they think it's research for another book. There may be some legends handed down from the earlier generations. Maybe one of those stories is true."

"What kind of legends?"

"Buried treasure."

There was another hesitation. "Oh, what the hell. I'll be in touch one way or the other. But if there are family legends about buried treasure, I'm using it in a novel."

"Done."

Bonder and Donna were waiting for me. He agreed to forward any information that came from his requests. I thanked him for his help and promised to let him know what we found out. Donna was slowly shaking her head as we got back in the car.

"What's next?"

"We're going to Morrissey's office."

Chapter Nineteen

We weren't expected but I didn't care. Donna had been there when we first got the case and interviewed the widow. She'd met Valerie Mann on Friday at the funeral. Valerie's mood was frosty when we arrived.

"Mrs. Morrissey is in a meeting."

"We'll wait," Donna said.

"It may be a while. There are a number of issues they have to discuss."

Unless they'd brought in barstools, I knew the meeting wouldn't last more than an hour. But we were on a roll. And I was impatient. A delay could be trouble. I'm not superstitious, but it was time to keep the momentum going. Valerie was standing in the hallway just outside the conference room. Her arms were crossed protectively over her breasts. The black cotton dress wasn't snug, but it didn't hide her figure. She fidgeted. I took a step toward her. Valerie's eyes widened in surprise.

"Why don't we do this the easy way?"

"What way would that be?"

"You knock gently on that door, ask Colleen for ten minutes of her time and keep her guests occupied while we have a quick conversation."

She stood a little taller, the frosty demeanor intensifying. "Or?"

"Or I send Detective Spears into the room to

interview the visitors and determine if they had any reason to kill Kyle Morrissey."

"You wouldn't!"

I was growing tired of playing games. "Don't fuck with me. In case you've forgotten, we're investigating his homicide. That outranks any meetings."

Donna turned toward the conference room. Valerie stepped in front of the door and dropped her hands. "I'll get Colleen."

In less than a minute, Mrs. Morrissey joined us in the corridor. She calmly extended her hand to each of us.

"What can I do for you, Sergeant?"

I was standing in front of the framed photograph that was in the center of the hallway. It was the only one that wasn't tied directly into the theaters. It was the same photo of the estate that we'd just viewed with Franklin Bonder.

"You can start by telling us everything you know about this picture."

Colleen let her gaze shift to the photograph. Then she nodded and turned toward her office. She motioned with her left hand that we should follow, just in case we weren't already planning to. Once inside Colleen closed the door and went to the phone on the desk. She dialed an internal extension that was answered immediately.

"Reschedule the meeting."

Obviously this was going to take a while. I noticed Donna shifting as she settled into one of the visitor chairs. Her right hand dipped into the pocket of her jacket. That's where she kept the digital recorder. She'd done the same thing when we met with Bonder at the construction site.

"Kyle wasn't a sentimental guy, but he always insisted we keep that picture." Colleen was speaking calmly, her hands laced together on the desk. "He said this was a memento, a reminder of what hard work could result in. Sometimes I think it was his goal to become rich enough to buy a place like that. Not that I'd ever want something so extravagant. We were quite happy with our home."

"What's the story behind it?" I asked.

"It was the last job. He'd done manual labor every year we were in college. The money was good. Kyle didn't want to get student loans so he worked while going to school. He lived with his family, didn't have to pay room and board. Almost every dollar he earned went for tuition and books. Occasionally we'd splurge and go out for burgers. Actually, we went out about once a week, but usually I paid. I was waiting tables at a bar in the Shores. We both paid our way through school."

"So why this particular photograph?"

She took a moment before answering. "Something about that last job changed Kyle. His attitude became more positive. He'd always talked about someday." Colleen smiled wistfully at the memory. "It was, 'someday we'll have a nice home.' And 'someday we'll start a business together.' And 'someday we'll have kids.' We talked about getting married after we finished school. I thought we'd find jobs, get a little apartment and start a life. An adult life."

Donna gave her a gentle smile. "Sounds like you had a few 'somedays'."

"We did." Her attention returned to me. "We had a lot of good days. The business, the kids, our home."

"Did he ever tell you what was so special about that estate?"

Colleen took a moment to consider the question. "No. But whenever Kyle was about to embark on another project, he'd stand in front of that photograph for a while. He said it was his lucky charm."

"I think it was."

"But why is it important? What does it have to do with finding his killer?"

It was my turn to consider the questions. In my peripheral vision I saw Donna turn toward me, her expression curious. As Jamie would say, 'what the hell'. "We're never sure exactly what's important when looking for motive. But money is often a factor. No one seems to know where Kyle got the capital to start the business. From what you've just described, I doubt he was able to save enough while going to school and working."

"The last semester was paid for, so he might have been able to earn a thousand or two, since he was still working."

"He ever tell you where the money came from when he bought the Shores Madrid?"

Colleen gave her head a negative shake. "It surprised me when he put the plan together and got the approval from the city. But Kyle was always persuasive. He'd set his mind on something and he'd figure out a way to get it. I just assumed someone he'd met along the way was impressed with his dream and bought into it. Literally bought into it."

We sat there quietly for a moment, each lost in our own thoughts. Colleen let her gaze fall to the family photos on the side of the desk. "He could be so charming. Sometimes I pictured him dancing with wealthy little old ladies, persuading them to invest in the company. Like that bit from the movie."

Donna didn't make the connection. I did.

"The Producers. Mel Brooks musical comedy."

"I'll have to check that one out."

"Get the remake with Nathan Lane. You'll enjoy it."

"Do you think he found something at that old mansion?" Colleen asked quietly, bringing us back on topic.

"It's possible. It would certainly help explain a sudden influx of cash."

"Maybe it was those jewels that were in the trunk."

I shook my head. "Even with a cursory examination, Jared confirmed that the diamonds had serial numbers on them. That's a process using a laser. The technology wasn't available forty years ago. He'll be tracing those numbers to determine their providence."

The quiet returned. No other questions came to mind. Donna and I stood and thanked Colleen for seeing us.

"When you figure out what he found, will you tell me?"

"Of course."

"Find out, Chene," she said in a voice harsh with determination. "And then go get his killer."

****

We needed direction. Donna was waiting impatiently for me to determine our next move. Suarez was camped out at the forensic lab, waiting for the report on the contents of the iced tea bottle we'd found in Morrissey's car on Saturday. Last night I'd reviewed notes on the case and realized we'd never dug deeply into the background on Nicholas Trent, the guy who had been comforting Colleen during our first meeting. Kozlowski and Laura were following up, rattling that cage to see if something fell out. Despite his claims of being a 'close family friend', no one recalled seeing him at the funeral.

Before I could make a decision, my phone buzzed. Olivia Sholtis from the television station.

"You have a sudden interest in history, Chene?" she asked sweetly.

"A continuing interest in crime. Any luck?"

"Not a lot of video footage, but a fair amount of backstory in the archives. You're going to owe me a manicure. I'll be scraping cobwebs out of my cuticles for at least a week."

"If it leads to something, I'll throw in a pedicure."

She laughed lightly. "I'm surprised you know what a pedicure is, Chene. Got a new girlfriend?"

I met Olivia a few years ago when she was first starting out as a reporter. She was very intelligent, with a sharp sense of humor. Our paths cross periodically. I've been an unnamed source on more than a few crime related stories. It dawned on me that she could qualify as a friend, which would crack Ted's idiotic statement of 'name six'.

"Let's stick to business."

"Oh, I sense a human interest feature. The romantic life of a dedicated homicide cop. The conflicts. The drama. The intensity."

She had me grinning. "Shut up."

Laughter bubbled from the phone. "Come on down

to the station, tough guy. I'll have everything ready by the time you get here. And you know my price is going to be a lot more than a mani-pedi."

"On our way."

When we got to the television station Olivia was waiting for us. She gave me a quick hug and brushed her cheek against mine. I introduced Donna. Liv cranked up her smile and led us back to a small meeting room. On one wall was a flat screen television showing the tail end of the noon newscast. She clicked a remote and brought up some old video footage.

"There was a string of clips from a number of charity events held on the grounds. A garden party for the cancer society. Another one for the heart association. There was even an event with classic cars spread over the grounds to support the Salvation Army. Lots of chrome and wax in that one."

We watched the brief video, listening to the reporter drone on about the crowd, the estate, the organization that would be the beneficiary of such generosity. Little was said about the family or the origins of the fortune. Most of the video was from the late sixties and early seventies. When the last clip ended, Liv tapped a button on the console and the screen went dark. She swiveled to face me and extended her palm, wiggling the fingers.

"Start talking, Chene. I know you're working the Morrissey homicide. What does this place have to do with it?"

"Maybe nothing. Maybe everything."

Laughter rose from her throat. "Oh, I love it when you're being cryptic."

After getting her assurance that nothing would be

used until we cracked the case, I explained our theory about the money. Olivia jotted notes on a pad using some form of shorthand that probably only she understood. Most of the time she kept her eyes on me. Occasionally she'd glance at Donna for verification.

"So you're digging for proof that there was something valuable hidden there that Morrissey found while working on the demolition project."

"Exactly. Anything else in the archives that might be worth a look?"

Liv smiled and tapped a narrow forefinger on the table. "I can have one of the interns do a little digging. She lives for research. A story that has its roots a hundred years ago will have her lit up like a pinball machine."

I mentioned our efforts with the local historical society and Jamie's attempts to reach the remaining family. There was no need to duplicate efforts.

"Whatever we find, Chene, I will send it along."

"You gonna bill me for that manicure?"

"Baby, if you're on the right track with this story, it could be worth a local Emmy award. A manicure would be nice, but I'm thinking a day at the spa would be appropriate." Olivia ran that forefinger across the back of my hand. "Or you could tell me about this new girlfriend."

"Seems to me your husband might be a little curious about someone else paying for your spa time."

"Charlie's a very understanding guy. Besides, if he reaps the benefits and it comes out of your wallet, he'll appreciate the results even more."

I bit back a grin. "Get to work."

As we got back in the car Donna's phone rang. She

switched it to speaker and propped it on the dash. Suarez.

"I got the lab results, boss. Pappy said to bring everyone in. He also said it's your turn to buy lunch. And no Hollywood vegan crap."

"We're an hour away."

"The man sounded hungry," Suarez said nervously.

"Call the others. We'll be there."

Donna hung up. Pocketing her phone, she gave me a quizzical look. I knew what would please Cantrell. I made a call. The place was right on the way.

****

Back at the post I carried a cardboard box into the meeting room. Cantrell was slowly swiveling his chair back and forth, the ever-present coffee cup close at hand. He raised an eyebrow as I set the box on the conference table and slid it toward him. Pappy dug out two submarine sandwiches and pushed the box to Laura. She grabbed one and passed the carton to Donna. I dropped into my chair as the box made the rounds. Suarez pulled out a sandwich and was about to grab a second one when Kozlowski wagged a finger in his direction.

"Not so fast, rook. How many are left?"

Suarez peeked inside the box. "Three."

"Which just stands to reason that one of those is for Chene and the others belong to me."

Sheepishly he withdrew his hand. I claimed mine and handed the other two to Koz. He nodded his thanks and began to unwrap his delicacy. Suarez was tentative.

"These are from Buscemi's, the best subs on the entire east side," I explained. "They've been in business for more than fifty years. Good pizza, but the subs are legendary. They're packed with meat, cheese and veggies. And if you hesitate too long, Kozlowski will make yours disappear."

Suarez glanced around the table. Everyone else was busy eating. He shrugged, peeled back the wrapper and sank his teeth into the sandwich. Donna passed around two large bags of chips. For twenty minutes we put homicide on hold. Friendly chatter followed. Kozlowski was the last one to finish. He walked around the table, gathering the wrappers and trash, stowing them back in the box.

"Break's over," Cantrell grumbled. "Obliged, Chene. So whatcha got?"

I glanced at Donna. She took a moment to gather her thoughts, then reported about our investigation. Cantrell shook a fresh cigarette from his pack but didn't light it up. Instead he slowly rolled it along his fingertips. When Donna finished, he shifted his gaze to me and nodded. "Follow dem bucks. Keep at it."

Suarez was up next. "Lab results on the iced tea confirm there were traces of nicotine in it. Also some other chemicals. Took them a little while to identify it. All the ingredients that you'd normally find in bug spray. It was diluted, but apparently enough to be lethal."

"Any fingerprints on the bottle?" Koz asked.

"They processed it for prints while the chemical analysis was being done. Several that were Morrissey's and what looks like at least three more sets, but nothing in the system to match them to."

"Stands to reason. Probably clerks stocking the shelves, cashiers ringing up the sale, maybe even the truck driver who brought the stock into the store," Koz said.

So now we knew how the nicotine got into his system. We kicked around ideas on the poison for a few minutes. I noticed Laura was unusually quiet. She kept stealing glances at Kozlowski, then shifting her gaze back to Pappy. Something was up. I wasn't the only one to notice.

"Spit it out, Girlie. Y'all lookin' like the accountant who works my taxes."

"We found a cover girl."

When the photos in Morrissey's phone had been discovered, Koz began referring to them as cover girls. Each one was in a similar pose. They were wearing a short skirt with a white or cream colored blouse that was unbuttoned all the way down. No bra. The young women appeared to be caught in the act of flashing their breasts at the camera. All of the pictures were taken at one of the bookstores or theaters, judging by the background. Each girl was pretty with a curvy figure.

"Keep talkin'," Cantrell said with a grin.

Laura flashed her own smile. "It was a fluke. We were at Trent's office, just finishing up our interview with him. As we were heading out, I noticed the receptionist was behaving strangely." She hooked a thumb at Kozlowski. "Of course, he noticed it first."

"Thought it was just my animal magnetism working its charms. When she started to turn away, I recognized her."

"Y'all been starin' at those pictures a lot?"

Koz nodded. "Every day. I kept thinking it was only a matter of time before we crossed paths with one of them. This happened to be it."

"So she was one of Morrissey's playmates?"

Donna asked.

Laura rejoined the conversation. "Not exactly. We took her into a conference room, figuring she must have seen Morrissey whenever he had meetings with Trent."

The cover girl's name was Darcie. She explained that a few months ago Morrissey bumped into her at a coffee shop down the street from the office. They chatted for a few minutes and then he made her an offer. If she was willing to pose and merely flash her chest for a couple of pictures, he'd pay her $500. No sex. Just the pictures. Morrissey assured her that the photos were for his use only and that they would never end up on the internet. He explained the concept of a racy calendar, where the models face would be obscured, with the idea that books and movies can be sexy.

Kozlowski picked up the narrative. "Darcie was a little hesitant but said that Morrissey was always charming her, paying little compliments whenever he stopped by. She admitted that the idea of being on a sexy calendar intrigued her. Darcie also said she would have done it for free, but when Morrissey offered up the money, she jumped at it."

"So there weren't no sex?" Pappy was obviously skeptical.

"Not with her," Koz said. "She was smart. Had a friend with her in the background, watching to make sure Morrissey didn't try something. He took the pictures, paid her in cash and gave her a kiss on the cheek. That was all. Darcie's friend was taking video, just in case. Her friend is going to send me that."

"Do you believe this story?" I asked.

He shrugged his massive shoulders. "Yeah, she's

bright. It was a smart move having a friend be a witness and film it. So the calendar story could have been legit."

"So maybe Morrissey wasn't such a scumbag after all," Donna said.

"Once a scumbag, always a scumbag," Koz said. "Maybe he just got a little more selective. And Darcie is pretty young."

"So you found a titty sister. What's that git us?" Cantrell growled. "We still ain't figured out who killed him. Scumbag or not. Y'all need to break this case. Ya gotta catch this killer."

Silence fell around the table. Gradually all eyes shifted to me.

"Let's recreate Morrissey's movements on that Saturday. Suarez, check his car and his phone for a GPS program. See if either or both can show where he went before arriving at the war games."

"Copy that."

"Laura, review those other cover girl photos. See if you can find a time stamp or anything that will help put them in chronological order."

"On it, boss."

Cantrell snickered but said nothing.

"Donna, review the materials we got from Olivia Sholtis. Something in there could give us a clue to the money."

"Right away."

The three of them left the room. Before I could go any farther, my phone chimed, indicating a text message. I glanced at the screen and saw Jamie's number and three little words. Cantrell crookedly raised an eyebrow. Leaning across the table I showed him and

Kozlowski the screen.

"Fuck me hard," Pappy muttered.

"Can't argue with that," Koz said. "So what's next?"

"You and I are going to see an old gangster."

****

Maximo Aurelio answered on the second ring. There was a lot of noise and wind in the background.

"What's going on, Chene?"

"I need to see him. Where are you?"

Max let out a deep throated chuckle. "Damn shame, buddy. We just left the marina for a cruise. Won't be back until late tonight. Or maybe tomorrow."

"You're running the boat?"

"Nah, the agency sent over a new captain. He seems to like this one, so what better way to test her skills than going for a cruise."

Kozlowski and I were standing next to my car, the call on speaker. Koz raised his palms in a 'what are you gonna do' gesture. Fuck that.

"Where you headed, Max?"

"The man said something about the Black River and Port Huron. That's a pretty nice ride from what I hear. Catch you later, Chene." The line went dead.

"Now what?" Koz asked.

I scowled at him. "We're going for a boat ride."

Chapter Twenty

Kozlowski stood on the dock as I undid the cover for the speedboat. Massive hands rested on his hips as he slowly shook his head.

"The hell did this come from?"

Folding the cover, I stowed it down below. "A favor for Ted."

"Which means there's a woman involved."

"Of course. Get the bow line."

"That's the pointy end, isn't it?"

Ignoring him, I turned on the blower to clear the engine compartment and went to release the stern line. The boat bounced and wobbled as Kozlowski stepped aboard. We drifted away from the seawall as I keyed the engine.

"He's got a half hour head start." Koz settled in the passenger seat.

"But he's probably doing fifteen knots. We'll be doing better than forty."

Koz tugged his sunglasses down his nose and looked over them. "You sure you know how to run this thing?"

"Bet your Polish ass I do."

Once we cleared the canal and entered the lake, I jammed the throttle down. I was tired of chasing leads and not getting anywhere. On the way to the house, I'd had a quick conversation with Jamie about her message.

"Three little words, Chene. Buried treasure: Prohibition. That sums it up."

"Got any details?"

"Two of the great grandchildren gave me the same story. One's in Kitty Hawk, the other is in Napa Valley. Legend had it that the family was famous for extravagant parties back in the early 1910s. Big money was just rolling in then. When alcohol was suddenly illegal, that didn't slow them down. Lots of drinking and carousing. Even some rumors about illicit affairs. Maybe a niece or a nephew being sired by a bodyguard. Or maybe it was by an uncle. Lots of lust in the dark. Now my curiosity is rising." Jamie's laughter filled the car. "I may do a tell-all on one of the country's most famous families."

"So what's the buried treasure?"

"According to the kids, there was a stash of Prohibition era alcohol somewhere on the property. They used to explore whenever they could. But they never found it."

"Interesting."

"Talk to me, Chene. Where is this headed?"

"When I know, Jamie, I'll tell you everything."

"You'd better deliver, cowboy. There's nothing worse than a pissed off redhead."

"Don't I know it."

Racing across the lake, I was glad that there wasn't much boat traffic. With the clear skies and bright sunshine, it was easy to see a long way out. Koz found a set of binoculars in one of the cupboards next to the seat. He was slowly panning the lake before us, looking for anything of size.

"Agonasti know you got this ride?"

"Nope. I'm hoping the element of surprise works in our favor."

"You sure they're headed for Port Huron?"

I shrugged. "Makes sense. We headed out that way last week. I mentioned a nice restaurant up there on the Black River that could accommodate his yacht. He probably wanted to see for himself."

We were flashing along, the sleek boat performing well. Ten minutes passed when Kozlowski jammed a finger ahead at one o'clock.

"What was the name of his boat?"

"Mikahla. And it's a yacht, not a boat. Must be over fifty feet long."

"Got him."

I coaxed a little more horsepower out of the engine. We closed the gap quickly. I could have used the marine radio, but wasn't sure what response that would generate, if any. Drawing alongside and matching their speed, I tapped the horn. Max and Agonasti appeared on the bridge's rail. Agonasti shook his head slowly in disbelief, then turned away. The yacht cut power.

"Now what?" Koz asked skeptically.

"Now we talk."

It took a little maneuvering, but we ended up boarding the yacht from the swim platform. I tied the speedboat's bowline to the yacht's stern cleat and gave it plenty of length to keep the boats from colliding. The yacht was barely moving. Ascending the ladder brought us into the aft salon.

Max greeted us at the door. He crushed my fingers in his grip, then slapped me on the shoulder.

"Gotta say it was a treat watching you drop that idiot in the water last week, Chene. Only wish we had video cameras rolling so we could watch it on instant replay."

"You mean your own video cameras."

"Yeah. The boss figures somebody in the alphabet must always be looking. Now what's so important that it couldn't keep?"

"Homicide. We need to talk with Leo."

Max shook his head slowly. His eyes shifted, taking in Kozlowski's bulk and demeanor. They'd met before.

"Hello, Giant."

"Hiya, shooter. Still wearing that Berretta in the ankle holster?"

"It's like an old friend. It keeps me company."

Kozlowski nodded. "I'll bet."

Leo Agonasti was standing in the center of the room. In the background the stereo was playing. Sinatra was gearing up with one of his greatest hits. A gentle breeze from the lake kept the cabin comfortable. There was a glass of something on the table beside a deep chair. Next to it was a thick volume about World War II. Despite the interruption to his cruise, he still offered me a smile as we shook hands.

"Jeff. Two visits within a week. That's got to be a record."

"Circumstances demanded it."

"Come in, have a seat." He turned slightly toward Koz. "Hello, Detective Kozlowski. It's been a long time."

"Indeed. Nice boat you got here." Koz remained in the doorway by the swim platform, taking in the room. Max crossed to one of the other doors that led below, resting a shoulder against the wall so he could keep an eye on us.

"Any progress on the Morrissey investigation?" Agonasti asked.

I took the chair beside his. "Bits and pieces. A case like this reminds me of that kids' game. A tower of wooden blocks where you pull one out slowly and see what happens. Hopefully you get the right one before the tower collapses."

"So which block am I?"

I took a moment to consider that. "You're a substantial one. Right along with the foundation. You have the connections and a love of history. We've often talked about events that have shaped the world, or our little corner of it here in Motown. Your interest in Morrissey's death was more than just a glimpse of something that appeared in the evening news."

Agonasti settled back in his chair. His expression was one of curiosity. "Go on."

"Throughout the case we've been puzzled as to how Kyle Morrissey got the business started. It requires some serious capital to take the plunge like he did, even fifteen years ago. He was a hustler, a hard worker."

"That's not exactly a bad thing."

"We've been pulling out blocks, trying to find a beginning. I think we're close now. Close enough that it might give us a new direction."

Leo Agonasti considered this. "And you're concerned that this direction may bring you to me. I assure you, Jeff, that I had nothing to do with the man's homicide. After all these years, I hope you know me well enough to believe that."

I nodded. "But we're talking about money. And if it was even a little bit of a gray area, perhaps you were involved."

"Tell me what you think." His voice remained smooth and calm.

I'd been working on this theory for days. Summarizing it was easy. "I think Kyle discovered something in that old estate in Grosse Pointe when he was working with the demolition crew. Something old, something so well hidden that nobody alive knew about it. Something he could smuggle out in the middle of the night. Something that a collector might pay a high dollar for. And somehow, that something made its way to you. Because you always had the pulse on this territory and nothing went on in the shadowy corners that you didn't know about."

Agonasti sat perfectly still. After a moment, he cut his eyes to Max. Agonasti gave a slight inclination of his head. Max walked out of the salon and descended the short flight of stairs to the galley and staterooms below. We waited in silence. The breeze from the lake stirring the air was invigorating. The yacht was still crawling forward. Behind it the speedboat followed, like a toy on a string. The background music shifted to Dean Martin. Max returned with a small cloth bag cradled in his hands. He set it on the table beside Leo's drink and resumed his post by the lounge door.

"That is one of only a handful of the remaining relics," Agonasti said quietly, a touch of reverence in his voice. He shifted his gaze to me, then slowly motioned toward it with his left hand. "Go ahead."

Carefully I lifted the bag and undid the drawstring at the top. There was movement behind me. Koz shifted, leaning in for a closer look. I widened the bag's opening and let the cloth drop to the base.

"Booze!" Kozlowski stared at the old squat bottle in my hand. "I'll be damned."

I was slowly turning the bottle around in my hands. It took an effort but I set it carefully on the table beside Leo's glass. The smile on his face was a combination of satisfaction and pride.

"Not just booze," I said. "Prohibition booze."

"You got that right," Max said from behind me. "That whiskey's priceless."

Agonasti broke into a broad grin. "That's impressive, Jeff. Even with your track record, I wasn't sure you'd put it all together."

"I've got a general idea. Why don't you fill in the blanks?"

He kept his eyes on the bottle. What followed was part history lesson, part connections, part relationships and a small part of luck.

Morrissey had discovered a chamber off the estate house that led underground. After the crew left for the evening, he came back to explore it. The chamber led toward the lake. What appeared to be a large room, perhaps even big enough to be a ballroom, was roughly dead center under the expanse of lawn between the house and the water. Here Morrissey found a storeroom that was packed with wooden crates. Each crate bore a dozen bottles, wrapped in burlap, of fine Canadian whiskey. Whiskey that had been smuggled in during prohibition across the Detroit River, probably by boat. There was a cave-in on the far side of the room, which could have extended to the boathouse.

"Morrissey recognized immediately what he found. He also knew that if he tried to peddle those crates all at once, the price would be a pittance. So he worked diligently all night, bringing up the crates and hauling them away." Agonasti paused in his story and waved two fingers at Max. I watched him open a small cupboard and remove four thick glasses. He lined them up on the table. Leo nodded. Max carefully opened the bottle and poured a couple of fingers of whiskey into each glass. Capping the bottle, he picked up two glasses and handed one to Kozlowski. Leo lifted the other two and passed one to me.

"What are you thinking, Chene?" Koz asked quietly.

I studied the amber liquid before me. "We're savoring a clue in the form of hundred-year-old whiskey. How often do we get to do that?"

"Not often enough."

Agonasti was holding up his glass, admiring the color in the sunlight. "You're not drinking alcohol, Kozlowski. You're sampling history."

I clinked glasses with Leo. He nodded and we took a sip. Max raised his glass in a silent toast.

After letting the whiskey slid off my tongue, I encouraged Leo to continue his story. Kyle Morrissey had hidden the crates in his family garage. Then he went to the library and did some research. There were stories in the old microfiche files of the newspapers about speakeasies and gin joints from Prohibition. What caught his attention was an article about an old family business, a liquor store in the Grosse Pointes that was still in operation all these years later. He approached them and learned that earlier generations had in fact been a clearing house for alcohol back in the day. Once he had formed a friendship with the current owner, Kyle brought in a single bottle.

"The owner knew what he was looking at. The family albums were filled with pictures of his grandfather and uncles handling countless bottles of alcohol from that period. And he wisely knew if there was one, there had to be more."

"How did he connect with you?" I asked.

Leo smiled knowingly. "I get around. Max and I still know a lot of people in a variety of...enterprises. And as you mentioned, I'm a fan of history."

"So he put you and Morrissey together."

"Yes. In the beginning, Kyle told me there was only a few bottles. I suspected otherwise. Max followed him and we found his cache." Agonasti shrugged and took another sip. "I made him an excellent offer. And enhanced that should he discover any additional bottles."

"How long before he makes the deal?" Koz asked.

Leo tipped a finger at him. "Very good. It was only a day or two later. Kyle was concerned that someone else might discover his treasure and take it away from him. He delivered. I paid handsomely. Part of the appeal was that I would be the only one to have this tangible piece of Detroit history."

I swirled the glass, watching the whiskey coat the inside. With a nod to Leo, I drank down the last of it. Who knew history could be so tasty?

"So that's where the money came from," Koz said.

"Does this create a problem for us, Jeff?" Agonasti asked.

I thought it over. "Don't see how. You didn't smuggle the booze back in the day. That was before your time. There's nothing illegal about owning alcohol now. You bought it a long time ago."

"Did Morrissey find any more?" Koz asked.

"Unfortunately no. He returned to the estate several times in the evening, and conducted additional searches of the basement. But if there was any more, it may have been lost in that cave-in between the ballroom and the boathouse."

Above us I heard footsteps. Conversation died as a small pair of feet began to descend the ladder from the bridge. Tanned shapely legs followed, ending in crisp white shorts and a white blouse with captain's bars on the shoulders. The tan extended to the arms and face, which was framed in honey colored hair.

"Sorry to interrupt, gentlemen, but we're coming close to the channel for the freighters and towing that speedboat may create a problem." She was looking at Agonasti at first, then her eyes widened and she swung to Kozlowski.

"Koz! Are you kidding me?"

He flashed a broad grin. "Hello, Cheyenne." Holding the whiskey glass to the side he spread his arms. The woman disappeared in his embrace.

Turned out Kozlowski and the captain dated occasionally. She had been focused on the yacht when we boarded and hadn't spotted him.

"Want to sample some ancient booze?" he asked. I noticed his was the only glass with about a finger's worth of whiskey left in it.

"Not while I'm working. I wouldn't want to do anything to put this lovely yacht or these gracious passengers at risk."

Agonasti nodded. "I'll be certain to pour you a taste when we reach our destination." He shifted his gaze to me. "Are we good?"

"We are." I set the empty glass on the table and stood.

Max gathered up the bottle and the cloth bag and stowed them in the cupboard. Kozlowski raised his glass in a salute to Agonasti and drained the last few drops. He hugged Cheyenne again and bent low to whisper in her ear. She laughed and pushed him away with both hands. All eyes were on her as she hustled back up the ladder to the bridge controls. I shook hands with Leo and Max and headed for the swim platform.

Once aboard the speedboat, I waited until the yacht increased power and rumbled across the lake. Koz dropped back into the passenger seat.

"So that part of the mystery is solved. But what does that mean to finding the killer?"

"You sound like Pappy."

He grinned. "Cantrell will be pissed he didn't get to sample that hooch."

"I'm not telling him we got to try it."

"He'll figure it out."

Chapter Twenty-One

We had just docked the boat when my phone rang. Suarez, with an update. I switched it to speaker and cranked up the volume.

"Boss, you were right. There was a GPS unit in his car. I put together a list of where he was during his last forty-eight hours. Laura found an app on his phone and matched it."

"Thought I told you to just track his movements on Saturday."

Suarez hesitated. "I know. But there wasn't much to it. That's why I went back two days. Looking for a pattern."

"Did you find one?"

"Yeah, I think we did."

Kozlowski grunted. "You gonna tell us, rook or are we playing guessing games?"

"He went to that bookstore. The one where we met the spaceman. Twice. The last time was the morning of the murder. He must have stopped there on his way to the war games."

"That of some significance?" Koz asked. "Seems only natural he'd be stopping at the different places of business."

"Let's go find out. Send me the details, Suarez. Dates, locations and times."

"You got it, boss."

It was almost six and traffic was heavy with commuters. Koz was quiet, which was unlike him. Usually when it's just the two of us, there's a steady flow of bullshit. Pulling up to a red light on Woodward, I turned and asked him what was going on.

"Reminiscing. I sensed that Cheyenne was the captain running Agonasti's boat. There aren't that many licensed captains in this area and when Max said 'her skills' it got me curious. It's been a year or so since we dated. She was still taking classes, studying for the exam. Then when winter set in, she headed down to Florida to work for the snowbirds." He chuckled and drummed his fingers on the door's armrest. "We had a lot of fun."

"Any reason you can't pick up where you left off?"

"I don't know. Guess that's what I was thinking about."

"You gonna get all sweet and sentimental? Because I'm not sure the world would be ready for that."

Laughter boomed from deep in his chest. "Oh hell no. But a few summertime romps would be very enjoyable."

"That's about what I thought."

We pulled into the parking area and found a space close to the store. There was a lot of activity. A sidewalk sale was going on, with display tables in front of each establishment. At the Imagination Station were a couple of tables with discounted books and posters. A gangly teenage boy in khakis and a denim shirt bearing the store's logo guarded the inventory. He confirmed Chelsea Coles was working inside. She greeted us as we entered. I introduced Koz, then guided her toward the same conversation area where we'd met last week.

Her hair was done up in a braided ponytail, dangling down her back.

"This is kind of a busy night. With the sale and the good weather, we've got a steady flow of customers. There's even a local author, a guy who writes mysteries, coming in at seven to do a reading."

"I don't think this will take too long. We just have a few questions."

Chelsea drew a deep breath and settled herself in the thick upholstered chair. "Okay. You know I want to help."

"When were the last two times you saw Kyle?"

She was puzzled. "Two times? I don't know. He was here that Saturday morning, right before we opened. Just stopped by for a minute."

"Think back. Wasn't he here the day before as well."

A flush of color touched her cheeks. Chelsea fidgeted. She turned and looked around the store, as if searching for someone. I'd spotted her brother when we came in. He was in the far corner, handing out pieces of candy. Her eyes flicked to me. Instinctively she flipped her head and the braided ponytail came over her shoulder. Chelsea caught the end and rubbed it between her thumb and forefinger. Realizing we weren't going anywhere, she started speaking quietly.

"Yes, Kyle was here the day before. It was late afternoon. He was very upbeat, beaming a smile."

"You talk about anything in particular?" Koz asked softly.

She glanced at him briefly. "Sales. Our numbers have been very good."

"Why does this make you uncomfortable?"

Chelsea hesitated, still stroking that length of hair. "It's difficult talking about him, knowing he's dead."

"You didn't have much trouble talking with me last week," I said. "Tell us what really happened that day."

"I don't remember!"

Kozlowski raised a massive palm as if he were directing traffic. "We think you do. We'd much rather have this quiet conversation here. But we can just as easily take you back to the state police post and hold you in an interrogation room for a while. It's your choice."

"Can we go to my office?" she whispered.

"Of course."

We followed her to the room at the back of the store. I watched her eyes dart as we walked. There was a steady hum of chatter from customers and staff as people wandered through the shop. Zack was busy, but I sensed he was aware of Chelsea. It was probably a type of familial radar, where he could find her in a heartbeat. We entered the small office. Some file cabinets, a student size desk with a computer and a couple of chairs. She took the chair behind the desk. Chelsea fidgeted to get comfortable, then drew her arms across her chest and hugged herself.

"Kyle was jazzed up. Some new project he was considering was coming together. He had just left a meeting that was close by. So he wanted to share the good news." Chelsea shuddered at the memory. "After more than a year, I thought we'd come to an understanding. I didn't want to be his plaything."

"What did he do?" Koz asked quietly.

"He got me back here in the office. We talked about sales and promotions and today's event. Well, I talked. He wasn't listening." Her hands were clutching her biceps. You could see her knuckles whiten as she squeezed. "He grabbed my shoulder and spun me around to face him. Kyle wasn't very tall, but he was strong. He pulled me close. One hand on my back, the other was lower." Chelsea's eyes were on the floor.

Koz had dropped into the guest chair, to make himself less intimidating. I leaned against the wall by the file cabinet. We waited in silence. Chelsea's voice was even softer as she continued.

"I tried to push him away. He laughed. He kept telling me how beautiful I am. How he was attracted to me. How natural it was. His hand was on my bottom. He kept pressing against me. Everywhere. I must have cried out. I just wanted him to stop. That's when Zack came in."

Koz glanced at me. "Her brother. He's the big guy that was giving out candy when we came in."

"Suarez told me about your last visit."

"What happened next?" I prompted Chelsea.

"It was like someone threw a switch. Kyle stepped back and was all friendly again. He assured Zack that everything was fine. Zack was upset. He could tell just by looking at me that something bad almost happened."

"So what did Morrissey do?"

"He nodded to me. Told me to 'keep up the great work'. Then he looked at Zack and said he wouldn't bother me. He knew how busy I was. Kyle walked out. Zack followed him. When Kyle left the store, Zack came back and sat with me for a little while."

We let it be for a couple of minutes. Chelsea kept her eyes on the floor. Kozlowski noticed a case of water bottles beside the chair. He removed one, twisted off the cap and gently handed her the bottle. Chelsea loosened the grip on her arms and took it in both hands.

"I'm sure this sounds pretty tame to you. But we were raised a certain way. You don't just hug and kiss people." Her voice was trembling. "I've never dated. Nobody ever wanted to get close to me, because of Zack. We look out for each other. And any guy who wants to spend time with me has to respect that."

"What happened on Saturday?" I asked.

She took a moment to gather herself. "Kyle stopped by early. We talked in the stockroom. I told him if he ever touched me like that again I would quit immediately. He apologized for his behavior. There were a couple of employees already here. Kyle was only here for about five minutes. Then he left."

"We need to talk with Zack."

Chelsea tried to speak but no words came out. I think she was waiting for me to explain. She saw how serious we were.

"I'll go get him," she said at last.

"Let's all go. The stockroom would be better."

Together we moved out into the main part of the store. Zack looked up as we approached. He smiled warmly at his sister. Kozlowski hung back. Zack nodded to me as Chelsea took his hand.

"Do you remember the policeman who was here last week?"

"Yeah. Do you want some candy?"

"No thanks, Zack. But we would like to talk with you."

He nodded quickly. "Okay."

Still holding his hand, Chelsea led him toward the back room. Kozlowski leaned against the door, so there would be no interruptions. Zack was sitting on a stack of boxes, lightly holding Chelsea's hand. He had a vague, pleasant expression on his face. I pointed at Kozlowski. "This is my friend, Koz. He's a policeman too. We're all friends, right Zack?"

The smile on his face widened. "I like friends. We don't have a lot."

"Friends are important, especially good friends." I glanced at Chelsea. She wasn't clinging to her brother's hand so much as squeezing it for support. "Was Mr. Morrissey your friend?"

Zack's face clouded quickly. "No. He's not a nice man anymore."

Chelsea started to interject but I held up my hand. "What do you mean, anymore?"

"At first, he was nice. He brought ice cream and cookies for me. But I didn't like him when he was bad."

"How was he bad, Zack?"

He slowly looked at his sister. "When he was trying to hold you. You didn't hug him, like you hug me. You pushed him away. You were mad at him. He was being bad."

"What did you do, Zack?"

His eyes studied the floor. "Nothing bad."

Chelsea clung to him protectively. Quietly she repeated my question.

"He told me not to worry. He said he wouldn't bug you anymore. But he wasn't smiling when he said it. He was mean. And he looked real mad."

"Did that bother you, Zack?" Koz asked.

"Yeah. He shouldn't have hugged Chelsea. She didn't like it."

"What did you do, Zack?" I asked again.

"He came back the next day. He always had a bottle of tea and he set it down right here. Then he said he wasn't going to bug Chelsea. But he still looked mad. He went out to talk." Zack was scuffing the toe of his right shoe against the cement floor.

"What happened?"

"I was putting my supplies away. I always put them away before the people come in to buy things." The toe kept moving.

Chelsea took her free hand and lifted her brother's chin so he would look at her. "It's okay, Zack. Just tell us."

"He said he wouldn't bug you. But he didn't mean it. You always tell me, we don't want bugs in the store."

Her voice was a whisper. "What did you do, Zack? Did you put something in his tea, Zack?"

He nodded. "Just a little. The spray works good on bugs."

"Why, Zack?"

"No bugs in the store, Chelsea. You always tell me that."

She hugged her brother tightly. "Yes, I do."

We were back in the office. Zack had returned to the front and was passing out candy again. Kozlowski was back in the visitor chair. Chelsea was blotting her eyes with a tissue, trying to regain her composure. I waited.

"What happens now?" she asked at last.

"Has he ever done anything like this before?"

"Never."

"Does he know Morrissey's dead?"

"Yes. We talked about that when it happened. Zack

understands about guns and that Kyle was shot." Chelsea fidgeted on her chair, trying to find a comfortable position. It was hopeless. She bounced to her feet and stood in front of me. "Will he go to jail? After the trial?"

"He's not going to jail. And there won't be a trial. You sit him down. Tell him that no matter what happens in the future, he must never do that again. If he has a problem with someone bugging you, he calls me. Or Kozlowski."

She shook her head as if to clear it. "I don't understand."

"There's nothing to be gained by pressing charges against Zack. The poison didn't kill Morrissey. Zack didn't shoot him. He just made him sick. We'll stop by occasionally. Make sure he's behaving."

"But we're going to expect you to keep a close eye on him," Koz said.

The tension drained out of her body. Chelsea gave us a relieved smile. "I will. Come back anytime. And thank you both, for understanding him."

She led us back into the store. Koz and I watched her walk over to her brother. She waited until no one was around then threw her arms around his shoulders and hugged him tightly. Their heads bowed together, Chelsea began talking to him. We left.

"No killer there," Koz said.

"Yeah, but one more detail resolved."

Chapter Twenty-Two

Little pieces were falling into place. We'd been able to identify the source of the money, as well as the nicotine in his system. The location of the cell phone purchase was another clue. But it felt like all these small bits were unconnected. If this was a puzzle, it was damned big one. Maybe Tuesday morning would start with some answers. We were in the conference room. Kozlowski and I updated the others on yesterday's late events. Donna reported about the research materials on the old estate. But since we'd figured out about the money, I wondered if that made any difference now. The heirs to the family fortune were no longer in the area. Did they even care about the booze? Or the money that came from it? I had my doubts.

Laura had been sitting there quietly, turning ever so slightly in her chair, giving each speaker her undivided attention. The corners of her mouth kept creeping up. She'd catch herself and resume a serious expression. I called her on it.

"Cover girls. I found two more."

Pappy gave her a wolfish grin. "Which uns?"

She pulled two photos from her notes and handed them over. One was a green-eyed blonde with a sassy expression, leaning forward in a quick flash, her hands pulling her blouse apart like Clark Kent in the old movies revealing his Superman outfit. The other was a dark haired girl, maybe in her early twenties. A pair of designer glasses were perched at the end of her nose. Her blouse was completely unbuttoned, the tails hanging over her skirt.

"How did you find them?" Koz asked.

"I decided to look for a pattern like we found with Darcie. So I started with the bank where Morrissey did most of his business. At my first visit, I met with the manager and he was very helpful. But I remembered a couple of assistants that were busy in the back, taking care of other customers."

"Y'all find more than one there?"

Laura explained that there were several young female employees. One was Maria, an assistant manager who had helped Morrissey many times over the years. She admitted to trading flirtatious comments with him but claimed it was never anything more than that. Laura indicated this was the brunette with the glasses in the photo. When Morrissey broached the idea of the photograph, Maria thought it was just a playful joke. He offered a hundred bucks to pose for a picture. She brushed it off. At his next visit, he upped it to three hundred. Maria told him to make it a thousand. He immediately agreed.

"She figured it was harmless. But she wanted a witness. So Maria recruited Tabitha, the blonde, to be there. Tabitha is her roommate. When Morrissey got a look at her, he offered her five hundred dollars on the spot. Tabitha went for it." Laura shrugged. "The girls got the cash, he got his pin-up photos. These are tame in comparison to what you can find on the internet."

"Y'all think this here calendar's for real?"

Kozlowski nodded. "Morrissey was always coming

up with new ways to get attention, to promote the movies or the bookstores. You could crop the photos to obscure the faces of these women. Maybe consider it artistic. Or even tasteful. He could have sold a lot of them."

"Knowing Morrissey's proclivity for charitable causes, he may have even tied it to support a program or two," I said.

"Y'all wanna keep lookin' for these girls?"

In the grand scheme of things, the pictures seemed tame and hardly a motive for murder. Laura was right. You could find racier pictures on the internet. I glanced around the table. Everyone else was watching me.

"Let's hold it in reserve for now."

I sketched out plans for the day. Donna and Suarez were going to follow up with Olivia Sholtis at the television station. She had left a message last night about some more information. From a folder I pulled copies of the photographs Pinky had given me of the guy buying the cell phone. I slid these to Kozlowski. He gave them a cursory glance and tucked them in his jacket.

"How many warriors did we fail to identify?" I asked.

"Six. Four men and two women."

"Take Laura and go back to the scene. Have them look at the photos, see if it trips any memories. Also find out if any of these mystery gamers are repeats. Someone shows up on a regular basis but doesn't want to use their real name."

"Got it," Koz said.

Cantrell cocked an eyebrow in my direction. "Whatcha gonna do, Chene?"

"Brainstorm."

He waved the others out. Every once in a while, he and I would do this. We would dump everything we knew about a case on the table and shake it up. Cantrell has an eidetic memory. He's also one of the smartest people I've ever met. On more than one occasion he's picked up a minor thread in a case that ended up leading us right to the killer. In his youth Cantrell pounded the pavement just like the rest of us. I trusted his instincts as much as my own.

Now he pulled a legal pad close and began scratching down random points on the case. I did the same. After a few minutes we compared notes.

"Y'all got a clusterfuck. Shit goin' in so many ways, ya can't hardly see straight. Money from booze, sexy women, jewels, movie business, bookstores and more women. Makes muh head hurt."

"Somewhere along the line, Morrissey pissed somebody off. Someone who didn't like his actions."

Cantrell thumped a finger on my notes. "Cyber doin' any good?"

"We've thrown more at them than usual. They're checking the videos from the war game and the funeral, Morrissey's computer and cell phone. And they were able to trace that threatening email. Yekovich and his crew are busy."

"What's next?"

Mentally I had a whole list of things to follow up on. Prioritizing them was the challenge. Before I could respond my phone rang. I didn't recognize the number but it looked like a business line, so I answered it.

"It's Jared Devonshire. I've got the analysis completed."

"That was fast." With that many pieces, I hadn't expected to hear from him before the end of the week.

"I was able to put a couple of gemologists on it. But I wasn't sure whether I should contact Mrs. Morrissey first or you."

"Let me call her. If she's available, I'll bring her to the store."

"Later."

Cantrell was tapping the end of a cigarette on the table. "Follow dem bucks. Sumthin' tells me y'all ain't at the end of that trail yet."

Colleen Morrissey was at home. She had a couple of hours free before a meeting at the office. She was waiting impatiently in front of the house when I arrived. Apparently she had been walking around the block, trying to burn off some nervous energy. Colleen was wearing a turquoise dress in a modest cut. Leather sandals and a thin gold chain completed her ensemble. A black leather purse dangled from her shoulder. She pushed a pair of small oval sunglasses up in her hair as she slid into the passenger seat.

"I didn't expect to hear from Mr. Devonshire so soon."

"Nor did I. He put some extra people on it. I'm sure his staff is the best. Devonshire's reputation is impeccable."

Colleen nodded. "I went there once, to buy some earrings. They treated me like royalty although I'd never been there before."

I couldn't hold back a grin. If they gave her the royal treatment before, I could only imagine how she'd be welcomed this morning. It didn't take long to find out.

Just looking at Devonshire's store on Mack Avenue gives you the sense of class, quality and exquisite taste. The door is secured and can only be opened when an employee buzzes you in. Apparently if you don't meet a certain standard, they ignore you until you give up and move on. There was probably a moment's hesitation as I rang the bell. But once they saw Colleen, you could hear the lock click open. We stepped inside. A half dozen sharply dressed associates, both male and female, were moving about the showroom, quietly taking care of the early morning customers. Jared approached, passed the gleaming display cases.

"Good morning, Mrs. Morrissey." He gently pressed her hand and tilted his head in a Grosse Pointe nod.

"Good morning." Her voice cracked with a tremble of nervousness.

Devonshire turned and extended his hand. "Hello, Chene."

"Looking good, Jared."

He smoothed down his silk tie. I had a feeling that little number was in the five-hundred-dollar price range.

"Let's go to my office." He offered his arm to Colleen. She hesitated, then took it. I followed behind, feeling like the bodyguard.

Jared's office was well appointed and tasteful. Offers of coffee, gourmet chocolates and pastries were politely refused. He settled in the chair behind the desk and opened a leather portfolio. On thick stationery was a detailed summary.

"As I surmised on Saturday, Mr. Morrissey had purchased a significant quantity of very fine jewels.

Many of those were listed on the receipts Sergeant Chene gave me."

"How far back do these go?" I asked.

Devonshire's dark eyes flicked to me. "Nine years. Each receipt was for a single stone. In the beginning, it was once a quarter. A thousand dollars here, two thousand there. Gradually the frequency increased."

"Did he buy them all from the same vendor?" Colleen asked quietly.

"No, ma'am. There were some repeated sales. A few dealers that specialize in emeralds, for example, reflected several purchases your late husband made over the years."

"Why would he do that?" she asked.

"Any number of reasons. He could have wanted to keep the sellers honest and not make it obvious that he was building a collection. Buying jewels in this form is definitely an investment."

"Tell us a little about how you valued the goods." I offered, hoping it would give Colleen a chance to collect herself. There were nervous tremors coursing through her body. She squirmed restlessly in her chair.

"Certainly. A small sticker was attached, indicating a number, to help make it easier to identify. Each jewel was weighed and measured, which is indicated in the catalog. Close examination was performed by the gemologists, where any imperfections or characteristics were indicated." Jared paused and turned to an adjacent wing on his desk. I hadn't noticed it before. There were six trays here, each draped in black fabric of some kind. He selected one and brought it to the center of the desk blotter.

"Here is an excellent example." Jared made a

selection with a pair of tweezers and extended it toward Colleen. "This is diamond number four, an exquisite pear shape with a very slight imperfection in the girdle. But the imperfection does not detract from its beauty or value. This weighs three quarters of a carat. It was purchased six years ago from a dealer in Montreal for nine hundred dollars."

Colleen cupped her palm beneath it. Jared opened the tweezers and dropped the stone in her hand. She rolled it between her fingertips and held it up to the light. From here I could see the sparkle as the diamond caught the natural light from his window.

"It's beautiful," Colleen whispered.

"Yes, it certainly is." Jared agreed.

She turned and offered it to me. I hesitated, then accepted it. Lifting it to eye level, the question jumped from my mouth before I had a chance to consider it. "You said nine hundred dollars six years ago. What's it worth now?"

Devonshire shot me a look, indicating I was being crass. Screw him.

"It has more than doubled its value. That particular one is now worth nineteen hundred dollars. Of course, the proper setting could make a difference, raising the price to three thousand dollars."

Gently I handed it back to Colleen. She pinched it between thumb and forefinger and set it back on the cloth covered tray.

"So what happens next?" Colleen asked quietly.

He laced his fingers together and rested his hands on the desk, with the tray of diamonds centered between him and Colleen, like a box of precious chocolates. "That is entirely up to you. If you have somewhere safe to keep these, I will return them immediately. Or if you prefer, I can keep these in our vault, until you decide another course of action. I will amend the receipt from Saturday to indicate the exact value of each lot."

"Should I sell them?"

"I cannot advise you in that regard."

"How much?" Colleen's voice had grown even softer.

"Three hundred and forty-two thousand dollars. As of today."

Colleen slumped back in the chair, stunned. "Excuse me?"

Devonshire offered her a gentle smile. From the leather portfolio he removed a copy of the list and extended it toward her. Colleen didn't move. Devonshire glanced at me and shifted his hand slightly. I took the list. Each page was a breakdown by category, listing the number, particulars and current value. On most of the items he had included the purchase price. Jared had been able to fill in some blanks, using serial numbers and contacts within the industry. At the bottom of each page was a subtotal for the collection. Mentally I did the math, although there was no reason to doubt his accuracy.

"Can I make a suggestion?"

Colleen turned to me eagerly. "Please. I'm having difficulty grasping all of this."

"Let Jared maintain the collection here. It's very secure. There's no reason to rush into a decision whether to keep them all or sell even a part of it. Talk it over with your personal attorneys or someone you trust."

Colleen gradually collected herself. "I'll expect you to invoice me for your services, Jared. The appraisals and the storage. And I may return for advice on what to do with it all."

"It will be our pleasure to assist you," Jared said with another Grosse Pointe nod.

"Send your invoices to the house. Let's keep this private."

"Of course."

Devonshire closed the portfolio. Deftly he returned the tray of diamonds to the wing table. From a drawer he removed a thick ivory envelope, embossed with the store's logo in the upper left corner. He passed it to me. I tucked the report inside and handed it to Colleen. Jared guided us out. We got back to the car without comment.

Colleen lowered the window. As I drove away, she pushed her right hand outside, letting the wind lift her fingers. She dipped her hand this way and that, as if it were a small bird, floating on the wind. A giggle escaped her lips. I glanced over as we rolled to a stop at a red light.

"Quarter to a half. That's what Detective Kozlowski said on Saturday. He was right. Three hundred thousand dollars." She giggled again. "It's like Kyle was playing the stock market and knew exactly what to buy."

"From what Jared's told me, diamonds never lose their value. Some of those other jewels I hadn't heard of, but if it's rare, it can demand a higher price. Kyle was onto a good thing."

"Did you learn anything more about that old estate?"

There was no reason not to tell her. I gave her an abbreviated version on the way back to her house. We pulled into the driveway as I finished. Colleen's hand remained out the window, her fingers resting on the edge of the door, no longer imitating a bird in flight. Once I'd started talking, she shifted, giving me with her full attention.

"It's like he was some kind of fortune hunter."

"Maybe in the beginning, he was. But Kyle must have been pretty smart too. He parlayed the money from the whiskey into the theater. Then you both worked hard to make it successful. One theater led to another. You created a very profitable business, adapting to meet the desires of your customers."

The car was off now. There was just enough of a breeze to stir her hair. "He was determined. I always thought Kyle was driven. He wasn't satisfied with just one theater. When he learned another old movie house was available, Kyle wanted it. But he'd learned from the experience with the Madrid. We spent a great deal of time, planning, developing the area, meeting with landlords and city officials.

"So what do you think I should do with all those beautiful jewels?"

I shook my head. "That's not an area I know much about."

"C'mon, Chene. If these were yours, what would you do?"

She wasn't going to let this go. "I'd get the advice from those with experience in investments. If you don't need the money right now, I'd keep them in the vault and let them continue to increase in value. If you're not comfortable having them at Devonshire's I'd secure a couple of different lockboxes, with different banks. Split it up amongst them. Get everything insured."

Colleen's eyes were dancing. The corners of her mouth tugged into a crooked smile, one I'd caught the occasional glimmer of over the past week. "That's boring. Nothing else?"

"I would have Jared pick out two emeralds and have him create a pair of dangling earrings for you. Something tasteful, not gaudy. That color would complement your eyes. And it would be a way of staying connected to Kyle."

There was a moment of hesitation. Then she reached over and pressed her hand to mine. "What a beautiful idea. You've got a touch of the romantic in you, Sergeant. That's nice to see."

"Easy to do with someone else's jewels."

We got out of the Pontiac. Colleen walked past the house and up to the garage. Her car was in the second bay. "The kids are on the run, spending the day with friends at the park. Things are slowly starting to get back to normal for them."

"It takes time."

"Dale took us for a ride in the Camaro last night. He couldn't stop talking about your drive on Friday."

I shrugged. "Seemed like the right thing to do. The car is a big connection with his father."

She opened the driver's door to her car and dropped her purse and the envelope on the seat. "I'd better get to the office. Thanks for going with me to Devonshire's. Just the thought of all those beautiful jewels is a bit unsettling."

"It was my pleasure."

She slid behind the wheel and touched a button on

the dash. The car purred to life. I closed the door and headed for my vehicle. Over three hundred thousand dollars in precious jewels. Morrissey kept them hidden. But had he let it slip? Was someone else aware of the collection? Someone else in the mix?

I circled the block, making sure Colleen didn't accidentally follow me. Back at Devonshire's I waited to be buzzed inside. Jared was assisting a silver haired matron who was examining a tray of designer watches. When I caught his eye he summoned one of his associates to step in for him. With a slight inclination of his head, that Grosse Pointe nod, we went back to his office. I noticed the wing on his desk was bare. The collection must be back in the vault.

"Is there a problem, Chene?"

"Just a quick question. Where did Morrissey have those jewels shipped?"

Jared eased into his chair and withdrew a file from the desk drawer. He began to page through the receipts. "At a glance, it looks like they were all sent to his office. Probably came in with the regular mail. Perhaps they were sent in a small box or a padded envelope. The return address is often a post office box and no name. No sense advertising the company name, in case someone got curious." He looked up at me. "Does this matter?"

"It's a homicide. Everything matters. The more information we can put together, the more complete picture we have of the victim. And that can often lead us to a suspect."

He closed the file and squared the edges against his desk blotter. Everything about this guy was neat and tidy. "Do you want the receipts?"

"I'll make copies. You should keep the originals. They give credence to some of the purchases."

"Wait one." Jared lifted his phone and made a quick call. A moment later, a young female associate entered, scooped up the file and disappeared. "We do have a copier here."

It was probably capable of toasting a bagel and making a latte. We talked about baseball and the standings. The Tigers were doing well. There was some question about the strength of the bullpen, but there was hope for another good season. Within five minutes his associate returned. She handed me the copies. Jared returned the originals to his desk drawer.

Heading out, I mentioned the suggestion to Colleen about having a set of emerald earrings made. Devonshire smiled and gave me that miniscule tilt of the head. "You've got a good eye, Chene. The right set would be an excellent accessory for Mrs. Morrissey."

So now I had one more set of details. But where did it lead?

Chapter Twenty-Three

Somebody had to know. If Morrissey was buying those jewels, how exactly was he making payment? By check, from a secret account? A separate credit card? Even that would need to be paid somehow? Was he mixing it in with receipts from the business?

As I was leaving Devonshire's my phone buzzed. Kozlowski.

"We may have something on one of the mystery gamers."

"Yeah?"

"Turns out that Kenneally's daughter recognized them."

"Them, as in plural?"

There were voices in the background, several people talking at once. To the side I heard Kozlowski snarl 'shut up!' Silence ensued. "It was a couple out here to play. And it didn't involve paint."

"Jenna Kenneally identify them?"

"Only the female. Jenna gave her up, but the witness is being reluctant."

Koz waited. He could sense what I was thinking. After days of chasing down leads and players, the frustration of not making more progress was getting to us all. "Bring her reluctant ass in. We'll do the interview at the post."

He chuckled. "Want me to soften her up a bit?"

"No. Throw her in the car and have Laura sit beside her. Give her the silent treatment all the way."

"Copy that."

It's not every day that we bring someone to the post for an interview. We usually have better results when the person is in their comfort zone, either at home or at work. But every once in a while, you need to shake some people up. Putting this reluctant witness in our playground may speed up the process. I got to the post about five minutes before them. Kozlowski and Laura escorted the petite young woman down the hall and deposited her in the interview room. The only word spoken was when Koz released her arm, jammed a thick finger toward her and snapped "sit!" before slamming the door. He and Laura joined me on the other side of the glass, watching our witness. She nervously settled on the chair and clutched the edge of the table with both hands.

"What have we got?"

Laura spoke first. "Her name is Heather Gaines. Twenty-three, works in customer service at an insurance company. Single. She and Jenna attended some classes in college together. Apparently she's been involved with a married guy since last summer. They get together every other week or so at Kenneally's for an afternoon frolic. She hasn't named the guy yet."

"And she saw something?"

Koz nodded. "Didn't come right out and admit it. But she did tell Jenna. It didn't take much pressure for Ms. Kenneally to give up her real name. We showed Jenna the pictures from the phone store. Those didn't trigger anything."

"How do you want to do this?" Laura asked.

"You and me. She may relax a bit with Koz out of the picture."

"He can be intimidating," she said.

Koz feigned surprise. "Me? I'm a teddy bear."

"Yeah, from a Stephen King novel."

We entered the room. Heather Gaines started to stand up. I waved her back down. Laura took a chair directly opposite her. I stood next to the table. Heather was tiny, maybe five-foot-tall with shoulder length chestnut brown hair. Dark brown eyes darted back and forth between us.

"I don't know why you had to bring me here." She had a high voice, almost a squeak. Part of that could have been nerves.

I didn't say anything. From a file folder I laid several pictures of Morrissey on the table in front of her. The first was a headshot from the company website. The next was of him on the ground, his features masked with traces of blood. Beside that was the photo from the store surveillance cameras.

"We're talking murder. This man was brutally executed during the war games on the Kenneally property. It's our job to find his killer. And by law we can use any means necessary to do that. So a little inconvenience to you doesn't really matter to us. Do you understand that?"

Her eyes were glued to the center picture of the dead body. With a shudder she turned it over and wiped her hands on her thighs. "Yes."

"So tell us what you saw." I dropped into the chair beside Laura.

"We've been going out there for a while."

"Who's we?" Laura asked quietly.

Heather blinked a couple of times, then sighed. "Frank Carmichael and I. We work together. About a year ago we started going out. A drink or two. He was friendly and easy to talk with."

Even though the session was being filmed, Laura had a notepad open on the table. She scrawled Carmichael's name on the top of the page, then thumped the pad with the pen. "Is he your boss?"

"No, he's one of the sales guys. Kind of charming. Funny too."

"Married?"

Another sigh. "Yeah, but he says it's no good. So we have a little fun, the kind of stuff he can't get at home. Nothing kinky. It's just hooking up. I didn't think it was a big deal."

"Walk us through it," I said.

Heather shifted her gaze to Laura. Maybe she thought another woman could understand her situation better. I didn't care, as long as she started talking. With another sigh, she did.

"Frank's a big guy, kind of stocky, you know. So when we get together, there's no way he can be on top. He'd crush me."

"So you do the cowgirl," Laura said.

"Yes. And it really turns him on. We found this spot out there a long time ago. It's over by that cluster of trees. There's a little hill, like on a golf course, where the grass grows up and on the other side, there's a dip in it. At the start of the games, we get with everyone else. Once we're assigned colors, we drift away to our secret spot."

"What's with the colors?" I asked.

"Each team is assigned a different color. Red is

against blue, yellow versus green. Once we know what color we're supposed to be fighting, we go and hide. Frank has pockets filled with the different colored paintballs, so after the round is done, we make it look like we've been hit by the other side."

Laura nodded. "That's pretty smart."

"It would raise a lot of questions if we came back at the end of the round with nothing more than grass stains."

Impatience kicked in. "So on that Saturday?" I prompted.

Heather blushed and kept her eyes on Laura. "We actually played the first round. A little delay tends to get Franky really turned on. At the start of the second session we drifted over to our spot. I kicked off my cargo pants, but kept my boots and shirt on. It was unbuttoned. Franky likes to see my little boobs dance as I ride him."

"So that's all you were wearing?" Laura asked.

"And my helmet. It's part of the turn on, that someone might see me bouncing away, but they can't see my face."

Heather explained that some warriors prefer the full helmet, which comes down over the face and gives more protection. Others stick with goggles and might wear a bandana over their mouth and nose.

"Anyway, it's kind of quiet out there, since few of the gamers went in that direction. Franky and I keep it quiet, just a few grunts and groans."

Laura bumped my knee with hers. In my peripheral vision, I can see her chewing on the inside of her cheek. Probably to keep from laughing.

"What happened next?" Laura asked.

Heather sighed again. "I heard somebody cough. Three times. Which I thought was weird, because no one was around. Franky's attention was getting to me. He was ready too. Anyway, with the spot we were in, I could barely see over the bunker of grass. And everything happened at once."

Both Laura and I remained quiet. Heather swept her hair back from her face and shifted just enough so she was staring straight at Laura. After a breath, she resumed the story.

"This guy came out from the willow trees. Franky was about to groan, so I clamped a hand over his mouth. We both finished, if you know what I mean."

Laura nodded. "Yeah we know. Tell us about the guy in the trees."

"He was only about fifteen or twenty feet away. I watched him to see what he'd do. But he headed back toward the base, kind of on an angle from where we were getting busy."

"Can you describe him?"

Heather thought about it. "He was average, maybe as tall as you." She pointed at me. "Thin, not real muscular. He had on camo gear, but it didn't look old, like maybe he bought it from army surplus or something. And when he got past the trees, he pushed his helmet back on his head."

Laura and I exchanged a glance. "Could you see his face?"

"Yeah. And I think I've seen it before."

"When?" I asked, "or where?"

"I can't remember."

****

Laura called in one of the tech people. Working

with the computer, they would make a composite of the details Heather could recall about the shooter. Kozlowski went back to the war games to find the love nest and determine the proximity to the grove of trees. I briefed Cantrell.

"Lemme git this straight. This girlie is gettin' her jollies, ridin' her boyfriend when the killin' takes place?"

"Yep. By her estimate she was within twenty feet of the killer."

"Next y'all be tellin' me she thought he'd join 'em."

I shrugged. Very little surprised me anymore. "Part of doing it in public is the chance of being caught. Adds to the excitement."

"Y'all speakin' from personal experience?" A grin flashed across his face.

"No comment."

"Whatcha gonna do next?"

"Laura's staying with the witness to make the sketch. I'm going to run down the boyfriend and have a chat."

He waved me out, slowly shaking his head.

****

A call to Carmichael's cell phone made it easy. He answered with a salesman's patter, probably expecting a potential client on the other end. After identifying myself, there was a long moment of silence.

"Heather Gaines told me we need to talk. I could meet you at your home in about twenty minutes."

Carmichael groaned. "Ah man, not my house. Anywhere else. Anywhere you say, just not there."

"Where are you right now?"

There was no hesitation. "I'm at the Renaissance Center. Just about to make a call on a client."

"Postpone it. Do you know where the Elwood Bar is?"

"By Comerica Park?"

"That's the one. Meet me out front in five minutes."

"Okay, but how will I recognize you?"

"Don't worry, Franky. I'll know you. Five minutes."

Heather had shown me several pictures of Frank Carmichael on her phone. Before making the call, I'd had the cyber unit ping his phone, so I knew roughly where he was. I'd headed in that direction before contacting him. I didn't want Carmichael to have time to work on his story. Parked in front of the Elwood, I got out and rested against the front fender, taking a moment to look the place over. The old saloon was one of Detroit's favorite haunts, a place filled with an art deco interior and a long history. Built in the 1930s, it enjoyed popularity for years on the corner of Elizabeth Street and Woodward Avenue, hence the name. In the late 1990s it was moved around the corner to its new location, making room for the luxurious new baseball stadium for the Tigers.

It was after the lunch rush and since there wasn't a game across the street, I took one of the few patio tables and ordered an iced tea. Carmichael showed up three minutes later. He was about five foot seven with a body that was quickly turning to fat. To call him stocky was being kind. He stood on the sidewalk, swiveling his head back and forth. I waved him over. Carmichael hustled up as quickly as his bulk allowed and hovered next to the table.

"Listen, I don't know what she may have told you…"

"Sit down, Franky."

He attempted to gain the upper hand. "I'd rather stand."

"And I'd rather we have this conversation at the state police post. Or at your home. I'm trying to do you a favor here."

Still he hesitated.

From the pouch on my hip, I removed the handcuffs and set them on the table. "Sit your ass down or put your hands behind your back. Your call."

"You can't arrest me!"

"Sure I can. Indecent exposure. Lewd and lascivious conduct. Having an extramarital affair. Take your pick."

He settled into the chair.

"Frank Carmichael, I am Sergeant Chene with the Michigan State Police. I'm part of the team investigating the murder of Kyle Morrissey. That homicide occurred at the Kenneally War Games site a week ago Saturday. Your mistress, Heather Gaines, has confirmed that you were both there, participating in sexual intercourse near the crime scene. What do you remember about that day?"

Carmichael had propped his left elbow on the table and was scrubbing his face with his hand. "I can't believe she ratted me out."

I let him sweat for a minute. "Listen, Carmichael, I don't care about your infidelity. What I care about is catching a killer. Tell me what you saw that day. Don't lie, because we will check the details. And if you fuck with me, I'll talk to your wife to corroborate your story."

"Jesus, not that. She'll bury my ass. My wife comes from money. I don't make enough on commissions to buy a decent cheeseburger."

Behind him the waitress came out to check on us. I gave her a slow shake of the head. She flipped me a little wave and stepped back inside.

"You're breaking my heart." I took a sip of tea. "Details."

He spilled everything. The affair with Heather Gaines, the romps at the war games, the occasional playtime after work. I let him ramble a bit.

"So let's get back to a week ago Saturday."

"Yeah, we were there. Played the first and last rounds, actually got shot with some paint." He shrugged. "I'm a big target. Easy to hit. Heather usually gets away longer into each round, her being so tiny."

"What about the second and third rounds?"

A weak grin started to show and he quickly tamped it down. "We did our play time. The spot by the trees. Heather's always on top. But I didn't see anything, other than her."

"Did she mention the guy coming out of the grove? It would have been during the second round."

"Yeah, but like I said, she was on top. All I could see was grass and sky and, you know, her. I wasn't really focused on anything else. Kinda hard when you think about what we were doing."

I ignored the obvious statement and let him sweat for a couple of minutes. "Did you see anyone you recognized during the course of the day? Someone beyond the staff. Maybe someone out of context, that you wouldn't expect to see at the war games."

Franky actually took a moment to think it over. "No. Really when we're up there, about the only thing I'm aware of is Heather. Either thinking about what we're going to do or what we just did. She's very…enthusiastic."

I had no other questions. Passing him a card, I told him to call me if he thought of anything else. Carmichael bolted out of his chair. He probably moved faster than he had in ten years as he scurried back to the street. I turned the menu over and switched off my recorder.

The waitress came back out. "Is your friend coming back?"

"That was no friend. Just someone I needed to interview."

It was too warm for a jacket. My badge was clipped on the left side of my belt. The holster with my weapon was on the right.

"Was he misbehaving?"

The comment made me grin. "Yeah, but he's not the one I'm chasing."

"That guy couldn't run very far if you were. Anything else I can get you?"

"Suddenly a cheeseburger sounds very good."

She flashed a big smile. "Ours are the best. Blue cheese?"

"Sounds great. Medium."

"Coming right up."

****

After enjoying the excellent burger, I sat in the sun for a few minutes, strategizing. I had calls to make, so there was no reason to go anywhere. Maybe being out in the fresh air was helping. Jamie answered on the second ring.

"I was about to send out a search party, cowboy. What did you learn?"

"That Prohibition whiskey is very smooth."

A burst of laughter greeted my ear. "You're shitting me!"

"Dead serious."

"Talk to me, cowboy. But don't describe the booze. I stopped drinking a couple of years ago."

It took ten minutes to give Jamie the run down and answer all the follow up questions she came up with. She admitted to being intrigued by the turn of events. In the background I could hear her fingers dancing on the computer keyboard. Probably taking some quick notes.

"You gonna fictionalize this, right?"

That was met with another laugh. "Of course. I'll probably combine this with another aspect of the story. Make it a subplot. Our use it as background. This is really great, Chene."

"So did you dig up anything else on the family?"

"Bits and pieces. I've been combing through society pages, doing some internet searches on even the shirttail relatives who were on the fringe of the family. There may be a few more skeletons in those closets. There's a chance a few of those loose connections will be happy to share stories with me."

"Good luck with that, Jamie."

"See you around, cowboy. And don't hesitate to call. You've obviously got my number." She laughed again and ended the call. Malone was a lucky guy.

Something Jamie said caught my attention. But I didn't know what it was. The waitress drifted back out, refilling my tea without even asking. She cleared away the debris from the burger. I thanked her and asked for the bill.

We were chipping away at the case. Each little detail we got nailed down seemed to lead to something else. I paid for my meal, leaving a generous tip. Maybe Laura had some success with the composite drawing.

Chapter Twenty-Four

It was nothing but a jumble of numbers. 3422734511. Pinky at the Cyber Unit was stumped. As was Yekovich. I thought it might be a phone number, but there is no area code 342 in use. This group of random digits had to have some hidden meaning, perhaps to Morrissey, but definitely to the killer. I'd been jotting notes on a legal pad. In the center of the page was that mixture of numbers. Every effort to tear it apart hadn't worked. Maybe I needed a distraction. Something to take my mind off it. My subconscious could work on it for a while.

I was at home, sitting on the rattan sofa in the back room. The sun had set a while ago. There was a flash of headlights in the driveway. Through the open windows I heard a car engine cut off. My distraction had arrived. She appeared in the doorway to the sunroom, her silhouette outlined by the dim lights in the kitchen. There was a single lamp burning behind me.

"Hello, beautiful."

"Hello, Chene." She hesitated in the doorway. "No kiss for a lady?"

I threw the legal pad to the floor and moved to her. Simone gave me a playful smile and shook back her hair as I got close.

"I've missed you." Her voice was a soft whisper as I drew her close.

"It seems like a month since I saw you."

"You saw me Sunday morning."

"That's still too long."

"Good answer," she whispered again. "Let's go get reacquainted."

****

It was well after four in the morning. I covered Simone with a thin blanket and slipped out of the room. After our time together I'd actually fallen into a contented doze for several hours. She'd been curled against me. Traces of her perfume hung in the air. I had no idea what awakened me but knew that there would be no more sleep this night. Breeze from the lake cooled the house. I drifted back to the sunroom. The legal pad slid across the tile floor when I stepped on it.

A comfortable rattan chair sat in the corner by the lamp and the window. I settled in. My mind drifted back to the homicide.

In ten days we'd made a lot of progress. This wasn't an easy case. It reminded me of origami, the Japanese technique of folding paper to create something artistic. We would determine a clue and find an answer. Fold and crease. The piece was starting to take shape. When we were done, it might be a crane, or a duck or a tree. Right now it was just a big sheet of paper, with creases and folds. I couldn't figure out what it would resemble when we got done. But we were getting closer. I could almost taste it.

I'm no artist. Drawing stick figures eludes me. I turned the page on the legal pad and began to sketch, making small doodles. What could have been a dog or a horse appeared. I glanced over my shoulder. The speedboat bobbed gently at the dock, waiting for me.

Maybe the lake held an answer.

The sky to the east was changing. Sunrise would happen within the next half hour. I went out and sat on the dock, letting my feet dangle toward the water. The only thing I wore was an old pair of jeans. Farther down the canal one of the neighbors loaded up his skiff and headed out to the lake for a little early morning fishing. I heard the click of the sunroom door. Simone came toward me. Her normal graceful stride was hindered, either by sleep or the lack of daylight. From my dresser she'd grabbed an old Patriots jersey. It never looked better. I offered a hand as she settled beside me.

"It's the middle of the night. What are you doing out here?"

"Thinking. It's almost dawn."

She kissed my cheek and rested her head on my shoulder. "It is very peaceful."

"Some would say it's the best part of the day."

She yawned and snuggled closer. "Mmm hmm."

"You should go back to bed."

"I was lonely. You could keep me company." Her fingertips danced across my chest. "Another hour of sleep would be nice."

My left arm went around her. Neither one of us spoke for a while. Out on the lake a cruiser went by, kicking up a good wake. A minute later the waves reached our spot, splashing cold water on our feet. Simone jumped, squealing in surprise. She'd dozed off in the stillness. I stood up and gathered her into my arms. Simone gave a little shiver as I carried her inside. I eased her onto the bed and slid in beside her. Once again she curled against me. Tenderly I stroked her back until sleep reclaimed her.

Mark Love

After a shave and shower, I checked the fridge. Breakfast sounded like a good idea. I pulled two skillets from the cupboard and got busy. In the background the shower started up. The food and coffee were ready when Simone appeared, brushing damp tendrils of hair back from her face. She wore a short terry cloth robe, a little perfume and nothing else.

"You made me breakfast?"

"No, I made us breakfast." I pointed to the table. Simone eased into a chair, tucking her robe beneath her.

"Chene, you missed your calling. You should be running a bed and breakfast somewhere."

There was a bowl of fresh strawberries and blueberries on the table. On the plate before her was a shrimp omelet with bean sprouts and mozzarella cheese. Small circles of fried redskin potatoes were around the rim. Presentation enhances the meal, so I've been told. I poured coffee for both of us. Simone tasted the food then put her fork down. She got up, took my face in her hands and gave me a long soft kiss. Then she returned to her chair and resumed eating.

"Think I'd get that response from customers at a bed and breakfast?"

She winked at me. "Maybe you'd better keep this our little secret."

"Unless the B & B only allowed beautiful women to stay there."

"Our little secret. I'm not into sharing."

We made small talk as we finished the meal. I was cleaning up the dishes when Simone brought the empty coffee mugs. She glanced down at the notepad on the counter. While the food was cooking, I'd retrieved it from the sunroom. It was back to the page of numbers.

316

My various attempts to crack the code covered the page. She turned the pad around, studied it for a moment.

"Secret combination?"

"Beats the hell out of me. It's from the case, but I can't figure out what it means." I put the last of the utensils in the dishwasher and turned the coffee pot off.

"Well, the first part almost looks like measurements."

I stared at her. My mouth probably dropped open.

Simone stepped close and put her arms around my back. Mine mirrored hers.

"Thirty-four," she said softly. Then she leaned back and pushed my hands down to her waist. "Twenty-four."

My eyes went wide. She wiggled a bit and pushed my hands to her hips. "Thirty-four. Just in case you were wondering."

Somehow I found my voice. "I will never forget that."

She darted in for a quick kiss. "I need to get dressed and go to work. Thank you for breakfast. And for letting me visit last night."

I released her hips and she headed for the bedroom. After a moment's consideration, I grabbed the pad. 3422734511. What if the first part was measurements?

Simone was stepping into a black skirt when I entered the bedroom. "Miss me?"

"More than words can say. I think you're onto something here. But what's with the extra numbers."

A turquoise silk blouse hung on a padded hanger. Simone must have brought these clothes with her last night. Studying my face, she saw how serious I was.

Moving close, she glanced at the pad again. A shy smile appeared. Taking my right hand, she lifted it to her breast. I could feel the warm soft flesh through the lacy bra.

"B cup. A is one, b is two, c is three. You know."

"Fuck me hard," I muttered.

She blushed. "Maybe tonight. I've got to work today. And I think you do too."

****

The smoke was thick in Cantrell's office. I moved to the casement window and cracked it wide open. He grunted in approval and pointed at one of his visitor's chairs. I dropped into it.

"Damn cleanin' crew keeps closin' dat window. Must think birds or sumthin's gonna fly in." He studied me. Pappy was leaving shortly for a meeting in Lansing with some politicians. It was one of his least favorite activities, but a necessary evil. "Whatcha got?"

I showed him the numbers, written on a clean sheet of paper. Then I broke it down into the measurements, using Simone's suggestion.

"So what's the rest mean?"

"I'm working on it. Maybe she's tall. Five foot eleven."

"Y'all come across a girlie that size yet?"

I shook my head. "Five eleven with those measurements would be memorable. Fashion models might be tall, but they're curvier than this."

"Y'all been spendin' time with fashion models?"

"Not me. But I seem to recall you with a couple."

He snorted a laugh and flipped the back of his hand at me. "Nothin' big. Just a couple of girlies from the auto show. They do grow 'em tall. So whatcha think it is?"

"I've got a few ideas."

"So whatcha gonna do about it?"

For a moment I considered the question. "I'm going to rally the squad and break out the tape measures."

Pappy gave me a sage nod. "Luck with dat."

****

Everyone was talking at once. The rest of the team was sprawled around the table in the conference room. I'd written the group of numbers on the white board, broken into sections. Koz was tilted back in his chair, his heels propped on the table. Cantrell had already left the building. I waited until the chatter wound down. Laura was slowly tapping a finger on the table.

"I hate to say it, boss, but it makes sense. Those could be measurements. 511 could be an apartment number or an address," she said.

"So, out of all the women we've met in this case, does anyone have those dimensions?" Koz asked.

"I can think of a couple of possibilities."

"And how do you propose to figure this out?" Donna asked. "Are we supposed to go visit anyone who would be close and come right out and demand their measurements?"

"I could just ask them," Suarez said. "It would be like a beauty contest."

"Do we need a warrant?" Laura asked.

Kozlowski started laughing. "I can just see the judge's reaction when you apply for multiple warrants to take the measurements of all the females Morrissey crossed paths with. That would be quite a list."

They all continued talking for a moment. Gradually

the room fell silent as the other four detectives looked at me.

"Think about this. We know from the store video there was a guy who bought the phone that was used to send the email. From the clip we've determined he is less than six feet tall, probably five eight to five ten."

"So we're thinking boyfriend or relative?" Laura asked.

"Maybe. Let's start closer to home. Colleen Morrissey instructed all of her employees to cooperate." I swung to Suarez. "Double check the pinup girls. See if any of them would approximately match the measurements. Also, check the date stamp on the photos. See if any of them were taken in May."

"Got it."

"Then check all the files. See if 511 is the address of any of Morrissey's properties. Look at those proposals he was considering. Then check the personnel information we got from his office. See if someone was hired on that date. Check if anyone has a birthdate of May 11."

I slid a list to Kozlowski and Laura. "These are half the properties. Do follow up interviews. If you see anyone who is even close to the dimensions we're talking about, you gotta ask."

Koz nodded. "I will be the model of discretion." He actually managed to say this with a straight face. Laura roughly smacked his arm. "You expect me to keep him in line?"

"I expect that you will probably have an easier time identifying anyone who might fit the bill."

"Hey, I'm good with figures," Koz said. He glanced at Laura. "I can tell you your measurements."

"You do remember that I carry a gun," she answered, getting up from the table. She folded the list and tucked it in her pocket.

He ignored her. "You checking out the other half?"

"Yeah. Donna and I will cover that. You make an ID, give me a call."

"Roger that."

****

We stopped at the Shores Madrid and the Grosse Pointe theaters. In both locations we didn't even have to ask about measurements. Nobody working at either site was close. Donna cut her eyes at me as we climbed back in the Pontiac.

"I get the impression you expect me to know women's sizes."

"Between the two of us, I think you'd do better at it that I would."

"Boss, this is one of the craziest things I've ever heard of."

I considered it. "We may be way off the chart here. But think how foolish we would be if this was the only clue we have to identifying the killer and we didn't pursue it."

"Do you think the killer is a woman?"

"Anything is possible. But I can't see a woman shooting Morrissey. Stabbing him would be more appropriate."

"From the reports, there are more than a couple of female employees who could have turned violent if he pushed it too far."

I parked in front of the office building on Woodward Avenue. Colleen greeted us as we stepped into the lobby.

"This is getting to be a daily occurrence," she said with a smile. "You'll be happy to know that I followed your advice."

"Oh?"

"Devonshire's will be designing a set of emerald earrings for me. With a matching pendant. Everything else will be kept in their vaults until the estate is settled."

"That sounds like an excellent choice."

Her smiled wavered a bit as she studied me. "So, what brings you by today?"

This is what the whole morning had been leading up to. From the moment Simone guided me through her measurements, I had an idea exactly who those numbers were describing. But I wanted time to think it through. Checking the others was necessary. God knows I've been wrong before.

"We have a few questions for Valerie."

Colleen's smile faded. "What kind of questions?"

"One's only she can answer."

She pointed down the hall toward the offices. "I'm going with you."

"Not this time."

"This is my business, Chene!"

I motioned to Donna. Her hand went into her jacket pocket, switching on the recorder. We walked to Valerie's office and stepped inside. She was busy entering data in the computer and didn't glance up until I clicked the door shut behind us. Recognition flashed as she looked from Donna to me. A nervous tremor shot through her hand as she rolled the chair away from the desk.

"What can I do you for you, Sergeant?" she asked

timidly.

"Stand up."

Valerie rose easily out of the chair. She was wearing a burgundy linen dress that barely reached her knee. A small gold chain dangled from her wrist. It twinkled as she brushed back her hair. In my peripheral vision, Donna nodded.

"Damn close," she said.

"Damn close to what?" Valerie asked.

I handed her one of my business cards. On the back was the list of numbers in the string. Beneath it was broken down by the segments. She stared at it for a long minute, then tried to hand it back to me.

"That's your measurements."

"I…this doesn't mean anything…it's just gibberish."

"Do I need to get a tape measure to confirm it?" I moved closer to her.

Valerie's face flushed scarlet. "That's insulting."

"How long have you known?"

"I don't know what you're talking about! You're scaring me!"

She was still holding the business card. I pointed at her chair and encouraged her to sit down. Donna and I remained standing.

"Let me run it down for you. On the morning Kyle Morrissey was killed, he received an email. The message read "Your turn to die!" It was sent from an account that was only used one time. The account was that list of numbers. Obviously they were supposed to mean something to Kyle Morrissey. They certainly were important to the killer. The first seven are your measurements. And I think we both know what the last three are."

Valerie was shaking her head robotically. "You can't be serious. You're trying to blame me for his death. That's crazy."

"You may not have pulled the trigger. But your actions definitely set things in motion. What was the date?"

"What date?"

"The date you and Kyle spent the night together. The date of your assignation, when you responded to all that pent-up sexual tension."

The shaking stopped suddenly as if I'd slapped her. Valerie's eyes narrowed and her features turned to a display of shock. "You said this would never be discussed."

"Unless it became pertinent to the case. Which it is. The date."

"You're an evil fucker!" she spat.

"It was May 11, wasn't it?"

Valerie started to rise as if she were going to fight. Donna stepped forward and put a hand on her shoulder, keeping her in the chair. "Stay."

I moved back, letting Donna be the buffer. "If you won't tell me, I'll ask Colleen when she took the kids to Toronto. That's all the confirmation I need. You can save her the embarrassment for a moment. But it's all coming together."

Valerie said nothing. She just sat there, gripping the arms of her chair. Her hair was disheveled now and her face was blotchy, a mixture of fear and anger. Donna was tense, standing just beyond her reach. Even if Valerie wouldn't verbalize it, she'd answered my question. There were a couple of ways to do this. I wanted to keep the pressure on.

"Read her the Miranda rights and put the cuffs on her."

Valerie's eyes widened in disbelief. "You can't be serious. I didn't kill Kyle."

Donna pulled her to her feet.

"We're going to take you to the post. If you have a lawyer, they can meet us there. Or we can have the public defender's office send someone over."

I waited until Donna had finished with the Miranda. Tears were streaming down Valerie's face, marking her with a trail of mascara. Somebody knocked impatiently on the door. Colleen stood there. Leaving them behind, I led the widow into her office.

"I'd like an explanation."

"We're taking Ms. Mann into custody. She may have inadvertently played a role in your husband's murder."

"Valerie? Chene, this is crazy!"

"We're going to find out."

Colleen's next statement surprised me. "Does she need a lawyer? I'll call one right away."

"Have them meet us at the post."

"Chene, what the hell is going on?"

Now wasn't the time to get into it. "I'll tell you everything, as soon as I can. But I can't do it now. We need to finish this."

Colleen took a moment to digest that. Slowly she nodded in understanding. Then she moved to the desk and picked up the phone. Colleen was dialing as I walked out.

Chapter Twenty-Five

Valerie cried all the way to the post. Neither Donna nor I said anything. Donna had propped her phone on the dash, switching it to video. It recorded everything on the way there, just in case Valerie started talking. Her face remained hidden in a veil of tears.

Inside we took the handcuffs off and placed her in an interrogation room. Donna gave her a bottle of water and a box of tissues. Valerie slumped in the chair while Donna stood in the corner, watching her. Suarez joined me in the observation room. Kozlowski and Laura were on the way.

"Start digging up everything you can on her husband. I want it all. Name, birthdate, job, vehicles, bank records, hobbies and physical description. Find out where he's working. Then start the paperwork for a search warrant."

"Right away, boss."

The crying had stopped. Valerie angrily tore tissues from the box and scrubbed her face. Defiantly she stared at the mirror, knowing I was behind it.

"You're an evil fucker!" She grabbed the plastic water bottle and heaved it at the glass. It bounced off and rolled across the floor.

Koz appeared behind me. "Doesn't sound like the newly elected president of your fan club."

"Surprising, isn't it? Where's your partner?"

He pointed at the door to the other room. It opened and Laura escorted someone inside. It was a young woman in her early thirties, dressed in a professional suit. Her honey blonde hair was styled to curl at her shoulders. Without missing a beat, she took the chair next to Valerie and put a reassuring hand on her arm.

"I'd like a few minutes with my client in private." Although she spoke to Donna and Laura, her eyes went to the mirror. Kozlowski reached over and turned off the electronics. The detectives left the room.

Laura handed me a card. The attorney was Holly Sutherland. She was from a large suburban firm that had a solid reputation of hiring only the brightest and the best. They were not cheap. Colleen definitely knew the right people. We waited in silence. When she was ready the attorney merely nodded at the glass. Koz turned the recorders back on. I took Donna with me. Introductions were made quickly.

"Are you charging my client with a crime?" Holly asked.

"Not yet. We have a lot of questions and no time for delays. If she cooperates, that will go a long way on what happens next. Did Mrs. Morrissey tell you much?"

"Preliminary details about her husband's murder. You have reason to believe Ms. Mann has some knowledge of the crime."

I settled back in the chair. Donna shifted alongside me. Holly Sutherland's face was calm as she jotted notes on a legal pad.

"During our investigation, Ms. Mann revealed that she had an affair with Kyle Morrissey. She said it was only one night, the culmination of several years of sexual banter. Ms. Mann claimed that she never revealed this information to her husband or anyone else, prior to discussing it with me and another detective."

Valerie's anger had not subsided. "You promised…"

Holly firmly placed a hand on her arm, silencing her. "Continue."

I described the message we'd found on Morrissey's phone and the clues to unraveling the code. Holly's eyes flicked to her client when I mentioned the measurements. Donna pulled the photos from the surveillance video and set them on the table. Holly Sutherland glanced at them and slid them in front of Valerie. Her anger faded.

"Do you recognize him?" I asked.

Words failed her. She nodded weakly.

"What do you need from my client?" Holly asked.

"Is that your husband?"

Another weak nod.

"I need details. Right now."

Valerie just stared at the photos. They were grainy but it was still clear enough for her to make that identification. "I never told him," she whispered.

"Ms. Mann is willing to cooperate."

I looked away from Valerie. "No more attitude and no stalling. I want everything. And I want it now. Right now."

Holly turned to her. "You need to answer all their questions."

Once Valerie got started, she talked for almost half an hour. Donna was taking quick notes. A couple of times Holly Sutherland prompted her for specific details on her husband. When Valerie was done, I made her go through it all again. After the second time she slumped in her chair. I was ready.

"When did you suspect your husband was the killer?"

Her jaw dropped open. "I never thought he killed Kyle. I still don't believe he did it."

"Bullshit. Your behavior alone should have given me a clue."

"What are you talking about?"

It was one of the things that nagged me from the beginning. "You ran polar opposites with me from one minute to the next. Friendly and helpful, then antagonistic. I never knew which version I would be talking to."

Valerie bit her lip. Her eyes kept darting back and forth between me and Donna, as if looking for an escape hatch. Holly watched her closely.

"The day of the funeral you were mad as hell that I was there. Then you relaxed after the service, only to accuse me later of manipulating Dale Morrissey. When I dropped you at your car, you looked like you were going to make a pass at me."

"I never…"

"Save it! Maybe you thought the stranger you behaved, the less likely I was to come around. If you were acting this way around your husband, he must have figured out about the affair."

"It wasn't an affair," Valerie whined, "it was just one night."

"The sex may have been only one night, but that was just icing the cake. The flirtations were a long running foreplay."

"You're an evil fucker!"

"So I've been told." I stood and led Donna out of

the room.

****

Suarez had the goods. We were in the bullpen, gathered around his desk. The day had flown by. It was already after three. Roger Mann was thirty-four years old. He was five foot seven and one-fifty-five with thinning blonde hair. From the driver's license photo, he looked pale and bland. Mann worked from a computer company that serviced small to mid-sized businesses across the state. According to his employer he was at a client's project out in Novi, on the far western edge of Oakland County. Barring any construction delays or traffic, it would take the squad at least an hour to get there.

I didn't want Mann to have any chance to slip by us. Remembering one of Cantrell's favorite maxims, 'steal help iffun ya need it', I punched up a number on my phone.

"This is Malone. What's up, Chene?"

"I need eyes on a suspect. He's in your part of town."

"Uniform or plainclothes?"

"Plain. Sooner the better."

There was no hesitation. "Send me the details and I'll make it happen."

"Thanks, Sarge."

Suarez sent the information to Malone, along with the photo of Roger Mann and the description of his vehicle. Koz raised his eyebrows rather than ask a question. He knew what needed to happen.

"Take Laura in your car. Suarez, you and Donna follow in a patrol car."

"By the numbers," Koz said.

"Damn straight."

Holly Sutherland appeared at my shoulder as the others were walking out. "What's by the numbers mean?"

"That means we do it exactly by the book. They will read Roger Mann his rights and put him in the back of the patrol car. He will be on camera the entire time for the ride here. And they will not engage in conversation with him."

"So is my client free to go?"

"Not yet. I certainly don't want her to warn him that we're closing in."

Holly leaned a slender hip on the corner of my desk. "Do you really think Valerie played a role in Kyle Morrissey's murder?"

"I don't think she's an accomplice. But I'd rather keep her under wraps until we bring her husband in."

"That makes sense."

"Are you representing Roger Mann as well?"

She gave her head a slow negative shake. "No, Mrs. Morrissey was very clear that I was only to provide counsel for Valerie Mann. Do you mind if I take her something to drink?"

I shrugged. "Be careful she doesn't throw it at you."

Holly gave me a gentle smile. "I doubt that. She doesn't think I'm evil."

"We all have our moments."

****

It was after six when they arrived. Kozlowski called me once they apprehended Roger Mann. He had been finishing up at the company in Novi when they arrived. Malone had sent two plainclothes troopers to keep him under surveillance. All six officers surrounded Mann as he was loading his equipment in the work van. Mann actually tried to run from them.

"Suarez did some fancy ass spin move and slammed him into a truck. Said he learned it from you." There was a trace of admiration in Kozlowski's voice.

"There may be hope for him yet," I said.

Suarez had read him the Miranda rights. Roger Mann was silent on the drive in.

I'd been busy during that time, finishing the paperwork for a search warrant. Fortunately Judge Conklin had been in his chambers when I called. He did a quick scan of the requests and signed with a flourish. The warrant included the Mann residence, garage, cars and any storage facilities. Additionally, I included his place of employment and company vehicles. Malone had sent a wrecker out to Novi to impound the van.

Now Suarez and Donna escorted Roger Mann into the interrogation room. They locked him in. The rest of the squad was waiting in the hallway. I'd updated Cantrell half an hour ago. He agreed with the plan. Pappy was known to have a lady friend in Lansing. I didn't expect him back until the morning.

"What's next, boss?" Laura asked.

"Kozlowski and I will conduct the interview. Take the others and go to the Mann residence." I handed her the search warrant. "Mrs. Mann and her attorney will be present. Play nice."

Laura grinned. "Which is why Kozlowski is staying behind."

"You're gonna hurt my feelings," he said with a frown.

"You don't have feelings."

"Baby, that's cold."

She pushed playfully at his chest. "Yes, but it's accurate."

He looked at me and shrugged. "I hate it when she's right."

I had already briefed Holly Sutherland on the search warrant. Koz and I watched as Laura guided Valerie Mann and the attorney out of the building. It was going to be a long night.

"You hoping for anything in particular to turn up in that search?"

"Murder weapon would be nice. Maybe a set of fatigues from the paintball game with a little blood on them. Details on Morrissey's movements."

"You ain't asking for much, Chene."

Koz and I entered the interrogation room. Mann was using the tip of a ball point pen to clean under his fingernails. He didn't say anything as we sat across from him.

"We have some questions. Are you willing to answer them without an attorney present?" I asked.

He kept cleaning his nails. "It won't make any difference."

"You're saying you don't need a lawyer?"

"Yeah, that's what I'm saying."

Koz and I glanced at each other. This wasn't unheard of, but with a homicide, it was fairly uncommon. I gave Koz a quick nod. He reached out quickly and snatched the pen from Mann's fingers.

"Okay, let's take it from the top," Koz said. "You have been brought in for questioning related to the murder of Kyle Morrissey. You've been given your rights twice now. You're agreeing to talk with us without an attorney present, understanding that anything you say can be used against you in court."

"Yeah, that's about it."

"Why did you kill Kyle Morrissey?"

His face twisted into a sneer. "Because he fucked my wife!"

"And how would you know that?" Kozlowski's deep voice took on a threatening tone. "Did they do it in front of you? How would you know that?"

"They might as well. I knew it was just a matter of time. They were always playing. Claiming it was only fun. She said neither one took it seriously."

"So you don't know if it happened or not," I said.

Mann snapped his head toward me. "Oh, it happened!"

"Why don't you lay it out for us?"

He straightened in the chair, drawing his shoulders back. Then he cleared his throat and explained.

"I've always had my doubts. Ever since we got married. I've seen the way he'd look at her whenever we were at some party or movie function. He would undress her with his eyes when he thought no one was looking. If she was wearing anything that showed her cleavage, or hugged the curve of her ass, he'd find a way to get a glimpse. More than once he'd bump into her, kind of accidentally on purpose. The longer we were at those events, the worse it got."

"Maybe you're a little paranoid," Koz said.

"Sometimes paranoia is just having all the facts."

Koz grunted. "Go on with your fairytale."

"I trusted Val. But I never trusted him. So I put an app on her phone. It let me track where she was. And I could also remotely turn it on, where I could listen in on her conversation. Even if she wasn't making a call. I could mute my phone and listen to every word. Every. Fucking. Word!"

"So what did you hear?" I asked.

"It was a night when I was out of town on an assignment. I waited until around ten and checked. It showed she was still in the office. That wasn't right. So I keyed up the phone to listen. I could hear them going at it. Lots of grunting and moaning and kissing and all that shit. He was calling her name. She was calling his. It went on for a long time. There was no doubt what was happening."

"You expect us to believe this?"

Mann's expression was one of pure hatred. He clenched his fists in anger. "It doesn't matter what you believe. I heard them fucking. Then the pillow talk that followed. Morrissey was catching his breath, telling her how long he'd wanted her. That he'd decorate her with jewels." I glanced at Kozlowski. He raised his eyebrows in a quizzical look.

"So you just listened? Why didn't you do something that night?" I asked.

"I was two hundred miles away in Muskegon on a job. We'd been out for dinner and drinks after work. So I started thinking maybe it was my imagination, just playing games on me."

"What happened next?"

Mann's face relaxed and he slowly flexed his fingers. "I knew what it sounded like, but part of me was still hopeful. Maybe it was wrong. Maybe I just imagined it. But I had to know for sure."

He dropped his head and stared at the table. No one spoke for a couple of minutes.

"What did you do?" I asked.

"I tried to ignore it. Somehow I finished the job the next day, probably made a bunch of mistakes. Then I drove home. It was around eight when I got there. I didn't know what to expect. But Val was home. She'd cooked a nice dinner, looked happy to see me. She made a big fuss over me, paying more attention than she normally would. Kept saying how much she really missed me. I'd been gone three nights."

"So then what?" Koz asked.

He glared at Koz. "Sex happened next. It was gentle and tender, like something out of an old Hollywood movie. I started to doubt what I'd heard. Maybe I was wrong. We fell asleep. But the next morning, I knew for sure."

"How's that?" I asked.

"When she was gone to work, I went out to the garbage can and took everything out. Opened the bags on the floor of the garage and sorted through it." His voice had dropped to a whisper.

"What did you find?"

"Proof. A pair of lacy blue panties, ripped apart. Stockings with big runs in them. And a box from the pharmacy for the morning after drug. They call it Plan B."

I'd heard of it. The intent was to use it after unprotected sex to eliminate a possible pregnancy. I glanced at Kozlowski. He nodded once. Mann continued his story.

"We talked about having kids. Tried for a while. Went for tests when nothing happened, even when we knew she was ovulating. Turns out I've got a low sperm count." He shrugged. "We were considering adoption, maybe doing the artificial method. But those are expensive. We hadn't made any plans yet."

"So the Plan B box…"

"Confirmed what I'd heard. Morrissey fucked my wife. He'd gone too far." Another brief shrug. "I had no choice. I had to kill him. Do you want to know the worst part?"

I couldn't imagine it getting any worse. "What's that?"

"I bought her those panties. To see them like that pushed me over the edge. It's like I paid for the wrapping but he was the one to get the prize inside."

Mann stopped talking. He turned his head and wiped his mouth on his shoulder. "You want to hear it?"

"Hear what?"

"That night. It's on my phone. I kept it in case I ever got up the nerve to confront her. There's no way she can deny it."

I glanced at Kozlowski. Without a word he left the room. When Mann had been arrested all of his personal possessions were taken and logged in as evidence. Koz returned a minute later with the phone. He handed it to Mann. Roger activated the phone and keyed it up.

The recording was just as Roger Mann described. I recognized Kyle Morrissey's voice from the recordings Jamie Richmond had made during the interviews. Mann slumped back in his chair, listening sullenly to the entire recording. I had no doubt he'd done this several times before. When it finished he passed the phone back to Kozlowski.

"Why not simply divorce her?" I asked.

Roger Mann shrugged. "I love her."

There was something still bothering me. I shifted and glanced at Kozlowski. His expression was blank but his eyes were locked on Roger Mann. It didn't matter anymore, but I wanted to know.

"The email. Why did you send that?"

A trace of defiance flickered in Mann's eyes. "I wanted him to sweat. To spend that whole morning looking over his shoulder. Wondering who it was that was going to end his miserable fucking life. We'd met a few times, but I doubted he'd recognize me, especially in that setting. It freaked him out. Otherwise why would he hide out in that grove?"

Kozlowski shook his head. "Too bad Morrissey never saw that message."

"What?"

"It went to his spam folder. Morrissey never opened it. Looks like it didn't arrive in the system until after he was already at the war games. So your plan of making him sweat didn't work."

"But he was hiding!"

"Nah, he was sick. Probably hoping it would pass. Then he'd join in or give up and drive home."

Confusion crossed Mann's face. I sensed he was replaying the events, tracking Morrissey into the grove, confronting him. Maybe some questions before he executed his wife's lover.

"You realize the email's what led us to you," I said.

"It was inevitable. Sooner or later someone would figure it out. It was bound to happen. I'd make a slip. Or the guilt would get to me. I thought Morrissey would see those numbers and know exactly what it was all about. You don't forget those measurements."

Chapter Twenty-Six

Roger Mann turned out to be the most cooperative murderer I've ever dealt with. He told us where to find the gun and the clothes he'd worn that day. They were stashed in a plastic bin in his garage, mixed in with various computer and telephone components from his job. He was booked on a charge of first degree murder and transported to the Macomb County jail.

At ten the next morning, Donna and I went to the Morrissey home. Colleen was waiting on the deck in the backyard. She fidgeted in her chair, trying to get comfortable. Frustrated, she got up and began to pace as we told her everything we'd been able to piece together.

"Valerie called me this morning and resigned. She said you weren't going to be charging her with any crime."

"That's right. Her husband's confession will be verified, but I don't think she knew what he did."

Colleen was dressed for the office in a short navy skirt and a white silk blouse. She leaned her hips against the deck railing and folded her arms across her breasts. "This is all so senseless. It makes me wonder if I ever really knew Kyle. So many secrets. So many lies."

"It's unfortunate," Donna said. "But now you know a lot."

"In some respects, he was just like a little kid. Kyle did whatever he wanted to do and left it all behind for someone else to clean up the mess," Colleen said disgustedly. She pushed off the railing and resumed pacing.

Stepping in front of her, I put my hands out, palms up. Colleen stopped in midstride. She gave me a small smile and placed her hands on mine. "I never met Kyle. But from what we've learned about him, there were some very positive qualities. Building two successful businesses, supporting local charities and communities. He seemed to be a good father to the kids. Had a nice home and a wonderful family. You should always remember that too."

"Thank you, Chene. You and your team got me the answers. Now I'll have to figure out what happens next. And put this whole sordid mess behind us."

"Just take it slow," I said. "Nobody is expecting you to solve all the problems in a single day."

"What about the media?"

"Captain Cantrell will be holding a press conference at noon." I had to bite back a grin at the thought of it. "It will be brief. He will ask that the press respect the privacy of the family and leave you alone. With any luck, they'll listen."

She squeezed my hands and nodded. "One can only hope."

****

I had a few debts to pay. So I made the call to Olivia Sholtis at the television station. She got all the details an hour before Pappy held the press conference. That would give her plenty of time to get the background information together for a feature story and a jump on the other stations.

"Chene, I still want to do a story on you. Trials and tribulations of an erstwhile detective. I can hear the applause from the award show even as I speak."

"Cute. But I'll pass. You know Pappy likes to keep us in the background."

"I promise to use a filter," she said with a giggle.

"Go away."

"Call me if you change your mind. Or the next time you're working on a juicy story. And don't forget my spa day."

"I'll keep you in mind."

Laura had taken six booking photos and arranged them in a plastic album page. She'd met with Heather Gaines and asked her to see if anyone looked familiar. Heather immediately picked out Roger Mann. Turns out Mann's employer serviced the equipment where she worked. He'd last been in the office the week before the murder.

I heard from the prosecutor's office that Mann was willing to plead guilty for a reduced sentence. There was a chance they would consider it. Maybe it would save the taxpayers some money on the expense of a trial. It didn't matter much to me. If it went to trial, I'd be called to testify. Other than that, the case was closed.

Pappy was pleased. He'd gotten high praise from his boss and the governor. At the press conference, he had included Ray Craddock from the sheriff's office. Pappy praised him and his department for securing the crime scene and the thoroughness of their work. A little positive PR could go a long way for Craddock in the next election.

But I still had another debt to pay.

****

"You didn't forget me, did you, Chene?" Jamie asked.

"I don't think that's possible. But it might be easier to do this in person rather than over the phone. I owe both you and Malone for your help."

She laughed, a deep throaty sound in my ear. "I've got expensive tastes."

"Malone working tonight?"

She laughed again. "Yes he is. Whatever do you have in mind?"

"Dinner and a long conversation."

Turns out Malone had Friday night off. I told Jamie where and when and a few other details, then ended the call.

Friday arrived without fanfare. I was in the kitchen, putting the steaks into a Caribbean jerk marinade when the doorbell rang. Simone had arrived a few minutes ago and had just changed into shorts and a tank top. She veered to the front door. Stevie Ray Vaughan's "Riviera Paradise" was on the stereo. I could hear strains of a muted conversation. It was too early for Jamie and Malone. Curious, I wiped my hands on a dish towel and headed for the front door.

"So nice to meet you, Miss Bettencourt," a raspy voice said.

"Thank you. But I didn't catch your name."

"I didn't throw it."

She was holding a small package. Simone turned as she heard me approach. Maximo Aurelio was on the front porch. He slid a pair of sunglasses down his nose, peering over the frames. A crooked smile played on his lips.

"Hiya, Chene."

I slid a protective arm around her waist. "Think this is over the line, Max."

"No harm intended. The boss merely wanted to express his gratitude."

"For what?"

"Bygones. Or whatever you want to call it."

I glanced at package. Only now did I realize it was a bottle of prohibition whiskey. "You know I can't accept gifts, Max. Especially from you or Leo."

The crooked smile widened. "Who says I gave you anything? That is a present for the lovely Miss Bettencourt."

"Tomato, toe-mah-toe."

He nodded and pushed the shades back up on his nose. "Something like that. See ya around, Jeff."

"Give my best to the man."

"Will do."

We watched him amble down the walk to the Bentley. Silently it purred away from the curb. Simone looked from the package in her hands to me. "You have some very interesting friends."

I thought back to Ted's comment about friends and his insolent request that I name six of them.

"Yeah, I guess I do."

A word about the author...

Yes, my name really is Mark Love. I am a Michigan native who up until recently lived in the Metro Detroit area, where crime and corruption seem to be at the top of everyone's news. So there's always the chance to find something that can trigger a story idea and enough interesting characters to jump-start your imagination.

I have worked in many industries and career paths over the years, but one of my passions has always been writing. I was able to parlay that passion for a while, working as a freelance reporter for a couple of newspapers in the Detroit area. Writing features and hard news helped me hone my talents. But while newspaper work was interesting and paid a few bills, it was a far cry from the fiction writing that I enjoy the most.

I'm drawn to mysteries and thrillers, the kind of stories that have a fast pace, that keep you moving and keep you guessing as to what's going to take place next. Mix those in with some elements of crime, perhaps a glimpse of the seedier side, and you've got me. So it's been one of my goals to write that type of story.

http://motownmysteries.blogspot.com

CPSIA information can be obtained
at www.ICGtesting.com
Printed in the USA
BVHW030210080922
646555BV00011B/301

9 781509 224104